when
the
dikes
breached

when
the
dikes
breached

martha attema

RONSDALE PRESS

RONSDALE PRESS
3350 West 21st Avenue, Vancouver, B.C. Canada V6S 1G7
www.ronsdalepress.com

Typesetting: Julie Cochrane, in Minion 11 pt on 14.5
Cover Design: Julie Cochrane
Maps: David Lester

Ronsdale Press wishes to thank the following for their support of its
publishing program: the Canada Council for the Arts, the Government of
Canada, the British Columbia Arts Council, and the Province of British
Columbia through the British Columbia Book Publishing Tax Credit program.

Library and Archives Canada Cataloguing in Publication

Title: When the dikes breached / Martha Attema.
Names: Attema, Martha, 1949– author.
Identifiers: Canadiana (print) 20230140564 | Canadiana (ebook) 20230140572
    | ISBN 9781553806745 (softcover) | ISBN 9781553806752 (EPUB)
    | ISBN 9781553806769 (PDF)
Classification: LCC PS8551.T74 W54 2023 | DDC jC813/.54—dc23

Printed in Canada.

To my children and grandchildren,
who will have to deal with the devastating
consequences of climate change.

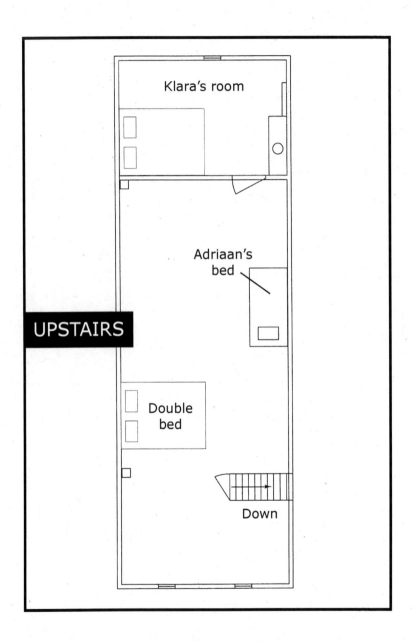

Klara's room

Adriaan's bed

UPSTAIRS

Double bed

Down

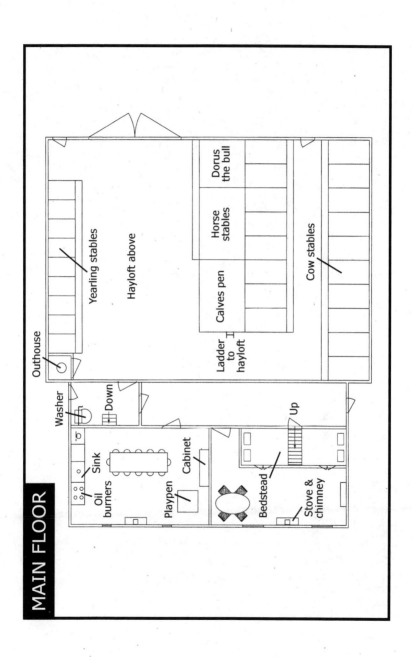

MAIN FLOOR

Outhouse

Yearling stables

Hayloft above

Dorus the bull

Horse stables

Calves pen

Cow stables

Ladder to hayloft

Washer

Down

Sink

Oil burners

Cabinet

Playpen

Up

Bedstead

Stove & chimney

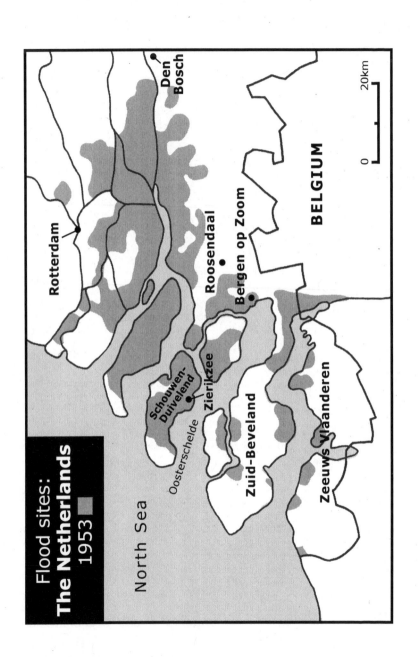

Flood sites:
The Netherlands 1953

Den Bosch

Rotterdam

Roosendaal

Bergen op Zoom

BELGIUM

Schouwen-Duiveland

Zierikzee

Oosterschelde

Zuid-Beveland

Zeeuws Vlaanderen

North Sea

20km

0

1

Klara

"KLARA! STOP DAYDREAMING! Those milk pails won't scrub themselves!" Father's head peeks out the barn door. He grabs hold of his cap as the strong January wind tries to snatch it from his head.

Startled, I reach for the brush on the ledge of the milk can rack; then I remember what I wanted to ask. "Father! Can I go with Dora and her mother to Rotterdam to buy textiles?"

My father opens the door wide. Watching the deep lines etched in his stern face, I know his answer.

"Why do you even ask?" He wags his index finger at me. "You know how I feel about the mainland. It'll poison your mind."

"But Dora and her mother go every spring and their minds haven't been poisoned," I plead.

"I don't want to hear about it!" Pulling down his cap, he turns and disappears into the barn, slamming the door behind him.

"I'm not going to be exposed to the evil influences of the mainland!" I yell at the closed door. "I'm going to buy fabric!" I kick one of the buckets. The sound of my wooden shoe hitting metal echoes in the yard. The pail rolls down the gravel until the mud slows it to a halt.

In all my sixteen years, I've never been off the island. We live on Schouwen-Duiveland, one of the islands in the province of Zeeland, in the southwest part of the Netherlands. The Oosterschelde, an arm of the North Sea, separates our island from the other islands and the mainland. This isolation is good according to my father.

I pick up the bucket, collect two more and drag them to the well. The January wind balloons my woollen skirt, chilling my legs. Moving the handle of the pump up and down, I fill the bucket and flinch when the cold water splashes my hands. I scrub the milk pails with angry strokes and don't care if they get clean.

I wish I were back at the Spinach Academy — what my friends and I call the School for Domestic Sciences — where we had cooking classes and learned to clean, sew and take care of children. I wasn't keen on learning the duties of future wives and mothers; I get enough of that at home. But I miss my classes in history and geography and, my favourite subject, Dutch poetry.

And I miss seeing Dora and the other girls. We used to giggle and gossip about people in our village and the teachers . . . and boys.

After I plunk the milk pails on the drying rack, I pause, take a deep breath and let my anger subside. My gaze and mind wander longingly toward the east, to the sea dike. I recite softly the words I wrote last night: "The call of the breakers, crashing the coastline, makes me yearn for faraway places where mysterious shores call my name."

In the fading light, I walk down the farm lane in the direction of the dike. If I didn't have chores, I'd go to my special spot. It's close to the water and sheltered from the western winds. There, I can hear the waves rolling onto the dike that protects our island like a mother's arm shielding her child. When the tide rolls out, I dream of riding with it, of landing in other countries and meeting people who don't speak my language.

It's not just the rest of the world I want to see but also the rest of the Netherlands. I could experience the big cities, get to know the people, discover the dunes and the beaches along the North Sea, trot through the forests in the eastern parts of our country to smell pine and spruce.

The people on the mainland, instead of being evil, are far ahead of us. Nobody there wears traditional costumes anymore, except in a few fishing villages along the Ijsselmeer. It's 1953, for crying out loud — not the Middle Ages.

On our island, everything is backward. I feel buried in this conservative community with its debilitating rules and expectations for girls and women. I was born on this dairy farm to a father whose narrow-mindedness forces us to live in the previous century.

I inhale the sea air, taste the salt on my lips and sigh. I'm stuck on an island that's slowly sinking into the sea, and I have no idea how to change the situation. I turn and drag my feet back to the farm.

Opening the door to the cow stable, I feel the warmth radiating from the animals' bodies. I walk to the first stall and step over the manure trench to check on Dina. She's ready to deliver her calf any day. I rest my forehead on her back and place my numb hands on her swollen belly.

"Where have you been? And tuck your hair into your cap." Using a pitchfork, Father spreads fresh straw underneath the cow beside Dina. "You need to get the evening meal ready. Your mother is resting."

"What about Rosa or Liesbeth?" I try.

"I asked you." His stern response makes me swallow hard.

"Not even a minute to warm up," I mutter to Dina before I step off the stall. "Why is he always picking on me?" As I hurry down the path behind the row of stalls, I barely miss the wheelbarrow full of steaming manure coming toward me, being pushed by my twelve-year-old brother, Adriaan.

"Open the door, please, Klara?" Adriaan calls.

"Sure." I pinch my nose to avoid inhaling the sharp, pungent smell and open the outside door.

Straining his body, he balances the wheelbarrow with its less than delicate load through the door.

"Where are Martin and Jacob?" I ask.

"They're helping Piet feed the chickens," Adriaan answers.

I notice a welt on his left cheek as he limps past me. "What happened to your face?" I call after him, but he doesn't hear me. I'm sure some kid at school beat him up because of his hobble. Even the raised sole of his customized shoe cannot hide his shorter leg. I watch Adriaan push the wheelbarrow down the path outside, behind the barn and up the plank. At the end, he tips the barrow, and its steaming load slides onto the dunghill.

After I close the door, I retrace my steps to the end of the cow stalls and find my seven-year-old brother, Martin, and Jacob, who is the same size but one year younger. Together they carry a sack of chicken feed with help from our German shepherd, Max.

"Why is Max wearing a scarf?"

"He's cold," Jacob answers.

"But Max wears a warm coat already."

"We know, but the scarf makes him happy," Martin replies. He drops his end of the heavy sack on the ground. "Can you bring some newspapers to the outhouse? I have to go, but there's no paper."

"Sure." One more thing to remember.

"Will you read from Paulus, the gnome book, tonight?" Martin asks.

I shake my head. "I've choir practice."

"Why do you always go out at night?" Jacob asks.

"To get away from chores, chores and more boring chores," I answer, sounding harsher than I intend.

"We do chores," Jacob pipes up. "We don't mind."

"I know. It's not your fault." I give my head a shake. I shouldn't take it out on them, I scold myself.

"No," Martin says with a grin that shows his missing front teeth. "You go to choir to see your boyfriend."

"Hey! Cut it out!" I feel the heat creep into my cheeks.

"When Klara kisses Luuc, we all have to puke," the boys sing.

"You little brats!" I throw up my arms and run into the mud-room, which connects the barn to the living quarters. The room is cloaked in darkness, so I switch on the light. The wringer washer stands in the corner to my right. I see that the hamper is already overflowing with dirty laundry, and a sigh escapes my lips. To my left, another door leads into the house, but before I can get there, a voice makes me turn around.

"I . . . hurt my hand . . . on the calves' pen!" Clasina runs through the door from the barn. My sister is only four, but she never misses a day to help feed the calves. Her wooden shoes clatter on the stone floor, and tears stream down her face.

"Show me." I scoop her up in my arms and carry her into the dark kitchen, where we're met by the wails of Sara and Neeltje.

The little ones are standing in the wooden playpen, desperately trying to climb out of their enclosure. Sara had her first birthday last week, and Neeltje is just one and a half years older.

"Just a minute," I tell the little ones. I lift Clasina onto the granite counter and switch on the lamp. Yellow light spreads across the long harvest table. I lay my shawl and woollen hat on the back of a chair and tuck my escaped curls inside my lace cap.

The girls reach for me, but I'll tend to Clasina first. "Hmm, that's a nasty scratch." I work the pump handle. "Put your hand underneath."

"The water stings," Clasina cries.

"Clench your teeth, and you won't feel the sting," I reassure her.

After cleaning the scratch, I reach for the first aid kit in the top cabinet above the sink. I cover the wound with a plaster, press a kiss on the injured hand and lift Clasina off the counter. She magically stops crying.

"Why is it so cold in here?" I shiver in my woollen cardigan and look at the cast-iron stove that sits between the two west-facing kitchen windows. "It must be dead," I murmur.

Lifting the rings off the top of the stove, I poke around until I stir up some sparks. I reach for the coal scuttle and fill up the black beast. Closing the rings, I wait for the fire to start. It doesn't take long before I see skinny flames dancing through the mica window.

The two little ones turn up their volume, but then I remember

Martin's request. I grab a stack of newspapers from the box beside the stove and run back through the mudroom to the barn. To my left is a wooden, closet-like structure with a built-in outhouse. Having it in the barn keeps it warmer than if it was outside. I drop the newspapers on the seat and jog back inside. I open the bread box and cut the crusts off a slice of bread.

Clasina hands Neeltje and Sara each a strip of crust. The girls plop down onto their bottoms to gobble up their treat.

With a cloth, I wipe their snotty, tear-soaked faces. *Where is Liesbeth?* I suddenly realize that my ten-year-old sister is missing. She's supposed to look after the little ones as soon as she comes home from school.

I walk over to the windows, stare into an almost dark world. The old apple tree scratches its branches against the windowpane as if it wants to come in out of the wind. Beyond the apple tree, the vegetable gardens are in winter sleep. In November, Mother and I harvested and canned the last of the kale, Brussels sprouts and carrots. The cans line the bottom shelves in the cold cellar.

Slowly, I pull the red and white gingham curtains. The heavy cotton fabric keeps the drafty cold winds out and the stove's warmth in. The grandfather clock on the wall beside the sideboard chimes once. It's five-thirty.

"I'll check on Mother," I tell Clasina. "You look after your sisters."

As I close the kitchen door and walk down the hallway, I hear Clasina sing, "All my ducklings are swimming in the water, fal-de-ral-de-rira, fa-de-ral-de-rara."

2
Mother

THE FRONT ROOM is cloaked in darkness. The forest green-velvet curtains that cover the two windows are drawn. I turn on the ceiling light. In two alcoves built into the wall across from the windows are the bedsteads where my parents and my sisters sleep. The doors to the bedsteads are open. My mother, covered under a quilted blanket, faces the wall.

"Mother," I whisper. "Where's Liesbeth?"

She turns slowly toward me and opens her eyes. Deep lines mark her tired face; her skin is the same colour as the bed linens, and her eyes are sunken with dark rings.

"Oma isn't well. Liesbeth went to help her after school." Mother sighs. Her voice sounds tired. "It would be so much easier if Oma came to live with us."

"It would help. We could keep an eye on her, and she wouldn't be so lonely," I say. It's hard to imagine that she's Father's mother. Oma Klara is the opposite of her son. She's always interested in our lives. Her stories about events from long ago show me a window into the past. And when she sings psalms and hymns in her rich soprano voice, she sounds like an angel.

"Will you get the evening meal ready and give me another half hour to rest?" Mother asks.

"You need at least a year, Mother, if you want to feel any more rested," I reply while I cover her gently with the blanket. "Do you remember what the doctor said after Sara was born?" I ask.

Mother doesn't respond but closes her eyes.

"He said, 'For your health, Mrs. van Burgh, this should be your last.'"

She briefly looks at me. "I know what the doctor said, Klara. I know."

"So why are you expecting again?" I can't help but feel anger rising in me.

"That's not for us to decide." Mother closes her eyes and pulls in her lower lip.

"God willing," Father had said. I remember how his stern voice had silenced the doctor. And here she is, pregnant again. I can't believe that at thirty-four she's expecting her tenth child; it should be her twelfth. After Jacob was born, there were two stillborns.

I shudder. Why is God willing to jeopardize my mother's health? At times I don't understand God's ways. I just hope I'll never have that many children.

I check the trundle underneath my parents' bed for soiled sheets. That's where Sara and Neeltje sleep.

My eyes come to rest at the cradle on the shelf at the foot of the bed, ready for the new sibling's arrival at the end of April, and I envision more diapers to wash — as if we don't do enough laundry.

The second bedstead, where Rosa, Liesbeth and Clasina sleep, holds a mountain of tangled sheets and blankets. Although it's not my job to make their bed, I quickly straighten their covers. I used to sleep downstairs in the front room, too, but Father remodeled the big room upstairs two years ago. He divided the space into two rooms, one for me and one for my three brothers. Their space is bigger, but I don't mind. My room is cozy, tucked into the slope of the roof above the eaves. The boys' room has two skylights close to the eaves, and I have a skylight above my bed to let in light and air. I love to look at the stars at night, and sometimes I can even see the moon.

The boys' space is open to the stairs that lead up from the main floor, but I have a door that I can close for privacy. Mother helped me decorate my room, which makes it feel more special. I love the soft cream-coloured wallpaper with tiny blue cornflowers in vertical rows. A wall hanging depicting a meadow with wildflowers, cross-stitched by Oma, hangs above my bed.

I walk back to Mother's bed. "I'll call you when we're ready to eat."

"I'm leaving too much up to you these days," she mumbles.

"I can do it."

I watch her turn back to face the wall. My eyes move to the cherrywood and glass cabinet that stands against the opposite wall. It holds our best dishes and silverware but also pictures of my mother's parents, the grandparents I never knew. On the bottom shelf stand nine photo albums, proudly lined up, their spines showing our names. Mother makes sure we all have a book with memories.

Before I turn off the light and leave the room, I trace the wallpaper with my finger. I follow the outline of the paisley pattern embossed in soft green velvet and dream of forests in their summer dresses. I watch my mother for a moment longer:

If only
I could erase
the tired lines,
colour your face pink,
put stars in your eyes,
make you dance with us around the kitchen table,
like you used to do.

3

Dora

FATHER LOOKS UP from the Bible. "Klara! Tuck your hair inside your cap." He continues reading aloud. "For if a woman is not covered, let her also be shorn. But if it is shameful for a woman to be shorn or shaved, let her be covered." Father points at the page. "It even says it here, 1 Corinthians 11.6." He closes the Bible and puts it back in the top drawer of his rolltop desk.

I shiver. "Yes, Father." I'm not doing this on purpose.

In the next moment, Father grabs his pipe and tobacco tin from the second drawer and turns on the radio for the seven o'clock news and weather report. Without giving me a second glance, he settles with the newspaper in one of the two armchairs beside the stove.

I glimpse at Rosa. My fourteen-year-old sister's straight brown hair never escapes from her lace cap. Neither does Liesbeth's or Clasina's.

Mother looks at me. Her eyes tell me to not take Father's comment too seriously.

Clasina grasps my hand. "Wish I had happy hair 'yike' you."

I press a kiss on her head and squeeze her hand.

"Martin and I would like to have jumpy hair like yours," Jacob adds. My brothers are both on their knees, bent over the comic strip in the *Zeeuwse Courant*. It's a story about an anthropomorphic bear named Oliver B. Bommel. He lives in Castle Bommelstein with his clever cat, Tom Puss.

"That's enough nonsense!" Father glares at the boys, who shrink back into their chairs. Next, his eyes rest on Adriaan's face. "Who beat you up today?"

"No one," my brother grunts.

"You need to stand up for yourself. If you don't hit back, they'll continue to pester you about your limp."

Adriaan's face turns beet red, making the welt even more visible.

"Ready for choir practice?" Rosa calls.

We dress in our woollen winter coats and drape triangular scarves around our shoulders. When Rosa opens the door, a forceful wind greets us. "No point riding our bicycles tonight!"

"Let's link arms!" I aim the flashlight ahead of us, as we struggle against nature's force during the two-kilometre trek into town. On the right, we pass the small house where Piet, our farmhand, lives with his wife, Jantje, and their children, four-year-old Grietje and her little brother, Casper, who just turned two. Every Friday morning, Jantje helps me wash all the windows inside and out while Grietje and Casper play with Clasina, Sara and Neeltje. The kids have become close friends, and Piet and Jantje have become family.

Closer to town, we walk by a cluster of five old clapboard houses where some of the men who work in the mud flats live with their families. Tonight, the curtains are drawn, and only tiny slits of light escape into the night.

"I wonder if there's dike watch." Rosa points at two men walking in the direction of the quay, their kerosene lanterns swinging with every step.

"The men always watch the dikes when it storms," I reply.

"Are you excited to see Luuc tonight?" Rosa nudges my elbow.

"Hmm," I murmur. Of course, I'm flattered that Luuc, the oldest son of a prestigious dairy farmer, shows an interest in me, but I'm not sure how I feel about him.

"But everyone says that he's such a great catch," Rosa adds. "Have you really looked at the van Borselen's farmhouse?" Rosa's voice sounds dreamy. "The living quarters have such tall windows and the entrance is flanked by huge white pillars!"

"I know," I say. "And the lane leading up to farm is lined with linden trees — like royalty lives there." I shake my head, as if I don't want to know all these details about Luuc's farm.

I also know that Luuc's mother mingles only with the upper class. Before our church was destroyed, Mrs. van Borselen would stride down the aisle as if she were the queen of New Port.

"I would love to live on that farm." Rosa sighs. "Nobody talks about our ordinary looking farm."

"You're right, and I suspect Mrs. van Borselen doesn't approve of her son's choice."

"That would be silly." Rosa moves her head to look at me. "It's Luuc's choice."

Maybe my sister is right, but I have my doubts about Rosa's statement.

When Rosa and I come to the Ring Dike, more young people

join us. My sister runs ahead to meet up with her friend Jopie, and I hook arms with Dora.

"I don't like this nasty cold wind." Dora shivers beside me. "I can't wait for spring to arrive."

We walk past the parsonage, which is under construction, and the ruins of the centuries-old church. In 1944, during World War II, the Germans blew up the steeple. Now all that remains is a pile of rubble and part of a brick wall that's still standing.

That was nine years ago, but when I close my eyes I can still hear the sound of exploding bombs and see the flames and black smoke spewing up into the air. The worst part was Father saying that the end was near, now that the enemy had destroyed God's house. I felt sick with fear; in the days after, I waited for the end of the world, but the only other awful thing was the flooding of homes and land on the east side of the island when the Germans opened the floodgates to prevent the Allies from liberating our island.

"As soon as the weather warms up, we can go for walks in the evenings with our boyfriends," Dora says.

When I don't respond, she nudges me and adds, "Luuc is the perfect boy for you. I can't wait for you to marry him."

I stop.

"You're going too fast." I look at my best friend. "Who says I'm going to marry Luuc?"

"Everybody in town does."

"I can't believe that people talk about . . ."

"There is one problem," Dora interrupts. "When you become Luuc's wife, I can't be your friend anymore because you'll be a member of the upper class."

I grab her arms. "How can you say that? You'll always be my

best friend no matter what class I'm in! We will be best friends forever." I take a deep breath and give her arms a gentle squeeze — her remarks confuse me.

"I hope you're right," she says softly. "We will stay best friends . . . forever and ever."

I drop my hands, and while I contemplate Dora's words, we continue our walk to the vestry. This is the building we're using until the church is rebuilt. She opens the door into the cloakroom. Winter coats line the walls. The aroma of wood-burning stoves and tobacco, mixed with the smell of farm animals, welcomes us inside. After we hang up our coats and leave our wooden shoes underneath the bench, we walk into the large room where church services, funerals and community meetings are temporarily held. All the drapes covering the small windows have been drawn. The coal stove at the back of the room glows with heat.

"I see him," Dora whispers.

Pretending to ignore Dora's announcement, I peek in the direction of the tall young man with straw-blond hair neatly combed to one side. His head turns toward us, and he winks at me.

Confused, I look away; my face burns. All of Dora's talk about Luuc's social class has further complicated my thoughts. I'm not sure how I feel about Luuc, I'm not sure I want to get married, and I'm definitely not sure I want to join a family who might look down on me.

"Shus," a boy behind me whispers. "Miss Sour Puss is looking right at us."

"Miss Nazi Lover is a better name for her," another adds.

I force myself to focus on Miss Poortvliet, our choir director, who takes her place behind the lectern, a signal for everyone to settle down.

I wonder if Miss Poortvliet heard the derogatory remarks, but if she did, she shows no emotion. In her brown woollen day dress and traditional white lace cap, she looks much older than her early thirties.

"Why don't they leave her alone," I whisper to Dora. "The war ended eight years ago. Hasn't she been punished enough?"

"She should have never fallen in love with a Nazi," Dora replies. "She can't expect people to ever forget what she did."

I shake my head. "I know what Miss Poortvliet did was wrong, but her boyfriend was killed by the Allies. If she loved him, she must be hurting."

"We'll start with the new hymn we practised last week, 'To God Be the Glory,'" Miss Poortvliet announces.

Dora and I both sing soprano, but it's Luuc's voice that fills the room with his deep, rich baritone. Soon I forget the world around me as our voices fill the hall:

"Music carries me away
  from reality,
  my monotonous life,
  chores.
  Just like words in poems,
  the soothing sound
  of the waves
  tossing,
  twirling
  against the dike."

4

Turbulent Thoughts

"I'LL WALK YOU HOME," Luuc says while I put my coat on. My heartbeat quickens. Luuc has talked to me several times after choir practice, but he's never walked me home.

"You'll come for tea on Sunday after church?" Dora says as she opens the door. "Bring your poems."

"I'd love to and I will," I answer.

I see that Rosa has joined Luuc under the streetlight. "We've been waiting for you!" she calls. I don't answer, but I notice my sister's glowing cheeks and sparkling eyes.

"Great choir practice," Luuc says when he takes my arm.

I glance at his profile. His head is tucked deep into his black cap, and when his dark blue eyes meet mine, I feel nervous. What is he thinking? What is he expecting? I've never been kissed. I shiver in my coat. I feel Luuc's arm tightening. Does he know my thoughts?

We don't say much but let the wild wind blow us home. As soon as we get there, Rosa disappears inside.

"Let's get out of the wind," Luuc suggests. "I've been thinking," he says as soon as we find shelter beside the front door. "Now that you and I are an item, we should go steady."

Go steady. What does it mean?

"Then we should get married next May."

"But . . . but I'm only sixteen."

Luuc chuckles. "But you'll be seventeen in October. Almost eighteen by next May! Why wait, Klara?"

"I . . . I . . ." I want to argue that he's moving too fast, but the words refuse to come. It feels like something is blocking my vocal cords. Perspiration trickles down my spine despite the cold evening air.

"Klara, we belong together. I don't know why you're hesitant?" He sounds annoyed.

"Do your parents agree that I'm —"

"My girlfriend?" Luuc finishes the sentence for me. "Oh, they'll come around. Who else can I marry?" he adds. "The farmers in this part of the island have sons my age, no daughters."

Who else can I marry? I can't believe what he just said. If there had been a girl from the upper class, then he wouldn't have picked me?

"We'll be good for each other, and you love children."

His comment makes me cringe. But he isn't finished.

"We can have many children, right? Our farmhouse is huge, and we'll want to fill the rooms. I know you like children. You're always carrying a baby around, and Clasina is like an extension of you." He places his hands on either side of my head, on the wall behind me, trapping me.

His words overwhelm me . . . his assumptions . . . as if I have a choice, carrying babies around.

"We . . . we don't really know each other," I say meekly.

"We'll have the rest of our lives to get to know each other. That's why we should start soon."

My mind starts spinning.

"Time for Luuc to go home!" Father calls from the front door.

"Mr. van Burgh," Luuc calls over his shoulder. "Do I have your permission to visit Klara Saturday nights?"

"Yes," Father answers in his usual curt voice.

"I . . . have to go inside." I worry that he's going to kiss me, and I don't know if I —

Luuc's face comes closer and without warning his mouth lands hard on my lips. His kiss lasts and lasts. He smells of cows and hay, and I taste pipe tobacco. I feel a strong urge to twist away, but as if he knows what I'm thinking, he increases the pressure and his teeth crush my lips.

My heart pounds wildly, and my brain reels. When he finally pulls back, I stumble and gasp for air.

"See you Saturday night, my Klara."

The wind blocks out the sound of his footsteps and takes away his smell, his taste and his voice.

I hang onto the door handle and rest my head against the door. My tongue tastes the blood on my lips. My eyes well up. My heart beats wildly in an uneven rhythm. My Klara! He acts as if he owns me already.

I fumble with the buttons on my coat and stay in the mudroom, pondering Luuc's words. Wasn't this exactly what the teachers at school had prepared me for? To get married and to have many children. . . . I wish I didn't have to face my family right now. Breathing slowly, I compose myself, hang up my coat and enter the kitchen where the warmth of the stove hugs me.

Spirals of smoke from Father's pipe circle his head while he's reading the newspaper. The younger children are in bed. Mother sits at the table mending a pair of trousers. Adriaan works on a jigsaw puzzle — a jungle scene with birds, flowers and animals in exotic colours. Rosa's knitting needles click in an even rhythm as yet another pair of socks grows from her hands. Liesbeth's face is burning, her bottom lip sucked in. I watch her struggle to keep the stitches on the needles.

Max snores in the basket beside the stove. One of his ears hangs over the edge.

As I pick up the sock I've been working on from the knitting basket on the table, I can't stop the trembling of my hands.

The wind howls, and the coals make settling sounds in the stove. The ticking of the grandfather clock accompanies these sounds in our otherwise quiet kitchen. I take a deep breath, glad nobody is talking, and even though I can feel Rosa's eyes scrutinizing my face, I focus on my knitting.

"Klara, pour the tea, please." Mother's weary eyes meet mine, and for an instant, I wonder if she knows of the turmoil going on in my head? My hand trembles, and I spill tea into the saucers.

"I wonder if there's a dike watch tonight?" Adriaan looks up from his puzzle.

"We saw two men walking in the direction of the quay," Rosa answers. She stares at me, but I avoid her gaze.

"They must have put up the flashboards," Adriaan adds.

"Do you mean those wooden boards in the openings of the dike, right in town?" Liesbeth asks.

"They only close those openings when they worry that the water level is going to be too high, like when there's a storm," Adriaan explains.

"But will the flashboards stop the water from coming into town?"

"The regulating gate is made with horizontal wooden planks. It can prevent the water from coming over the dike into town, right Father?" Adriaan asks.

"You're right, Adriaan." Father folds the newspaper. "But we should be all right. It's not spring tide until Saturday night, when there's a full moon."

"Let's hope we won't have a storm at the same time." Mother's face shows many worry lines.

Slowly, I drink my tea, washing away the taste of my first kiss.

Nine chimes signal bedtime for my family.

I tuck in Martin and Jacob when I get upstairs. They always seem to wrestle with the blankets before falling asleep.

Adriaan's bed is placed against the wall. Open shelves hold the boys' clothes, sheets and blankets. On the top shelf, Adriaan keeps his model sailboats. He has spent hours building the vessels out of tiny pieces of wood.

Pieces of driftwood have been added to the shelf by Martin and Jacob.

Two framed black and white pen drawings of a clipper and a schooner adorn the wall opposite the open shelves.

I look at the two small skylights near the bottom of the sloped roof and remind myself that I need to sew curtains when I have a spare moment. Father has already nailed two curtain rods above the windows.

After I close the door of my small refuge, I change into my

flannel nightgown but keep my woollen stockings on. The small lamp on my nightstand casts a soft light. I close the blue curtains and hop under the covers on my double bed. I pull the quilted blue and white striped blanket that Oma made up to my chin. Brrr . . . I should've prepared a hot water bottle.

While the wind rattles the tiles on the roof, Luuc's words come back to me. If it is God's will and we are destined for each other, then I have no choice but to marry him. That's what my family, everybody in town and even Dora expect me to do. But the thought of marriage feels like a jail sentence.

"Dear Lord," I whisper, then pause to search for the right words. "If it is your will that I marry Luuc and stay on this island, then . . . please make sure we don't have many children. Five is plenty. Luuc seems to think . . . but he's wrong. His mother bore three children, Dora's mother had five, Oma had three, but my mother . . ." I feel sick with worry when I think about my mother. I roll into a tight ball and pull the covers up to my chin.

"Please, Lord, look after Mother. She's so frail. I'm so afraid to lose her. And I'm so confused about my feelings for Luuc. . . ."

Tears choke my voice when I whisper, "Amen."

I turn onto my back. The breeze blows through the gaps in the tiled roof above me. Even the curtain that covers my skylight moves slightly. I'm too upset to sleep so I get up to write in my notebook.

One big question keeps coming back to me. Luuc's kiss . . . wasn't I supposed to like it? Dora can't stop talking about kissing Bas. It makes her float up to heaven. My first kiss didn't promise anything I had imagined. Slowly my emotions make their way from my heart to paper:

A kiss holds a promise,
a yearning for more.
The heartbeat quickens.
The body becomes weightless,
afloat.

The alarm startles me, but I don't want to get up from my warm cocoon. It's still dark, and I can hear the wind howling, rattling the roof tiles. I switch on the lamp on my nightstand. Digging my clothes from under the blankets, I quickly dress in my underskirt, woollen day dress and apron. The cardigan that Oma knit for me last winter hugs my body. From the built-in closet, I grab a triangular shawl, which I fasten with a silver brooch designed in the traditional Zeeuwse knot. I make the bed before I dip the face-cloth into the freezing water in the bowl on the washstand and hurriedly wash. A tired face stares back at me from the gilt-framed mirror above the washstand.

Beside the washstand is my dresser. A picture of me when I was younger, holding baby Clasina on my lap, sits beside the jewellery box and my hairbrush. I pick up the brush and start pulling at my tangled mass of unruly curls. "Ouch!" I cry. No wonder Father always makes comments about my hair. It looks like the untidy nest of a raven. Curls always jump out, even when I secure them with hairpins and tuck them under my lace cap.

I glance longingly at the shelf above my dresser, which holds my treasured collection of three books. These books, by Dutch poets Joost van denVondel, Adriaan Roland Holst and Bertus Aafjes, were gifts from my Aunt Neeltje, who shares my love for poetry. I keep my notebooks with my own poems in the bottom drawer of my dresser. How I wish I had time to curl up in one of the armchairs beside the stove and read. I'd love to lose myself in the music of the language of others. But my chores are waiting, and I tuck away my yearning thoughts.

When I leave my room, I find Martin and Jacob in a deep sleep, but Adriaan's bed is empty. He's already down in the cow stable helping Father and Piet milk the cows.

Downstairs, I tend to the stove in the kitchen, grab a bowl and a large spoon from the shelf above the sink, then go down to the cellar. My breath floats out in puffs in the cold air. I glance at the shelves that line the walls. The top ones that hold the canned produce from last year's vegetable garden are getting bare.

From a large tub, I skim the cream off the milk, carry the bowl upstairs to the kitchen, pour the cream into a glass bottle and start shaking until the heavy cream turns into butter.

In the meantime, Rosa sets the breakfast table.

As soon as I hear Mother's voice accompanied by the babble of the little ones, I pour the tea and spread fresh butter and brown sugar on open sandwiches for the little ones.

Rosa butters slices of bread and adds cold cuts for her lunch at school.

The door opens and Clasina rushes into the kitchen and wraps her arms around my legs. "Mm . . . bread with sugar." She smacks her lips.

Neeltje and Sara mimic their sister making smacking sounds.

"Don't spoil the girls so much," Mother reprimands, but her face shows a weak smile.

"Here's your tea." I move my mother's armchair closer to the stove.

"Now you're spoiling me."

With a loud commotion, Martin and Jacob barrel into the

kitchen and, like every morning, argue about who will be first at school today. Liesbeth enters, rubbing the sleep from her eyes.

A few minutes later, Father and Adriaan enter the kitchen. Instantly, the kitchen is filled with the sound of scraping chairs, clattering cutlery and voices all trying to make themselves heard.

"We pray first!" Father's voice silences the early morning chatter as he opens the Bible.

"This is from Deuteronomy, chapter twenty-six, verse seventeen. 'Thou hast avouched the LORD this day to be thy God, and to walk in his ways, and to keep his statutes and his commandments, and his judgments, and to hearken to his voice.'"

Soon my thoughts drift away from my father's droning voice praying for obedience to God.

"Klara! Your hair!" Father's sharp words bring me back to the harsh reality of the kitchen, and I tuck the escaped strands under my lace cap.

Rain and wind batter us for the rest of the week. By Saturday, the rain has moved on, but the strong wind decides to stay.

"Will you see Luuc at Bible study, tonight?" Rosa asks while I put on my coat.

"I think so," I answer.

"It must be so exciting to be in love." Rosa's cheeks turn pink.

I don't answer but leave the mudroom, walk down through the barn and find my bike in the machine shed.

Remembering the kiss and Luuc's words about marriage and babies makes me nervous.

"Here," says Dora as she points at the chair beside her when I enter the room in the vestry. Many young people have already arrived, but I don't see Luuc.

When Miss Poortvliet reads to us from the Bible, she mentions that God is loving, that his word is powerful, sovereign, but also reasonable and loving.

Those words give me hope, but before I can reflect, a commotion at the door makes me turn.

Luuc walks in and finds a seat at the back of the room.

5

Oma

"I'LL TAKE YOU HOME," Luuc says after Bible study.

"Oma isn't well. I'm going to see her," I say quickly.

"But it's Saturday night!"

"I know."

"Tomorrow afternoon, then!" He sounds impatient.

"Sunday afternoons I always visit with Dora," I say, knowing well that I'm pushing my boundaries. "We'll have lots of time to visit."

"You think you can change the rules whenever you feel like it?" His eyes narrow into slits. "Once we're married you'll have to obey your husband — the Bible says so!"

"We're not married!" I hear myself say. I've been taught to never talk back; this is the first time and I feel terrible, but what he says next makes me feel worse.

"Temper! Temper!" Luuc spits. "It's that red hair of yours! Time someone reined you in!" He stomps away, leaving me standing on the cobblestones. My face is on fire.

When Dora catches up with me, she asks, "What's with your flushed face? Did you and Luuc already have your first fight?"

I look away. "It's . . . nothing."

She stares at me. "I'm your best friend. No secrets, remember!"

I wish I had Dora's confidence. She never questions anything. That's what I like about her.

"No secrets," I say softly.

Dora's eyes sparkle when she talks about her Bas. Why can't I be like her?

"Klara, do you think it's a sin that I enjoy kissing so much that it's the only thing I can think of?"

"You like being kissed?" I answer with a question.

"Don't you?" Dora's eyes narrow. "What aren't you telling me?"

I feel cornered. "If you must know, I don't like it when Luuc kisses me."

There, I've said it.

"But Klara, Luuc is amazing. Every girl in the area envies you!" Dora's face clouds over with disappointment.

"Maybe I haven't tried hard enough," I say quickly. "Forget I said that."

"You're not in love with Luuc?"

"I don't know." I look at my shoes. "I need to see Oma."

"You're destined to marry him. Remember, if you don't love your husband at first, you might learn to love him over time."

"Might?" I repeat. "You believe that?"

"Don't question everything. Accept what comes your way!" With those words, she turns and walks down the street in the direction of her home.

I watch her go and worry. If Dora tells her mother, soon

everyone in town will know and then Luuc will find out, too. I should've kept my thoughts to myself. But Dora is my best friend. *Best friends have no secrets.*

A movement behind one of the lace curtains of a nearby house reminds me that in a town of six hundred, not much stays secret, even when the curtains on the windows are drawn.

I shiver in my warm coat, then hurry to Oma's house. Her street is off the Ring Dike, closer to the harbour. The streetlights on Juliana Street guide me to Oma's place. Lights in the windows depict a picture-perfect street with gabled houses on either side. Here, the windows are washed every Friday, stoops scrubbed on Saturday mornings and clotheslines billow with laundry on Mondays.

When I stop in front of my grandmother's house, I notice that there is no light coming through her window, and the curtains are open. I hang up my coat and shawl in the hallway and enter the front room. I'm surprised how much light comes in from the street.

I look at the bedstead at the back of the room and meet Oma's warm smile.

"Why are you in bed?" I turn on the light and close the heavy velour curtains. "It's cold in here!" I shiver.

"That's why I'm in bed. I couldn't get the stove going. The drawer is full of ashes."

"Let me fix that."

After emptying the tray outside, I open the door to the coal shed and fill up the shuttle. Back in the front room, I start a fire, and it doesn't take long for the stove to start purring. Soon, the room feels warm and cozy. Next I go into the kitchen to make tea.

"I'm so glad you came," Oma says when I return.

I grab my grandmother's arthritic hands and rub them gently until they feel warmer.

I check the stove once more before my eyes travel to the black and white photographs that line the mantel. The first one shows Queen Juliana in full regalia. It was taken in 1948 during her coronation.

Oma keeps a scrapbook that holds photos of the royal family. That's why ten-year-old Liesbeth loves coming to Oma. The two of them share pictures about the royals. I can't resist a smile when I look at the photograph of Princess Beatrix holding baby Margriet in her lap while her sister, Irene, stands beside her. The photo was taken during the war when the Royal family had fled to Canada. I still find it so amazing that the government of Canada granted the room at the hospital in Ottawa extraterritorial rights, so that the new princess would be born Dutch and not Canadian.

I pick up the family photo of Oma, Opa, Aunt Neeltje, Father, Uncle Hendrik and their white dog, Kees.

"Did Father always look so stern when he was young?" I ask. I notice that Uncle Hendrik has a big smile that reaches his eyes. The more I look at his face, the more I feel like smiling back at him.

"Yes," Oma interrupts my thoughts. "Neeltje and Jannes were the two serious children, but Hendrik's mischief got him into trouble more times than I like to remember."

"Poor Neeltje." Suddenly, Oma is overwhelmed with grief, telling me again that when I was little Aunt Neeltje lost her husband and her two boys, aged four and two, to tuberculosis. She blows her nose several times before she tucks her hanky into the sleeve of her day dress.

I often think how sad Aunt Neeltje's life is. She lives on the mainland in a flat, all alone. Twice a year she visits us. I understand why Oma is so sad for her and grieves for her two lost grandsons.

I change the subject. "Father never talks about Hendrik. Why did he go to America?"

I put the picture back before I get the tea.

When I return, Oma is standing in front of the stove, the photograph in her hands. "When they got older, they didn't get along," she says. "Jannes was jealous of Hendrik. Hendrik sometimes took life with a grain of salt." Oma leans forward and studies the faces. "Jannes was going to inherit the farm, as is the birthright of the oldest son. That responsibility weighed heavily upon him." She places the photograph back on the mantel. "That picture was taken long ago. Where did the time go?" She sits down in one of the two armchairs in front of the stove.

I hand her a cup of tea. "I wish I'd known Opa and Uncle Hendrik."

"They probably could have worked the farm together after Opa died if they hadn't gotten into a big fight. That's when Hendrik decided to try his luck in America. He left on a ship. For months, I never heard from him. . . ." The teacup rattles in the saucer. Oma's eyes fill.

I take the cup and saucer from her. "You must miss him. What was the big fight about?"

Oma wipes her eyes and nods.

"Jannes has a temper. The two brothers were so different." Oma shakes her head. We drink our tea, my mind overflowing with thoughts of Uncle Hendrik in faraway America and how different the land must be from our island.

"Mother and Father will take you to church tomorrow morning," I say, topping up the stove once more before I leave. Then I think of Oma all alone once I'm gone. "Will you live with us? We can look after you and you won't be so lonely."

"I'm not lonely, Klara," Oma answers. "The Lord keeps me company."

On my way home I look up at the night sky, which is lit with a million stars. I raise my arm, point at the sky and say in a clear voice:

"Imagine if I were a star,
I'd watch every ocean,
the north and
south pole,
the continents.
I'd check on Uncle Hendrik,
let Oma know how he is doing."

6

Chilling Sermon

THE NEXT MORNING, my parents load up the old station wagon with the older children to attend church, like they do every Sunday morning. Clasina, Martin and Jacob love to go as they get to colour pictures, listen to stories and sing songs.

I change and feed Neeltje and Sara and entertain them by singing hymns while I peel the potatoes for the midday meal.

After the noon meal, Rosa and Liesbeth and I leave for the afternoon service. We walk because Father thinks it's sinful to ride our bicycles on Sundays. In the morning, my sisters helped Miss Kievit with Sunday school activities, which are held in a small room at the back of the vestry.

"You're so quiet, Klara," Liesbeth says.

"I miss school. You two have so much to talk about, but my days are filled with chores. I wish I could go back to school and study languages."

"What for?" Rosa pipes up. "It's just a waste for us girls to study."

I keep my thoughts inside. There must be something wrong with me because not even my own sisters understand.

"You're such a dreamer," Rosa turns toward me. "It's not healthy. You should dream about Luuc instead of those crazy studies," she adds.

Best not to respond, I think, and without talking, we follow more parishioners to the vestry.

The room has been set up with rows of chairs. I look at a painting on the wall depicting our church before it was destroyed. The tower with its spire stands proudly against a blue sky.

Dora and her mother approach us. I watch my friend closely, remembering our discussion from last night.

"You're coming for tea, right?" Dora asks as soon as she sits down.

Relief warms my thoughts.

The room fills up quickly, and Miss Poortvliet plays a familiar hymn on the organ. Even though I like the sound, I can still remember the large pipe organ in the church. The rich sounds made me dream of distant places.

As soon as the minister takes his place behind the lectern, the congregation falls silent.

The Reverend Potter is a tall, skinny man in his late fifties with a bald head and black-rimmed glasses. I've never seen the man smile, and I'm certain he is convinced that all the people of New Port are sinners and evildoers.

"We'll start this afternoon with Psalm 69," he begins. In his dark voice, he shouts, "Save me, O God, for the waters have come up to my neck! I sink in deep mire, where there is no foothold, where the floods overflow me." He lifts his gaze and scans the congregation.

I shiver and look at Dora. Her expression is serious.

"'I am weary with my crying. My throat is dry. My eyes fail looking for my God.'" The minister's words fill the room with dread. I stare at the hymn book in my lap.

"I have strained my eyes, looking for help." Reverend Potter waves his arms as if to draw attention to his plight.

His voice becomes loud and intimidating as he yells, "'God, you know my foolishness. My sins aren't hidden from you.'"

People shift uncomfortably. Chairs scrape on the wooden floor.

"Let us pray," the minister says in a much softer voice. "Let us ask for forgiveness."

I take deep breath and realize I had been holding it.

"'O Lord, don't punish me. I will confess my sins to you; I will not conceal my wrongdoings, and you will forgive me all my sins.'"

He pauses to catch his breath. "'We will pray and confess our sins. Please forgive us, LORD. We will pray to you in times of need and when we are in trouble. We trust in you LORD. You are our refuge. We sing of your salvation, because you protect us.'"

"Amen," my voice quivers.

After the service, Rosa and Liesbeth walk home. I watch my sisters. They giggle about something and don't seem to be bothered by the reverend's words. But they weigh heavily on my shoulders.

"That was a depressing sermon," Dora's mother says as we walk down the street to their house. "For heaven's sake, who wants to think about flooding and drowning? We've barely recovered from the war. And the people to the east of us are still suffering the consequences of the controlled flooding that the Germans inflicted."

"God will protect us as long as we ask for help and confess our sins." Dora touches her mother's arm.

"I agree, but his words scare me," I add.

Mrs. Timmer looks at me. "Those words scare me, too, Klara."

The large family kitchen at Dora's house is warm and cozy, and I inhale the smell of burning wood and baked goods. Her three younger brothers crowd around the kitchen table, waiting for a slice of cake.

Dora's mother shoos them away from the table. "Wash your hands at the pump."

The three of them scramble to the sink, fighting each other to be first. After they've washed their hands, Dora hands them each a plate. *Jan, Kees and Teun are the spitting image of Dora's father*, I think, *whereas Dora and her older brother, Simon, look like their mother*. Mrs. Timmer is known for her laughter, homemade cakes and pastries and gossip. People come for coffee and the latest news, which Dora gladly passes on to me.

"Let's go to the front room," Dora whispers when we've finished our tea and a slice of the most delicious spiced raisin cake. "The boys are such pests."

"I can't stay long," I remind her. "My chores are waiting."

The front room at Dora's house is bright due to the large windows. I love the lace curtains her oma crocheted. They show a pattern of sailboats at the bottom.

Along the wall sits the family's organ, which Dora and her father both play. I wish I could play an instrument.

Dora closes the door. I sit down beside the organ, and Dora walks over to the bench.

"Did you bring your poems?" she asks.

I nod. "Please play something first," I beg.

Dora turns and faces me. "What did you mean last night when you said you didn't know if you loved Luuc?"

I fold my hands in my lap. "I don't know what I am supposed to feel."

"You shouldn't question it. You should accept life the way it's presented to you. Luuc has been presented to you. So accept it," my friend insists.

"You sound exactly like our teachers. Don't you ever long to be something other than a wife and mother?"

"Don't tell me you're still having dreams about travelling? You need to stop those thoughts. They're ridiculous." Dora gets up and raises her arms and sits down again. "All right, let's sing the hymn 'God Gives His People Strength.'"

I read the words from the hymnbook while Dora plays. The rich sounds of the organ accompanied by our soprano voices liven up the room.

"That song helps us feel better after today's gloomy sermon." Dora smiles at me. "Now it's your turn to read me a poem."

"Remember that Sunday afternoon last summer when we were laying in the field, and it was sprinkled with meadow daisies?"

"I do," Dora says. "We looked at the clouds and turned them into princes on horses."

I nod and open my notebook:

Friends,
lying on our backs,
we watch clouds sail by.
A whale,
two dolphins
and an elephant
drift overhead.
Next,

a castle,
two handsome young men,
smiling down at us.
Giddy with anticipation,
our hearts beating,
we dream of
princes
taking us away
on cloud-white steeds.

Dora claps her hands. "You are so talented. I wish I could write like you."

"But you're so good at playing the organ, and I wish I could play like you." I close the book.

"We were so romantic." Dora places her hand on her heart. "We were dreaming of our princes, and look at us now, we both found our prince. I found Bas and you found Luuc."

"I don't think I found Luuc," I answer. "I think he found me."

"But he is the prince of your dreams, right?" Dora's eyes scrutinize my face.

"I'm not sure yet." I don't know if I can explain my doubts, and I stare at the window. I try to think of some way to fill the silence. "How was your Saturday night?"

Dora's face flushes, and I notice the red mark on her neck.

With sparkling eyes, she says, "I hope I'll be forgiven, but when Bas kisses me, I feel like I'm in heaven, and I never want to leave."

So much for changing the subject. I wring my hands in my lap. "I really don't like it when Luuc calls me *my* Klara. It makes me feel like I'm his property."

Disbelief floods Dora's face. "First you belong to your parents, and when you marry you belong to your husband. It's so simple."

"It doesn't feel simple to me," I say softly. "Do you ever question God's ways?"

"What!" My friend's eyes turn dark. She stands up and looks down at me. "You question God?"

"It's not that I'm questioning God," I say, "but I'm confused about everything I have to accept. I don't know where I'm heading. Unlike you, I don't find life simple."

Dora wraps her arms around me. "You make life too complicated. Just accept and follow, and it'll all work out. And . . . God knows the journey you need to take before you do."

"I wish I had your confidence." I sigh loudly.

Dora shakes her head and stands up. "Can you believe that Princess Beatrix is going to turn fifteen on Saturday? Just imagine the kind of dress she's going to wear." Longing shines from her eyes. "Not the drab dress I'm wearing." She looks down at her navy blue Sunday dress. "Women on the mainland wear the latest fashion. Colourful fabrics and beautiful styles. No one wears traditional costumes like us. You must come with us, Klara!"

"I wish." I sigh. "But my father has made up his mind that everything off the island is evil, and I can't ever change his mind."

"Not that my mother lets me buy colourful dresses." Dora looks wistful.

"But at least you get to choose your dresses. I have to wait till the peddler comes and choose fabric from his boring selection."

When the clock downstairs strikes four, I get up.

Dora follows me. "Don't question everything. Accept, remember."

She's probably right. I ponder my friend's words all the way home. Why can't I feel like Dora? Why don't I find life simple?

Suddenly the words pop into my head:

I know somewhere there is a window.
Through that window shines a light,
but it's too high for me to reach;
for now
it is beyond my sight.

7

High Tide

THE SHUTTERS RATTLE. Upstairs the beams creak, and the roof tiles clatter in the storm on this last day of January.

During the evening meal, the little ones chatter while they eat their bread, but my parents and the rest of us listen to the whistles and howls of the wind.

"We learned in school that when the sun and the moon are in one line, and it's a full moon, the two work together and cause a spring tide," Adriaan says.

"A strong northwestern storm at the same time will blow the water from the North Sea in our direction." Father adds, "It becomes dangerous." He turns on the radio. "Let's listen to the weather report."

I stop eating as the newsreader warns about a strong northwestern wind with gusts up to one hundred and forty kilometres an hour.

"That's a hurricane!" Adriaan cries.

My heart skips a beat.

The voice continues. "The Ministry of Waterways and Public Works issues a warning regarding the spring tide. Water levels could reach higher than normal. Due to the storm, several ships in the North Sea have been experiencing trouble. The life-and-rescue boat *Wilhelmina* has been assisting ships all afternoon."

Mother shudders.

"Will we still go to the wharf tonight?" Adriaan asks.

"After we visit the barber, we'll check the water levels," Father replies.

"Bring Oma back with you," Mother says. "I'll telephone her."

"We will bring some of her clothes, too." Father lifts the heavy kettle with boiling water off the burner and empties it into a large galvanized tub. A screen has been set up around the tub for privacy. After cold water has been added, it's Clasina's turn to take a bath.

"Jacob, you'll be next." Mother points at the boys playing under the table.

"I don't need one. I just took a bath last week," Martin complains.

"Your skin will peel off if you take too many baths, Martin!" Adriaan teases.

The look on Mother's face tells Martin that he has no chance of getting out of this weekly ritual.

"Adriaan, Klara, Rosa, let's tie everything down." Father opens the kitchen door.

Just like in every other storm, we secure windows, shutters and doors and tie down everything that might blow away. Milk pails and cans have already been stored inside.

After Father and Adriaan leave for town and the little ones and

Martin and Jacob have been scrubbed clean and put to bed, Rosa, Liesbeth and I knit socks, and Mother makes tea.

Saturday nights, when it's just the four of us, are my favourite. Sometimes we listen to a radio play or a concert.

"I want to keep the radio on," Mother suggests, "just in case there is an update on the weather and the water levels. It's your turn in the bath, Liesbeth."

"Can we listen to the special program to celebrate Princess Beatrix's birthday?" Liesbeth disappears behind the screen. She feels privileged that she was born on the same day as Princess Margriet, January 19, 1943.

"I'm sure they'll interrupt the program for weather updates, but let me telephone Oma first." Mother dials the number.

"Liesbeth or Rosa will sleep with Klara," she says after she hangs up. "One of you will sleep with Oma and Clasina."

"I'll sleep with you, Klara," Liesbeth calls from behind the screen.

"I'm going to check on Dina." Mother opens the door to the mudroom. "She should've calved by now."

Over the radio, a brass band plays the national anthem, and a children's choir sings "Happy Birthday." A young female voice reads a poem in honour of the oldest princess. But the celebrations can't keep out the sound of the raging storm.

I shiver when I think of all the people who are outside tonight, like the fishermen in their small vessels bobbing on the waves and the men walking the dike on watch. The hurricane winds can easily blow them into the sea.

Mother returns from the cow stable.

"Is Dina in labour?" I ask.

"I'm worried it'll be a breech birth. I must phone the vet on Monday." She picks up her knitting and sits down.

"I wonder what kind of dresses the princesses are wearing?"

Liesbeth has finished her bath and picks up her knitting. "I know that Princess Margriet likes yellow. I'm sure there will be a picture in Monday's paper. Aah, I dropped a stitch!"

"Hold it still," I say. "I'll pick it up for you."

"I hate knitting!" Liesbeth cries. "Why do we always have to knit socks?"

"Because we have so many feet in this family." Mother gets up and strokes Liesbeth's hair.

While Rosa takes her bath, we listen to the voice of the princess thanking everyone who's made her fifteenth birthday so special. Her speech is followed by more music.

I'm the last one in the tub and decide to wash my hair. "Rosa will you rinse out the shampoo?" I ask.

"Hold your head still." She lifts the kettle and slowly pours the water over my long curly mass.

After I dry myself and put clean clothes on, I ask Rosa to help me clean up. First, we fill buckets with the dirty bath water and empty them into the sink. Next, we carry the tub and empty the last of the water. As soon as everything is cleared away, we return to . . . knitting socks.

I listen to a symphony orchestra on the radio and treasure the moment. Suddenly, I remember that Luuc might return with Father and Adriaan, and my happy mood vanishes like snow on a spring day.

Tree branches smack against the side of the house. The curtains are drawn, but I remember the worried look on the face of the full moon when I was outside tying down the shutters.

"Is Luuc coming tonight?" Rosa turns to me.

"I don't know," I answer. I feel nervous. He hadn't walked us home after last Wednesday's choir practice. "Absence makes the heart grow fond," he'd said.

I felt relief at the time but also guilty for feeling relief. That night I prayed I would try to accept Luuc and that a fondness for him would grow in my heart.

When the kitchen door opens, Oma walks inside, assisted by Father and Adriaan.

I get up and help her settle into an armchair. "I'll get you some tea."

"It's bad in town," Father says. "The men are using wood from Mr. Timmer's shop to reinforce the flashboards to hold back the sea."

"How dangerous is it?" Mother's voice sounds anxious.

I pour tea and Rosa cuts the spice cake she baked this afternoon.

"There were so many people at the quay," Adriaan says. "After my haircut I helped fill sandbags."

"People in the barbershop talked about the state of the dikes," Father says. "Since the war ended, the government hasn't done any upgrades, let alone repair them where needed. There are many weak spots."

"That's why we placed the sandbags at the weak spots in the dike," Adriaan adds.

"Do they expect that the water will come over the dike?" I ask.

"Let's hope we will be spared." Father lights his pipe.

A cracking sound tells us that another tree branch has snapped off. I imagine the old apple tree close to the kitchen wall is taking a hard beating.

"I'll never get used to these storms," Oma says.

"Jasper, the old farmer who lives close to the dike, said he noticed this afternoon that the water in the well in his field was bubbling up, and he'd never seen anything like it," says Adriaan.

His words worry me.

"As long as the dikes don't breach." Rosa hugs herself.

"God willing, we'll be safe." Father looks around the table. "One of the ferry captains said that the water in the Oosterschelde was muddy and full of debris. The last ferry ran at four this afternoon. It had trouble mooring due to the high water levels." He looks at the closed curtains and shakes his head.

"We should bring some important stuff upstairs," Mother suggests. "Just in case."

"It wouldn't hurt," Father answers. "Girls, Adriaan, take flashlights and the oil lamp that's in the cupboard in the mudroom in case we lose the electricity. Bring blankets and some food upstairs."

"What about the little ones?" I wonder.

Mother's hands rest on her belly. "Take them upstairs, too," she says in a choking voice.

In a rare tender gesture, Father rubs her shoulders, then sits down and resumes his smoking.

While Oma talks about the floods of 1906 and 1911, I get blankets and sheets from the front room. Adriaan carries the small oil stove. Rosa holds a kettle and two flashlights.

Liesbeth fills a pail of water from the pump and grabs another bucket "to do our business in."

I collect jars of food from the cellar. *Thank goodness, we will always have fresh milk*, I think.

We take all the goods upstairs. Liesbeth turns on the light and looks at Martin and Jacob. "I can't believe the boys don't wake up."

"We'll move them over, so Clasina, Neeltje and Sara can sleep in the bed with them," I tell her.

Half an hour later, everything we can think of is upstairs,

including coats and boots for everyone. The little ones hardly stir when they exchange their trundle for the bed upstairs.

"Adriaan, let's check on the animals. They were restless when we came home." Father gets up. Max follows them out into the stable.

The grandfather clock chimes ten, but no one gets up to go to bed.

"What do we do when the dike breaches?" Liesbeth asks, panic in her voice.

"We all go upstairs." Mother answers.

"I hope that won't happen." Rosa clears away the knitting basket.

"The sea has powers no one can stop," I remind her.

The ringing of the phone startles us. Mother motions me to answer.

"Van Burgh," I say, surprised the telephone is still working. "Yes, Luuc, we're all right. . . . Where are you? . . . No! Cut the animals loose? But . . . where will they go? . . . In the dark? . . . I'll let my father know," I whisper. Tears fill my eyes when I hang up.

"Luuc's in town. He's at the telephone office. He's letting all the farmers who have a telephone know how bad the situation is. He says the water's already higher than the flood-line mark."

I swallow a lump in my throat. "People predict . . . the dike won't hold."

"What about the animals?" Mother asks.

"He said we should cut them loose and open the doors, so . . . they can get out. And if we can take them to the dike, we should." I can hardly speak the words. "But the animals won't see anything in the dark."

"They won't leave the warm stable," Mother says. "I'm thinking of Dina, who still hasn't calved. We won't do anything until Father and Adriaan come back from the cow stable.

"Liesbeth, you go to bed. You're ready to fall off the chair. I'm going to see if we can put Dina in the pen with the calves. She seemed restless when I checked on her earlier tonight."

I'm glad Mother sounds a little like her old self, giving orders and being in charge.

"I should have brought my photographs," Oma says. "I'm grateful I'm wearing my double string of red coral beads that Opa gave me for our engagement." She fingers the necklace.

We sit quietly until Mother returns. "Dina is too agitated to give birth," she says.

"My house will be swallowed by the sea." Oma dabs her eyes. "It's so close to the dike."

"Let's pray it won't come to that," Mother says. "I'm sure the men will do everything they can to protect the dike."

"Will you come to bed?" Liesbeth stands at the door.

"Yes," I answer. "I'll bring the jewellery box upstairs."

"Bring the money safe from the cabinet as well." Mother leans against the table.

I carry the jewellery case and the metal box that holds money and important documents upstairs. By the time I'm back in the kitchen, Father and Adriaan enter, followed by Max.

Poor dog. I watch him pacing back and forth, whining.

"It's terrible out there," Father says. "It's even worse since we came home."

"Luuc is contacting every farmer in the area to tell them to cut loose the animals and take them to the dike," I say. "They predict that the dike will breach."

"No," Father says. "We won't cut them loose. The animals won't even go outside. I'll stay up and keep watch. Go to bed. I'll call if I need your help."

Adriaan and I trudge upstairs and Mother joins Rosa and Oma in the front room.

Liesbeth is fast asleep, but she hasn't left much room for me in the bed. I squeeze in beside her but keep my clothes on just in case. I close my eyes and pray.

"Please, God . . . calm this horrible storm. . . . Turn it into a breeze . . . or light wind, so men and animals will be safe. . . . If only we can survive the night . . . at least by morning we'll be able to see what's happening. . . . Amen."

8

First Night

AN ENORMOUS CRASH catapults me out of bed. I hit the floor and for an instant I'm confused. Then I remember the water. The wind, sounding like a freight train roaring by, hurtles branches or other debris against our house. My room is pitch black, but I realize that Sunday morning has arrived.

I open my bedroom door and walk across the boys' room. The hallway light is still on and spreads a dim light that reaches the second floor. For a few seconds, I watch the little ones sleeping, unaware of the racket outside, then hurry down the stairs and into the kitchen. Father is asleep, his head on the table.

"Father!" I cry. "Something crashed!"

He lifts his head, looks at me for a second, his eyes not yet focused. Suddenly, he shoots up from his chair. "What time is it?"

The hands on the grandfather clock show five minutes to five.

"The animals!" he yells. "Call Adriaan! It's time for milking."

I rush back upstairs to wake Adriaan. "Time to milk the cows!" I shake his shoulder when he doesn't respond.

"How's the storm?" Adriaan murmurs.

"Bad." I don't wait for him but run back down and hurry into the mudroom. Father follows me. At the cellar door I pause. "Listen — running water?"

When my father opens the door, I gasp. Water gushes into the cellar through the broken window.

I want to go down to save some of our food, but Father holds me back. "We need to cut the animals loose, now!"

"What about milking them first?" Adriaan has come downstairs and he grabs Father's arm.

Father shakes his head.

"I'll get Rosa." I bolt into the front room to wake my sister, who shares the bedstead with Oma.

Armed with knives from the kitchen, Rosa and I rush into the cow stable where we are met by lowing cattle, nervously stepping back and forth in their stalls.

Max barks and runs ahead to the door but returns moments later, whimpering.

Father has cut loose some cows already. The poor animals look at us, their eyes rolling in confusion. They have no idea what to do and even when my father pushes them out of the stalls, they turn around and walk back in.

I quickly run to Dina's stall. She still hasn't calved. I know Mother worries that she might have a problem. It's a challenge to cut Dina's ropes, as she is too nervous to stand still. I caress her head and murmur soothing words, but she doesn't seem to hear me.

"How will we find them for milking?" Adriaan shouts when

the last cow has been freed. Most animals stay in their spot; only some step out onto the path that runs behind the stalls.

My brother forces one of the doors open in the cow stable, but the wind immediately blows it closed.

"They'll stay around!" Father yells at us. "Did you see Piet out there?"

"No!" Adriaan shouts back. "I couldn't see a thing before the door closed."

The two Belgian horses whinny and snort, their bodies trembling. Father and Adriaan try to calm the two giants while setting them free.

"What about Dorus?" Adriaan watches the steer thrashing and pulling his chain.

"He can't be loose," Father calls out. "Too dangerous!"

The twelve yearlings, last year's calves, tramp around, mooing.

"What about the calves?" I call. Their eyes are rolling and showing the whites.

"Just open the gate!" Father yells.

As I run to the calves' pen, I can see the chickens flap all over their enclosure, feathers flying. I open the wire door, but they stay inside.

I feel like I'm in a madhouse with the wind roaring and the animals howling. A primal scream coming from the barn doors chills me to the bone and makes me look up. It's Adriaan.

"Noooo!" he screams again.

I race to join him. Together, we look down in horror as the water, which has entered the barn, covers our wooden shoes.

"What now!" I cry.

Father comes running. Immediately, the water reaches his ankles. "Wake everybody and send them upstairs!"

I don't remember running into the front room. Panic has caught me in its grip. "Water! Everybody upstairs!"

Mother and Oma collect winter coats and blankets before heading to the second floor.

I run into the kitchen, where Father tries the telephone — no connection. The lines are down. The lights are still on, but it's only a matter of time before we'll lose power.

A heaviness I've never felt before presses on my chest. I take a deep breath and follow Father. He opens the door into the barn and water rushes inside the mudroom. As he tries to close the door, the strong current pushes the door wide open.

Defeated, he follows me down the hall and up the stairs to the second floor.

When I look back I see water flowing down the hall, reaching the first tread. The storm blasts and rages, but I'm relieved that everyone is upstairs.

Liesbeth comes out of my room, rubbing her eyes. "Why is everyone up here?"

"The downstairs is flooded," Mother answers. She and Oma, wearing their coats, are sitting on Adriaan's bed, and Mother tucks blankets around herself and Oma. "We'll be warmer if we cuddle together."

Standing at the top of the stairs, I watch in astonishment as the water rushes up to the second tread.

Behind me I hear Oma praying, but I doubt if those words to God will help keep the water at bay.

"Max! Where is Max?" Adriaan comes to stand beside me and in the next instant rushes down the stairs, and I hear him sloshing through the water in the hallway. Standing on the third tread to keep my feet dry, I peer around the corner of the stairway into the hall and see him enter the mudroom. The light bulb on the ceiling dances, casting a bouncing light on the rippling water. Wooden shoes float down the hall, together with a bucket and Sara's porcelain doll.

I watch Adriaan wade through the mudroom, only to be met by a wave of water pushing him back.

"Max! Max!" He hollers.

"Maybe Max is in the kitchen!" I yell.

"No, I just checked. He's not in there!" Adriaan cries. "I have to save Max!"

"Don't, Adriaan. It's not safe down there!" But he ignores my words. Fighting the current, he disappears into the barn.

I run back up to the second floor. "Father, help us. We need to save Max! Adriaan went back into the barn to look for him."

"No!" Father yells. "It's too dangerous — the water is too strong. The dog will find a dry place, but Adriaan won't." He takes off his coat, and in a few strides he crosses the room and runs down the stairs.

From the staircase, I watch him slog along the hallway and into the mudroom before he also disappears into the barn.

"Adriaan! Father!" But the churning water swallows my voice. I watch in terror as the angry water submerges the fourth tread, like a sea monster clawing its way up the stairs.

"Father! Adriaan!" I call even louder. My eyes peer into the murky water, but all I see is straw, a bucket and a broom. "Adriaan! Father!" I scream at the top of my lungs and debate if I should follow them.

The water swirls and gurgles. What if Father can't find Adriaan? What if Adriaan . . . ?

A hand touches my shoulder. Mother pushes me down on the stairs and sits down beside me.

"Father will find him," she says in a shaky voice.

"Please, please let them come back." I grab my mother's hand. Panic almost chokes me.

High-pitched screams pierce the air. Adriaan? Father? Then it hits me — it's the cries of panicking animals. My stomach heaves.

"Oh, dear God!" Mother cries. "Poor animals!" She covers her face with her hands.

I crane my neck until I spot a movement at the door. "FATHER! ADRIAAN!"

My father labours through the rising water, carrying Adriaan's still body in his arms.

"Is . . . is he dead?" I call while Mother and I move back up the stairs.

Father climbs the stairs, wavers and almost loses his balance. Stumbling, he makes it to the second floor, where he drops Adriaan. He leans against the wall to catch his breath.

Mother is on her knees on the floor beside Adriaan. At that moment my brother starts coughing, choking, spitting, releasing the trapped water inside of him.

Suddenly, Father seizes his arms and lifts him up. He shakes him. "You could've drowned!" he says in a trembling voice. "Oh, God." Father drops my brother and covers his face with both hands.

I get towels from my room, hand one to my father, while Mother uses the other one to rub Adriaan dry. "Get out of your wet clothes. Both of you!"

"I couldn't find Max," Adriaan sobs.

"I'm so sorry." Mother's eyes fill.

I grab underwear, pants and a sweater for my brother from the shelf beside his bed and hand my father a pair of pyjamas that are too big on Adriaan.

After Mother helps Adriaan dress, she tucks him in under the blankets, using part of the bed that she shares with Oma.

Father puts his coat on and takes off his trousers and underwear before he dresses in Adriaan's pyjama bottoms. After he changes, he walks over to one of the skylights.

I grab my winter coat, wrap myself in a blanket and settle on the floor, leaning against the bed. Sitting in this spot, I can keep an eye on the stairs. I wonder how high the water is going to rise. While I listen to the bellowing wind, rushing waters and the thrashing sounds coming from downstairs, I feel numb with worry and stare into nothingness.

I must have dozed off.

A thundering sound wakes me. My body feels stiff and cold, and I slowly stand up. The hall light is off. We've lost power. The room is shrouded in a greyish light that tells me it's still early. After my eyes adjust, I check on my family.

Martin lays on the edge of the double bed, with Jacob curled up beside him. Sara has wriggled to the foot of the bed and Neeltje takes up the middle section, while Clasina hugs the pillow. The door to my room is closed. Liesbeth and Rosa must both be asleep.

Oma and Mother sleep sitting up, leaning against the wall and each other on the corner of Adriaan's bed.

Father's silhouette stands outlined against one of the skylights in the sloped roof.

"Floating farm equipment is bumping into the walls," he says, when I stand beside him. For a moment I stare into a mad world I don't recognize. The storm that rattles the roof tiles and swirls the water inside my home makes me angry. I ball my fists. I want to fight the mighty force of the sea, but the sea is stronger than us, and nature's elements reign.

The shattering of glass announces the rush of water through the downstairs' windows.

I walk back to the stairs. By now there are only four treads before the whole staircase will be submerged.

Downstairs the water will have almost reached the ceiling. Fear holds me in its grip as I try to imagine the chaos and destruction of our cozy kitchen and all the valuables we keep in the front room.

What will happen if the water reaches the second floor? The next high tide comes in about twelve hours . . . the water will rise until . . . we have nowhere to go. Twelve family members trapped on the second floor can't possibly go onto the roof. The skylights are too small for the adults to fit through. Our house has no attic. This feeling of helplessness makes me sick to my stomach.

As daylight slowly lights up the island, I return to my spot on the floor, leaning against the end of the bed, the blanket draped around me.

Suddenly Adriaan sits up, wide awake. "We've lost Max!" he cries.

Not just Max, I realize, but all our animals — Dina and her unborn calf, the horses, calves, even the two barn cats and the chickens. A numbness settles in my heart. I can't even cry. "Adriaan, come here," I urge. "We can share the blanket."

Adriaan looks at me. He wipes his nose with the sleeve of his sweater, then crawls off the bed and walks toward me. I drape the blanket around both of us. He leans against me. His body heaves with sobs. After a while he grows quiet; his weight settles on my shoulder as exhaustion claims him.

I wonder about the animals, and words fill my head:

What did the animals feel
when the waves hit them?
Did they sense
the end was near?
Did they feel
the wall of water
violently
attacking them?
Choking them?
Drowning them?

9

Destruction

A PALE LIGHT CREEPING through the two skylights wakes me, and I realize that I must have dozed off. Now the new day begins. I immediately hear the roar of the storm, accompanied by the thunder of angry waves, which sound like the freight train barrelling through Harbour Town, where I used to go to school.

I notice Father has fallen asleep sitting against the foot of the bed. Gently, I move Adriaan, drape the blanket around him, get up off the floor and walk over to one of the windows.

Oma is awake. "What do you see?" she whispers. Mother is still asleep, sitting beside Oma on the bed. They're both leaning on the wall, wrapped in blankets. I turn back to one of the skylights and, at first, I don't recognize anything. I blink my eyes to make sure what I can see is real and not a nightmare. The water has reached the eaves. Hills of manure float by. Bales of straw bob up and down. Tree branches, pieces of wood, buckets and barrels swirl in circles, then rush past.

My eyes try to find New Port. I can make out some of the rooftops, but the fields, pastures and road into town are gone. Telephone poles are the only indicators of where the road once was. The land before me has turned into one big sea.

Yesterday, our island had the protection of the dikes; overnight, the sea transformed into a fierce monster swallowing those same dikes and the land inside them.

I don't see any movement from neighbouring farms. Suddenly I gasp. Piet and Jantje's house! I rub my eyes but it's . . . gone! There's not a single reminder that a house had even been there. It has just vanished! Piet, Jantje, sweet Grietje, little Casper . . . Did they escape, have they been rescued or did the sea just sweep them up, house and all? Bile rises in my throat.

But what's that? In the water below . . . something is floating . . . a body and then another. Cows! The animals that drowned during the night are now floating out of the stable. I close my eyes; afraid I might see Max float by. I fold my hands in prayer. "Oh, God! Why? Why all this?"

"Klara," Oma whispers again. "Come here." She raises her hand slowly so that Mother won't wake up.

I turn away from the skylight, slump onto the floor beside the bed and let my head sink onto my grandmother's lap. Ice-cold hands caress my hair. My tears run, but my voice has lost its sound, as if the sea has taken it.

"Ma!" the sharp piercing cry of Sara's voice wakes everyone in the upstairs space.

Mother stretches her body after her uncomfortable position during the night.

Neeltje, Sara, Clasina, Jacob and Martin sit up, surprised to find they're all in the same bed.

"Why are we all here?" Martin asks.

"Why can't we go downstairs?" Jacob gets up and walks over to the stairs. "I can see the water!" he cries. "Is everything downstairs flooded?"

"What about our animals?" Martin now stands beside his brother and they wrap their arms around each other.

Mother rushes over to the boys and hugs them tight. In horror, she looks down the staircase. "The animals have drowned," she says softly, her face wet. They stand in silence, a solemn statue.

Father gets to his feet and resumes his post at one of the skylights.

I watch him closely as he takes in the destruction. He puts his hands on the wall and lowers his head. "Oh, God almighty!" he whispers. "It looks like the devil himself stirred the sea!" His words silence even the little ones.

I get up, wipe my face on the sleeve of my coat and hustle the boys from Mother's arms, back onto the bed with the promise of something to eat. In the corner I've set up an area for food. I fill the kettle with water from the pail and light the oil stove with a match. "There's no cutting board or bread knife."

Mother picks up the breadbox. "I'll give everybody a small piece because we don't know how long we'll be up here."

After what I witnessed outside, I don't feel hungry.

Father refuses to eat, too. He tears his gaze away from the window, grabs the Bible from the shelf and reads in a thundering voice, "The LORD saw that the wickedness of man was great in the earth, and that every imagination of the thoughts of man's heart was continually only evil. The Lord was sorry that he had made man on earth . . ." He closes the Bible and I see his lips move as he murmurs a prayer.

I look at my mother. She avoids my gaze. I silently question Father's choice of scripture. *How are we to blame for this?*

Neeltje climbs off the bed.

"We better block the stairs before anyone falls in the water," Adriaan says. He moves his clothes off the shelf above his bed and takes the now empty plank off the wall supports and secures the opening at the stairs so the little ones can't go down.

"When can we go to our kitchen?" Clasina asks.

"When the water is gone," Mother answers.

"How will people in the village know we're here?" Jacob asks.

"Everybody in the village is stranded upstairs just like us," Liesbeth cries. "Nobody can get out!"

"What about our cats and the chickens?" Clasina asks.

"They're gone. Max is gone, too," Martin says in a sombre tone. He slumps down on the bed and covers his face in his hands.

Liesbeth runs into my room and slams the door.

Max was our loyal companion for the last ten years, a member of our family.

Rosa sits pale-faced beside Neeltje. "She's soaking wet, Mother!"

Mother shakes her head. "I can't believe we forgot to bring diapers upstairs. Get a sheet and rip it in squares," she suggests.

In my room, I take the top sheet off my bed and rip it in half. I rip it again and again until I have squares the size of diapers.

When I return, I scoop Neeltje off the bed and carry her into my bedroom.

After I've changed her, I deposit a dry, clean-smelling Neeltje onto the double bed. I take the dirty diaper, which we can't wash, to one of the skylights, open it and fling the diaper outside, where it whirls away with other debris. Father has already emptied our bucket twice.

The room is lit up now that morning has come, but the sky is still a threatening grey, and the storm roars relentlessly.

While I wait for the water to boil on the stove, I walk back to the window. More swollen cows' bodies float by. Something else catches my eye. On our neighbour's, the Smids, farm a man has climbed onto the roof and is waving a white flag. Who is he waving at? I don't see anything going by. Please, send some boats . . . but then . . . how are we going to get into a boat?

No matter where my thoughts go, I realize we have no chance of getting out of here unless the water retreats as quickly as it came. The breached dikes will let more water in, and the tide is still high. So far, the water just stays beneath the second floor, but if it keeps rising . . . I try to force my thoughts in a different direction.

"Let's heat up some carrots from the cans," Mother suggests. Her face has taken on a greyish pallor and her eyes have sunk even deeper into their sockets.

I fill the pot with carrots. "We'll have to eat from our teacups," I say. "I forgot to bring up the dishes."

"I yike eating from teacups," Clasina pipes up. "It's yike playing house."

Yeah, just like playing house. I wish I could imagine like Clasina, but the images I see in my mind are of swollen animal cadavers. I can't even think of Max, with his trusting eyes. My mind wanders while I stir the carrots. I think of Dora and her family, of Ms. Poortvliet, the baker and his wife, who just had a baby two weeks ago. Are they all stranded on their second floors or in their attics? Some of the houses in town are close to the dike or even below it. *Stop thinking about these horrible scenarios,* I scold myself.

"Dora," I whisper, "please be safe." I quickly turn off the stove when I smell burned carrots. "Clasina, gather all the cups for me."

I fill each cup. "You can hand them out."

By afternoon the carrots are forgotten, and everyone is hungry.

"We don't have much food left," Mother hands me the canned beets.

"I wish I had brought more bread," I say when I look in the breadbox. "I didn't think the flood was actually going to happen."

"Nobody believed it would happen," Oma says.

"I believe we are all going to suffer." Father, who has barely spoken all day, startles everyone.

"Now, Jannes," Oma says. "I think you're wrong."

Sara has fallen asleep, and Clasina and Neeltje babble away, playing finger games. Adriaan stands at the skylight. Liesbeth and Rosa are sitting on the edge of the double bed, holding hands. But Father's ominous words hang in the air like sharp knives.

"A plane!" Adriaan shouts excitedly. "It looks like a Tipsy Junior, the Belgian plane!"

Rosa, Liesbeth and I scramble to the windows. Martin and Jacob stand up on the bed. We watch a small plane coming from the direction of White Church, flying toward Harbour Town.

"The pilot must be checking out which parts of the island are flooded!" Adriaan says. "I wonder what he can see?"

"Water and chaos," I answer.

When the plane disappears from sight, we all sit quietly, unsure what will happen next.

"Let's hope that plane will return or send help." Mother rubs her eyes.

After many long empty minutes, Martin and Jacob sit back on the bed and look at the pictures in their gnome book.

I stare at the cluster of five houses close to New Port. Are there fewer houses or are my eyes playing a trick on me? I gasp for air as I watch the farthest of the five houses fold like a cardboard structure and disappear completely. I know that family. They have five children. Cora, the oldest, went to school with me.

"It's high tide again," Father announces. "God knows how high the water will rise this time."

Disbelief clouds my eyes as I watch water enter the second floor and submerge the stairs.

"Everyone put your boots on or stay on the beds!" Father commands.

I walk into my room, take out my notebook and pencil and sit down on the edge of my bed. In the fading light, I write as the words enter my mind:

Fear,
uncertainty
will accompany us
this second night.
Cooped up on the second floor,
twelve people,
no hope,
only water.
My heart hurts with angst,
dread,
hopelessness.

10

Longest Night

"WILL YOU READ TO US?" Martin touches my arm. Jacob looks at me and smiles.

"Let's all sit on the double bed," I answer. "Clasina, Neeltje. Come sit with us. You can look at the pictures."

Adriaan carries the two girls from his bed and they squeeze in beside me.

"What kind of garbage have you been reading to them?" Father grabs the book from Martin.

"Aunt Neeltje sent that." Martin looks up at Father, tears in his eyes.

My father looks at Oma, then hands the book to me.

"One evening, Paulus, the forest gnome, opened the door of his hollow tree. He lit the pipe that he had made from an acorn shell and looked at the sky. . . ."

My voice fills the upstairs room, distracting children and adults with the magical world of the kind gnome.

When the outside light dims and the words become too hard to see, I close the book. Adriaan has been watching the outside world. Suddenly he points and at the same time we hear the sound of propellers.

"It's a helicopter!" Adriaan hollers.

"How will the pilot know we're up here?" Rosa yells. "It's too dark for him to see us!"

"We need something to flag him down!" Adriaan hops from one foot to the other, while the rest of us, except Oma and Mother, stand up on the beds to see the helicopter.

Mother pulls the case off one of the pillows. Father takes down one of the bare curtain rods. With a piece of wet twine found under his bed, Adriaan ties the pillowcase onto the rod. We watch in anticipation as my brother thrusts the window open and Father holds out the white flag. By the time the pillowcase flaps in the strong wind, the helicopter is nowhere to be seen.

"Maybe it'll come back," Adriaan says, but I see the hope fading from his eyes.

"It's getting too dark," Father answers. He pulls the rod inside and closes the window.

Defeated, we sit down on the beds, keeping our feet above the water, which has now reached about ten centimetres above the floor.

"First light tomorrow morning we'll try again." Father rolls up the pillowcase and puts it on top of the remaining shelf.

Mother pulls on a pair of boots and stands up to light the oil lamp on the small table between the beds. The soft yellow light makes the room look a little friendlier but not a degree warmer.

The cold is settling into my bones and when I touch my feet, they feel like clumps of ice.

"We'll pray," Father announces.

"Maybe we won't feel hungry when we pray," I add. "We only have bread for tomorrow morning."

I bow my head and fold my hands, but just as I'm about to ask God to get us all safely out of here, Father's words stun us.

"Dear God. I know you want to punish us for Mother's sins."

Mother's sins? I sit up straight. What's he talking about?

"Jannes!" Oma stands up in the water.

I look at Father in shock.

"You will not speak of the past!" Oma points a finger at her son.

"Jannes! Please! The children!" Mother pleads.

"It's time for the children to know!" Father glares at Mother.

"They won't understand!" Mother covers her mouth.

"Neither do I!" Father yells. He's facing the black skylight. With one quick turn, he confronts us, his expression far beyond this world. He looks like a stranger ready to address the congregation.

My heart pounds wildly. I've seen Father angry before, but at this moment, he seems possessed, as if the devil has taken over his mind!

"Yes, my children!" He looks from one sibling to another but avoids me. "A long time ago your mother was a sinner!"

My proper mother, who never raises her voice, who has the patience of a saint . . . who cares for people and for animals . . . a SINNER?

He points his finger at her. "We are being punished for your sins!" Mother shrinks back as if she were struck by a heavy object. Oma wraps her arms around her daughter-in-law, rocking her like a child.

Wide-eyed and silent, the rest of us look at Father.

The soft light from the oil lamp throws our shadows on the walls — statues frozen in horror. Rosa and Liesbeth hold on to each other. Adriaan looks confused.

I'm scared.

"You shamed our family!" Father rages. "You humiliated me! Now we're all being punished because that's how God deals with sinners! You all know the story of Noah!"

"Father! Please!" Without thinking, I slosh through the water, walk toward my father and hold up both hands as if to physically stop him.

"You! Get out of my sight!" He turns around and faces the darkness where the wrath of God is boiling over in the wild fury of the sea.

Mother motions me to leave.

I stumble to my room but not before I turn and look at her ghostly face. "Whatever you did, Mother, it could never have been so bad that our whole family and the rest of the country is punished for it!"

"Curb your tongue!" Father commands. "God makes no distinction between one person or people as a whole!"

"Well, what did the animals do to deserve His wrath?" I don't wait for his response but close the door and fall onto the bed. My fists hit the mattress hard, over and over again, until my hands hurt.

"Klara!" Two arms wrap around my shoulders.

"Oma."

We sit together in the darkness of my room. I feel angry, confused and numb all at the same time.

"Don't ever question God's ways," Oma speaks softly.

"I'm not questioning God. . . . I'm questioning Father's sermon. What did my mother do that is so bad the whole world has to pay for it?"

"Your father can't think straight right now." Oma strokes my hair. "If God didn't forgive sinners, the heavens would be empty. Don't think about it now because we have many more urgent matters to deal with. How will we get out of here? Even if the pilot of that helicopter saw the pillowcase?"

She wipes her eyes. "I have faith that God knows when the need is greatest, salvation is near. Be kind to your mother, Klara," she says, patting my knee, "and have patience with your father, especially under these difficult circumstances." Oma kisses my cheek.

"I know that life has not been easy for Mother."

Oma takes my hand. "She never knew her mother. Your grandmother died when your mother was born."

"Why did Grandmother Rosa die?"

"There were complications. She was already forty-five when she gave birth." Oma sighs. "It wasn't easy for your mother's father to raise your mother by himself. But . . . she was a smart little girl. She helped your opa on his rounds to the farms. Your mother was really good with animals. If she'd been a boy, she could have studied to be a veterinarian like her father."

"What happened to Opa Martin?"

"He had a heart attack when your mother was only fifteen. Her great-aunt looked after her until she was eighteen, and then she married Jannes."

I had not known this. My mother talks very little about her childhood.

We sit in silence. I wish Oma would tell me more, but she stays silent, and I decide not to ask, she has so much on her mind right now.

When she gets up and leaves the room, my mind feels detached, as if it's floating away from this catastrophe. Was it just yesterday that I complained about the never-ending chores on the farm? Now I wish I could have all those chores back and more. And to top off the misery, we now have a mystery in the family — my mother's dark secret that made her a sinner. Today has been the longest Sunday I've ever experienced, and I fear for an even longer night ahead.

"Klara?" Rosa walks into the room holding Sara in her arms. "She needs a change if we have any diapers left."

Except for Neeltje and Sara we all wear our boots.

I count the squares of cotton sheeting. "They can each have a clean one tonight and then there's one left for tomorrow." I reach for my little sister.

"I'll get Neeltje," Rosa announces.

"Bring Clasina, too. They can all sleep in here, and I'll stay with them." I change Sara into a clean diaper.

"I don't know what got into Father." Rosa returns with Clasina and carries a crying Neeltje in her arms.

"He's devastated and out of his mind by the loss of the animals and the farm." I don't look at my sister.

"Why did he take it out on Mother?" Rosa deposits Neeltje on the bed, while Clasina takes off her boots before she joins her little sister.

"I'm sure Mother has done nothing wrong!" I assure Rosa as I change Neeltje and hug her tight.

"I wanna go home!" Clasina sobs.

"We are home."

"I mean our real home," Clasina insists.

"We all want to go downstairs, Clasina, but the water is too deep, and we'll drown."

No matter what I say, my little sister is inconsolable.

I turn the three little girls sideways on the bed and tuck them in. Then I take my notebook and pencil out from the drawer, place them at the headboard, perch on the edge of the bed and cover myself with part of the blankets.

"There's no room for me on the double bed." Rosa is back. "Oma and Mother are in Adriaan's bed, and Father and the boys are on the big bed. I'll call Liesbeth, too."

Liesbeth brings another blanket, which she drapes around my shoulders.

"The three of us can sit against the headboard," Rosa suggests. "We'll move the little ones closer to the foot of the bed."

Here we are, six sisters filling the double bed on this long second night. When the little ones finally stop crying, they fall asleep from exhaustion.

Rosa and Liesbeth sag against me.

I grab my notebook and pencil.

"For heaven's sake. Do you need to write poetry now?" Rosa scolds.

But the words flow from my pencil:

Listen to the constant fury
of the howling storm,
the smashing waves.
I agonize about
what is to come,
while Father's accusations
torment me.

11

Second Day

A THUNDERING SOUND wakes me out of a restless, disturbed sleep.

"What's that?" Rosa sits up and nearly pushes Liesbeth off the bed.

"Ssh, don't wake the little ones," I rub my eyes. "Their day of hunger will start soon enough."

Grabbing my boots, I slip into them. The water holds the bedroom door back, and I force it open. Crossing the room, I head for one of the skylights. The pollard willows at the end of our garden are bending their heads as the unforgiving northwestern storm forces them eastward without their consent. Next, my eyes follow the line of telephone poles — until I spot something moving. My heart lifts.

"I see a raft, and it's moving toward town."

Rosa and Liesbeth have pulled on their boots and joined me at the window.

"I see people on it!' Rosa calls.

"We need to wave our flag," Liesbeth adds.

"How can all of us be saved by that little raft?" Rosa questions.

I know that's impossible, but I keep that thought to myself.

"What's going on?" Father calls.

"There's a raft," I tell him.

"But it's too small to save all of us." Rosa's voice is sad.

"Maybe it could save some of us," Liesbeth says, "but . . . I don't mean that some of us shouldn't be saved."

"We know what you mean." I squeeze her arm and open the window. Rosa sticks out our flag, waving it up and down. We wait and watch, but the raft doesn't seem to come any closer to our farm. It even passes the Smid's farm, which stands on higher ground.

In the next moment, I see where the raft is heading. "There! Look at that telephone pole! Someone climbed it."

Adriaan and Father watch from the second window as the person is helped down from the pole onto the raft. Now the vessel moves back in the direction of the Smid's farm.

"Maybe, if they saw our flag, they'll come here next," Rosa says, hope filling her voice.

"Where will they take the people they rescue?" Liesbeth asks. "How long will it take before they're back?"

"The centre of New Port, where the church and the school are, is higher than the rest of the town," I answer. *There can't be too many dry places*, I think. "It'll take a long time if they rescue one person at a time." For as far as I can see there's only water.

Sounds coming from my bedroom make me rush back there.

Once the little ones wake up, they will want to get off the bed. Rosa and I change them into their last diapers.

I pause and look at my sisters. "At last the longest night has ended, and the new day starts with a tiny scrap of hope."

The last breadcrumbs vanish in seconds. All that's left of our food supply is water and tea. I wonder how, where and when we will be able to get food.

We spend the morning watching out the two skylights for rescuers.

Clasina sings and plays peek-a-boo with the little ones, but after a while, Sara and Neeltje both have had enough of being confined and start to crawl around the bed.

Oma and Mother sit on Adriaan's bed, each draped in a blanket. Mother's eyes are closed. I wonder what she's thinking now, after Father's terrible sermon. My eyes turn to Father, standing at the window staring out into our ravaged world. He hasn't spoken much since his outburst last night. I wonder how we can go on from here. How can Mother recover from his rage, from his insulting, hurtful words?

I touch my mother's shoulder. "What do we do for food?" I whisper.

"Pray that help is on its way," she says in a heavy voice.

I nod. "Let's hope they drop food from planes, like they did during the war."

Mother doesn't respond, and I watch the boys play with small pieces of wood, pretending they are fishing boats until Martin suggests, "We should rescue people who have fallen in the water! And Mother, we are very hungry."

"We're all hungry, Martin," Mother responds. "We're hungry, but we also have hope that we'll be rescued soon."

"And then we will get food, right?" Jacob adds. "Martin, we need to rescue people with our boat." My brothers' imagination and logic make me smile.

Without realizing what I'm doing, I start collecting sweaters for my family to wear under their coats, in case a rescue boat shows up here.

Martin and Jacob are dressed in their church clothes, and I've shared my clothes with Mother, Oma and my sisters. I hand Father his almost dry pants. His coat covers him while he slips off Adriaan's pyjama bottoms and pulls on his own pants. He hands me the pyjama bottoms. I roll them up to use as diaper material, which Neeltje and Sara will need later in the day.

"Another plane!" Adriaan opens the window and waves the flag frantically up and down.

We watch it circle the area and then disappear.

"The pilot must have seen our flag," Adriaan cries. "And I see the Smids waving theirs."

Tension fills the upstairs room.

I make the boys wear warm sweaters and hand Mother my cardigan. "If they come, we won't all be able to go at the same time." I clear my throat. "Oma and Mother and the little ones should go first."

"Who will be next?" Liesbeth plucks at her sweater.

"It depends how many they can take at one time," Father answers.

"I'll stay with Klara." Clasina grabs my hand.

"All right." I look into her anxious face. "You can stay with me."

Hope does funny things to people's minds, I realize. We've

planned for our rescue but have no idea when, how or in what we'll be rescued.

"How will we get through the skylights?" Adriaan sizes one of the windows with his hands.

"We can take down the panelling and make a hole below this window," Father suggests. "We'll be closer to the boat or raft because the water is now up to the eaves."

Adriaan checks underneath the skylight. "We need to remove the panelling — break the slats and throw off the tiles." He immediately tries to pry one of the planks loose, but no luck.

"Use one of our rescue boats." Martin hands a piece of wood to Adriaan, who after a few attempts, finally gets a grip.

Father helps Adriaan dislodge the first plank from the panelling; the next one is easier to get out, but a freezing wind blasts into the room through the opening. Father takes one glance at his shivering family. "Let's close the opening until our rescuers are here." He tries to push the panelling back in place the best he can, without the availability of nails or any tools.

Monday morning slowly passes with crying babies, hungry children, boredom and tea. Fear, cold and anxiety keep us all company.

We take turns looking out the window, but all we see is water, destruction and debris, and all we hear is the relentless raging wind. Maybe it has lost its hurricane strength, but the strong northwestern storm is just as damaging.

By early afternoon, the hope we felt earlier is quickly fading. I continue to gaze in the direction of the town, willing my eyes to see some movement. I keep worrying about the families in those vanished houses. Where are they? That question leaves me with a lump in my throat.

All at once, I spot a movement. I'm not sure. . . . Is it . . . a boat? . . . Is it coming our way? I turn and look at my family, beaten and defeated. I turn back, waiting to see if the boat heads toward our farm before I make the announcement. At last, I can make out two men rowing, and I point.

"There's a rowboat coming in our direction."

"Are you sure it's coming here?" Adriaan jumps up. "I'll wave the flag!" he shouts, as he grabs the curtain rod and opens the window. "Over here! We're up here!"

The wind blows away his words, but after what seems like hours the boat arrives below the skylight.

Father sticks his head out the window.

"How many?" a voice calls.

"Twelve!" Father shouts back. "Two are toddlers! My wife is . . . with child, and my mother has difficulty getting around!"

"We'll take the most critical people first," the man calls. "How will they fit through the skylight?"

"We'll open it up beneath the skylight!" my father answers.

Adriaan rips out the panelling, hands the planks to me, and I pass them to Martin.

Father has broken some of the slats so that he can remove the roof tiles.

A cold blast enters our shelter.

"Mother, Oma, put your coats on and take a blanket." I'm ordering my family around, but I feel an urgent need to get everybody out.

A young man dressed in an oilcloth coat climbs inside the attic. His eyes scan the space and take in the number of people who need to be rescued. "The rowboat is too small to carry all of you."

His eyes meet mine, and for a split second I look deep into the dark eyes of my rescuer. In that moment, I notice his unshaven face, dark with stubble, and the black knitted toque worn by fishermen.

My mind stops working; heat creeps up my neck and face. Confused, I look away.

"My wife and my mother . . . and the little ones must go first." Father takes Mother's arm and helps her up from the bed.

"Where will you take them?" his voice is filled with anxiety.

"We can't go to New Port. The dike breached right in town, creating a long gap," the young man answers in a deep voice. "We'll go up to White Church. Church Street is dry, but the church is overflowing with people. We've heard that the café is now taking people in."

"Henk!" the young man calls through the hole. "Oma is coming out first. You grab her from me. Keep the boat stable."

"You need to go back into the rowboat," Father orders. "Your friend can never keep it from tipping."

The man looks embarrassed. "I don't have experience rescuing people." He looks at me and smiles. "It's my first day on the job."

I notice that he's the same height as Father. His accent tells us that he comes from the island of Walcheren. It's impossible to guess his age, but his smile . . .

"What's your name?" Father asks.

"Machiel," he answers. He points out the window. "That's Henk. We're fishermen from West Bay. We were fishing close to New Port on Saturday when the storm hit. We thought we could wait it out, but when the dikes breached, we sailed through one of the openings into town. We moored the boat in one of the streets. This morning, we found a rowboat and decided to help."

"We're grateful you came to rescue us, Machiel," I finally find my voice.

"I haven't rescued you yet," he says, smiling at me before he lowers himself into the rowboat.

Oma hugs us all. "Be strong, Klara," she whispers. Father helps Oma get her legs over the ledge.

Machiel holds out his arms while Henk steadies the boat by holding onto the roof. Fear ties around my heart when my grandmother slides down into the rowboat, which rocks up and down in an angry sea.

After Oma, it's Mother's turn. "I don't want to leave you here," she says. Her voice is choked with tears. "I need to stay with the children," she protests.

"No, you need to go to a safe place," Father's voice is gentle.

I'm surprised to see tenderness in Mother's eyes when she looks up at him.

While I watch my mother slide down, Clasina holds onto my legs. The boat wobbles and struggles with Mother's weight. My mother and grandmother sit at opposite ends of the small rowboat.

Sara and Neeltje scream hysterically. I hand Machiel two blankets. He tucks the little ones in, Sara with Mother and Neeltje with Oma. I'm touched by the way he makes sure they're all right.

The young men take their place on the middle seat. Huge waves make it difficult for them to manoeuvre backwards through straw bales, wooden crates and the swollen bodies of animals.

I place my arms around Rosa and Liesbeth while Clasina clings to me. Adriaan stands quietly, struggling not to cry.

Martin and Jacob hold onto Father, their faces wet with tears. My father blows his nose as we watch the rowboat and its precious cargo for as long as we can. Nobody speaks after the boat disappears into a cruel, unknown sea:

Tears choke my thoughts,
as I imagine
the wild current
rocking, bashing
the small vessel.
Will the waves swallow
this precious cargo,
just
like everything else
that crosses their path?
My thoughts turn cold,
my life is on hold.

12
Second Effort

"DO WE HAVE ANYTHING TO EAT?" Jacob asks in a small voice.

"We have tea." I release myself from Clasina's arms. "I'll make some." I hope the tea will calm down the rumble in my own stomach and warm us up a little.

Adriaan and Father close the hole with the planks, but without the roof tiles the wind blows in through the gaps.

The hot tea gives a five-minute reprieve, and then the minutes turn into another hour as the cold numbs our limbs and minds. All I can think of is Mother, Oma, Neeltje and Sara in that small rowboat bobbing up and down in the cold, wild water.

Machiel's words about the breached dike in New Port fills my mind with dread. How can I find out if Dora's family is all right? Ironically, we can see the town from our windows but have no way of knowing how bad the destruction is. The area around the church and the school are higher, and I hope people have found refuge in the school and the vestry.

Every now and then, Adriaan gets up and looks out the window. Just past three o'clock he announces, "I don't know what's coming, but it's bigger than a rowboat!"

We rush over to the window.

"It's one of those flat-bottom boats." Father says. "If it comes here, we can all go!"

Once more I check everyone's clothes, making sure buttons on sweaters and coats are done up. Next, I gather more blankets.

After what feels like an eternity, Father opens the window and talks to the men below.

"How many?" a voice asks.

"Eight," Father answers.

"That's too many." I hear the man say. "Six at the most! Five would be better!"

Father looks at us. "Adriaan you'll stay with me."

Adriaan swallows hard, fighting back tears.

"I'll stay," I say in a tight voice.

"We need to get going," the voice calls. "In about two hours, it'll be too dark! There's a rowboat right behind us."

"Father, go with the boys!" I take Martin and Jacob's arms and guide them to the window. "Take Rosa and Liesbeth." I feel a strong urge to push my family out as fast as possible.

"I'll stay with Klara!" Clasina yells.

"Go!" I help everybody get through the hole, except for Father.

"No," he says. "I'll go with the rowboat. You and Clasina go first!"

"Get in!" the man yells. "There's no time to argue!"

Father hesitates.

"You need to catch up to Mother and Oma ... and we'll be right behind you," I plead. Father grabs his pipe and tobacco pouch, sticks both in his coat pocket and climbs through the hole.

I lift Clasina in my arms, press her close to my chest to push away the panic. Together we watch the rest of our family move away through the debris. The roar of the wind makes it impossible to hear the engine.

"Just the two of us," I whisper:

"Just the two of us
  on a lonely,
  forgotten island,
  surrounded by
  an enraged sea."

After many attempts, we watch the rowboat reach the opening in the roof. I'm surprised to see the same two fishermen. "Where are Mother, Oma and the little ones?" I call, putting Clasina down while we wait for one of the men to climb through the opening.

Machiel steps into the attic and stands in front of me. He places both hands on my shoulders. His dark eyes bore deep into mine. "Don't worry. They are at the café in White Church. Listen. It's late. It'll be dark soon, and it'll be too dangerous to get you to safety."

He lets go of my shoulders and instantly I feel bereft of the warmth of his hands and closeness of his body. I turn away from him and pull a sweater over Clasina's head.

"We heard that the flat-bottomed boat couldn't take all of you, so Henk and I decided to come back."

His face is still close. I can feel his breath caress my skin. I have trouble breathing. My heart does funny things. I button Clasina's coat and pull a hat over her ears.

"I told Henk I must save the angel with the wild red hair."

"I . . . but . . ." I stutter while I button my coat. I know we have to get out of here, but Machiel's nearness is so distracting.

"The flat-bottomed boat will get to White Church much faster than us. Let's go," Machiel orders. "Get a blanket. You go first and I'll hand you the little one. Do you have any flashlights?"

"Ah . . . yes . . . I . . ." *What's wrong with me?* For the first time since this whole ordeal began, I don't know what to do first or how to talk. I dash to my cooking area and grab a flashlight, then rush back to the opening.

"Come. Get into the boat." Machiel guides me through the opening until my feet touch the bottom of the boat. It wobbles violently, and I can hardly keep my balance.

"Just sit on the seat in the middle," Henk says. "She'll be more stable." He steadies the boat with a long pole in the water and with one hand on the roof.

Next comes Machiel with Clasina in his arms, wrapped in a blanket.

"My name is Clasina, and my sister is Klara," I hear her say while they slide into the boat.

"I like your name," Machiel says. "But I also like Klara and her name."

Henk struggles to keep the boat balanced, and Machiel teeter-totters to stay on his feet. The boat almost tips when Machiel and Clasina sit down beside me.

"Klara, crawl to the stern!" Machiel orders.

On hands and knees, I reach the back seat while the waves try to tip the little boat.

Machiel crawls toward me and deposits Clasina onto my lap. He drapes the blanket around us and touches my face just for a second. The imprint of his fingers lingers on my cheek. "Keep her safe, Clasina," he whispers before he turns around.

Henk pushes off, and the two young men sit down on the middle seat. They each grab an oar and start rowing.

13

Heroes

I LOOK AT OUR HOME of which only the second floor is visible. Our safe sanctuary seems to be drowning. The barn is immersed to the roof. I shudder when I think of our animals.

Clasina holds onto me, her eyes wide with fear. Her bottom lip quivers. "I'm scared." Her voice trembles.

"Me, too." I press her close.

"Where are we going?" she asks.

"To a warm café. We need to sit very still so we don't make the boat tip." I tighten my arm around her while holding onto the seat with my other hand.

"Klara, you need to watch for large obstacles!" Machiel calls while he glances over his shoulder.

I nod. The men are facing the back as they row, so it's hard for them to see what's coming toward the boat.

Where once our shed with farm equipment stood there's nothing, just water. Two swollen calf cadavers bob up and down with the waves until they hit the roof of the barn.

Chunks of manure from the dunghill are caught between the wall and straw bales. For a moment, the strong odour fills our nostrils, then passes.

"Are those cows dead or are they swimming?" Clasina asks.

"They're dead. Close your eyes." I pull the blanket over her head.

My hair blows around my face, and only now do I realize that I've lost my lace cap somewhere between Saturday night and now. Father's annoyed face flashes into my mind.

The boat bumps into a large piece of wood, and Machiel and Henk use their oars to push away from it. "Klara you need to warn us!" Machiel repeats.

I nod and try to concentrate on keeping my eyes peeled for obstacles.

Now that I face my rescuers, I have a chance to take furtive glances. They're both wearing black toques and look about the same age — eighteen, nineteen or twenty. Heavy oilcloth coats and large rubber boots keep them dry.

Machiel's unshaven face makes him look more like a pirate than a fisherman, except I remember how kind and gentle he was when he helped Mother, Oma and . . . what he said about me being a red-haired angel.

The rowboat leaves what used to be our farm property. Out in the open water, the waves are even higher and the wind stronger. Wet snowflakes lash out at us. The dark water swirls and churns angrily. I don't recognize our land or the safe home I've lived in for sixteen years. I scan the waters, but there's no sign of the flat-bottomed boat with our family.

Machiel and Henk turn the boat north, in the direction of White Church.

"We're following the telephone poles," Machiel yells over the sound of the waves, "so we know approximately where the road is! You need to keep us on track! The wind will try to push us east!"

I can tell from the strain on their faces that our two heroes are exhausted; they have been rowing since this morning.

One time, we hear a military plane fly over.

Houses along the way show the terrible destruction — roofs ripped off, walls missing and curtains flapping through broken window frames like flags. We pass two farms that are totally destroyed.

To the right, I notice a row of nine houses standing on top of the sea dike. For some mysterious reason those houses and that part of the seawall are untouched.

Furniture, crates, logs, doors and a bed frame float along with us, heading in the same direction. Several times I call out when sections of abandoned buildings block our path, like ghostly monsters rising from the sea. The men try to steer the boat out of the way to avoid collisions.

We pass a horse standing on higher ground. It looks like it has walked on water to get there. My thoughts go to our loyal mares and how frightened they must have been before they drowned.

"Watch out!" I yell, when a large sideboard comes our way and bumps up against the boat. Henk grabs the long pole and pushes against it while Machiel tries to stay on course, but the wind forces us away from the telephone poles.

I point at a bicycle, a wooden clock, a cradle and a cat sitting on top of a floating door, to distract Clasina.

"I hope the cat finds a safe, dry place." Clasina says. "Cats don't yike being wet."

Machiel and Henk work their arms hard, trying to beat the rising water and threatening darkness. Every once in a while, Machiel smiles at me before his face frowns with tension of hard labour.

It's almost impossible to row between the bouncing straw bales, parts of walls and the many, many animal cadavers. I try to give directions, but these obstacles are everywhere and slow the boat almost to a stop. With their oars, the men push through the sea of rubble, and slowly we move ahead. "I'm trying to warn you," I yell. "But there's too much debris around us!"

"You're trying your best," Machiel yells back.

Darkness approaches fast and makes it even more challenging to find our way out of the chaos. When there is less debris our heroes can pick up speed, but my eyes catch sight of a shed racing toward us from the left. "Watch out!" I yell, but it's too late. The wooden building hits our rowboat, almost tipping us into the waves. I hang on for dear life.

"We need to stay closer to the telephone poles!" Machiel calls over the roar of the water. "Klara, make sure we stay close!" He pulls a flashlight from his pocket and aims it at the poles. "We're way off course."

"My tummy hurts," Clasina cries.

"We're almost there. We'll get food at the café in White Church." I hope and wish with all my heart that it's true because my stomach is screaming for something to eat, too.

The rowboat narrowly misses the first telephone pole, and Henk hits it with his oar.

"We're good!" he calls.

For a while we move along without incident. The men roll the oars through the water, synchronizing their strokes. The rowboat scrapes by another telephone pole, but with just a little wobble we move along. In the next moment an enormous wave makes our vessel rock up and down, soaking us in the process. I struggle to hang onto the seat and hold onto Clasina.

"Don't give up, Klara!" Machiel shouts as if he can read my thoughts.

Just when the words leave his lips, the boat jolts out of the water. I lurch off the seat, and as I reach out to steady myself a second bump hits the boat. Clasina flies out of my arms, hits the edge of the boat and tumbles into the icy water.

"Clasina! Clasina!" I scream in terror.

Frantically, I crawl to the side of the boat and reach into the water, groping desperately for my sister. It doesn't even cross my mind that I can't swim; I'm ready to go after her.

Machiel has already taken off his heavy coat, kicked off his boots and dived into the freezing waves at the spot where Clasina disappeared.

The boat struggles, trying to find its balance.

Henk grabs the flashlight and aims the light into the waves. Nothing! He aims at the pole, which is right beside us.

"Hang onto the telephone pole to keep the boat from moving away!" Henk shouts.

Climbing to my knees, I follow his orders and wrap my arms around the pole, fighting the waves that try to make us rush on. "Clasina! Clasina!" I cry as if I'm hanging onto her with my voice.

The wind howls, rain slaps my face and the strong current tries to push us ahead. I'm afraid I can't hang on much longer. I bite down, closing my eyes just for a second.

When I open them again and look down into the murky water, I see no sign of my little sister or Machiel. "Oh, God, please help," I sob. "Let this be a really, really bad dream."

A hand clutches the rim of the boat. Henk grabs onto it and pulls. I let go of the telephone pole, stick both my arms in the water beside him until I feel my sister's body. Pumped with adrenalin, I lift Clasina, heavy with water, out of Machiel's arms and into the bottom of the boat. I roll her onto her side.

"Thank God," I whisper when she coughs and a mouthful of water escapes.

While Henk pulls one of Machiel's arms, Machiel holds onto the rim of the boat with his other hand. The waves now have full rein. They push the boat away from the telephone pole, dragging Machiel along.

I crawl over Clasina and reach for Machiel's other arm. Together, Henk and I pull him up over the edge while the boat rushes ahead.

Once Machiel's upper body is inside the boat he's able to swing his legs over. He rolls onto the bottom, beside Clasina's quiet body.

"Grab the blanket!" Henk orders.

I cover them both and Machiel starts gasping.

"Grab Machiel's oar and help me row!"

My teeth chatter, and I crawl onto the seat beside Henk and grab the oar. I try to think how to work it, but my mind stumbles. I start by lifting the oar and rolling it back until it hits the waves. Dragging it through the water from the back to the front, I repeat the motion.

"We're off course!" Henk tries to match my uneven rhythm.

I cast a quick glance at Clasina and Machiel, not knowing if they're alive. It's impossible to pray, because I have to keep my mind focused on the movement of the oar. Even when my muscles scream in pain, I push on.

"A-live! A-live! A-live!" I chant with one powerful stroke after another, and I imagine a place of warmth and safety coming closer and closer.

14
Café Westwind

A LIGHT MOVES BACK and forth. "I need help!" Henk calls at the top of his lungs. He aims the flashlight at the moving light.

The light waves back.

"Thank you, God," I murmur.

"A few more strokes, Klara," Henk says beside me.

In the next moment, the boat rocks and a man in hip waders grabs my arm. I drop the oar. "Take my little sister and Machiel," I cry. "They almost drowned!"

The man lifts Clasina in his arms. "Oh, you poor little thing. You're colder than an icicle." He disappears into the dark with my sister in his arms.

Henk helps Machiel up on his feet. Another man offers to carry him on his back. "You two will have to walk," he says. "Take the boat with you or it'll drift away."

Using the flashlight, Henk grabs the rope and climbs out of the boat. He takes hold of my arm as I stagger over the edge. My arms are shaking. I can't feel my feet. The ice-cold water slashes into my legs like shards of glass. I'm holding onto Henk, who pulls the rowboat behind him. We slosh through the water until our feet find land.

I look up through the pouring rain to see our salvation. CAFÉ WESTWIND, the sign reads above the door of the building. A man with a beard and moustache waves to us from the porch.

"I'm Lou." He holds out his hand and helps me up the steps. "Come inside, you two."

Gradually my eyes adjust to the soft light of the two small oil lamps standing on the wooden bar. "Go upstairs," Lou says. "It's dry and there's a stove."

Henk helps me up the stairs, and I step out of my wet boots and socks. The room is smoky and my eyes water. The smell of wet clothes, cigarette smoke and people is very strong. With both hands, I grab onto Henk's arm and close my eyes until a wave of dizziness passes.

Someone slides a chair underneath me. I take a deep breath, open my eyes and search the room for familiar faces. Where's Clasina, Machiel, my family? The space is overcrowded with people and their belongings.

"Klara!" Rosa wraps her arms around me. "What took you so long?"

"Wh-wh-wh-where's C-cla-a-sina?" My body shakes and my teeth chatter when I try to speak. "I-is sh-sh-she a-a-al-live? I ne-ne-ne-need to se-see her!"

"Mother is changing her and rubbing her cold body. Somebody gave us dry clothes." Rosa helps me get up and pushes me ahead while people make a path.

I stumble toward my mother, who's holding Clasina in her lap.

Just the sight of my little sister takes my breath away, and I am beyond grateful.

"We are so fortunate." Mother's face is wet. "We're all safe now, but so many others . . ." She clears her throat. "Whole families drowned in their sleep. . . . I'm so thankful! The Lord has looked after us . . . all of us."

It suddenly dawns on me that God spared our family despite my mother's sin.

I touch Clasina's face, her hands, her hair, finding it unbelievable that she was submerged in the claws of the icy, angry sea only an hour ago. "Machiel saved her, Mother," I whisper. "But he's so cold. I'm worried that he'll die of hypothermia."

Mother nods through her tears. "We are forever in his debt."

"Klara, get out of your wet clothes." Rosa holds up a blanket like a curtain.

She's found me a dry skirt and blouse and cardigan. I strip off my damp clothes except for my undergarments, but I can't stop shivering. As soon as I'm dressed, I scan the room, looking for Machiel. I spot him wrapped in blankets beside the stove, so I make my way over and kneel beside him.

Machiel's trembling body shifts toward me. My hand brushes his face. His coarse unshaven skin caresses my hand. "You saved us!" I whisper. I feel a strong urge to hold him — to warm him.

He opens his eyes and whispers, "Angel!"

"I'll look after him, Klara." Henk helps me up.

"Come." Rosa has followed me. She takes my hand and pulls me back to my family.

My grandmother sits on a wooden chair wrapped in a blanket. She looks like a little mouse with only her wrinkled face sticking out. "Klara!" Oma pushes away the blanket and takes hold of my cold hands.

"Klara! Klara!" Martin and Jacob throw their arms around me. "We all thought you drowned, just like Max." Jacob hugs me tight.

I kiss Oma's cheeks and hug my brothers. I want to cry, but my tears are stuck.

"We were so afraid." Liesbeth's face is wet with tears. "It took forever for you and Clasina to come here, and it was so dark outside."

I throw my arms around her and realize how close we've come to death. "Clasina almost drowned," I tell her, my voice shaking. Finally, hot tears find their way down my cold cheeks. Liesbeth keeps hugging me, and I hug her back.

"Where's Father?" I scan the room. "Sara? Neeltje? Adriaan?"

Mother points at a table near the window. I find Adriaan, who's trying to feed Neeltje soup from a bowl with a spoon, but Neeltje grabs the bowl with both hands and drinks the soup.

The smell of that soup assaults my senses, making me sway, and I hold onto the table.

"I'll get you some soup." Father's voice startles me. "You'll feel better after you get something warm inside you."

Sara is standing on his lap, but once she sees me, she reaches out with both arms.

"Come sit down." Father plants Sara onto my lap. I sit down and feel the warmth of my sister's little body. I can't stop hugging her.

"People are very generous," Adriaan tells me. "They bring food and dry clothes to the café, and Lou, the owner, is a saint. He's giving away everything he has."

Father returns and hands me a bowl. "They've run out of spoons." His voice is kind, and I glance at him.

"I'm so grateful our family survived," he says in a choked voice. He takes Sara from me and lets her play with his cold pipe.

I close my eyes and inhale the smell of the warm liquid before I take a sip. Cabbage, turnip and potato — a river of warmth fills my stomach, heating my insides. It hurts but feels so good. Sharp pins pierce my hands as they cradle the bowl. If only my feet would feel something.

"Do you need socks?" Adriaan asks, looking at my bare feet. "I'm wearing two pairs. Someone gave them to me." He puts Neeltje down and takes off his socks. Next he reaches for my feet and places them on his knees. He starts rubbing my feet with his hands.

Slowly, a tingling sensation spreads from my toes to my ankles, followed by sharp pains as the blood tries to find a way through my frozen veins. Tears run down my face and the pain is almost unbearable, but I'm grateful that the feeling is returning to my feet.

I turn to Father. "Machiel jumped into that ice-cold water and saved Clasina. It was like a whirlpool and we couldn't keep the boat still."

"We'll pray for him," Father says.

"He needs soup and dry clothes, not prayers." My eyes fill with tears of frustration. Doesn't anybody realize what we've been through?

"I see that his friend is looking after him." Father looks over where the boys are.

No matter how hard my father prays, I need to find a way to help Machiel, to make sure he's going to be all right.

The dry socks give some warmth, but my feet won't stop throbbing, as if they're being stabbed with a sharp tool. I get up and cringe when I put weight on my feet. I hobble over to Father and lift Sara from his lap. With a sleeping Sara in my arms, I stumble over to Oma. She takes my little sister and holds her close.

Mother is rocking Clasina. Martin and Jacob sit on the floor and talk to a little boy, whose family is sitting near them.

"Do they have an outhouse here?" I ask.

"You need to put boots on," Mother answers.

I make my way to the stairs. Henk is sitting at a table. "How's Machiel?"

"He's so cold, can't warm up. I've changed his clothes. He doesn't talk, and that worries me."

"Did he eat?"

"No," Henk answers. "His bowl is here, but the soup is cold. You try."

I refill the bowl with warm soup from the pot on top of the stove. Kneeling down beside Machiel, I lift his head onto my knees and cradle my arm around him for support. "You need to get warm," I whisper.

As soon as Machiel places his hands around the warm bowl he groans, but then he slowly drinks the warm liquid.

"Your insides will get warm," I whisper when he finishes the soup.

"A kiss . . . will warm my heart," he murmurs.

Heat spreads inside me, and it feels so good to hold him. I don't even consider the consequences when I bend my head and brush Machiel's lips with mine. I want to stay like this forever, hold him close, caress his face and kiss him until he feels alive. His skin smells of sea and fish. His lips taste of salt water and a hint of tobacco.

"What are you doing?" Father thunders.

Startled, I realize what I've just done — kissed a stranger. Quickly, I cover Machiel with the blanket and get up.

"I fed Machiel soup." I look straight at my father. "He refused to eat. I don't want anything to happen to him after he risked his life for us."

Father stares back at me. There's no warmth in his eyes now, and he turns without speaking another word.

"Can I borrow your boots?" I ask Henk, hiding my confusion. "I need to go outside." I don't know what to do. My emotions are out of control. Did I lose my mind, kissing a stranger?

The boots are way too big for me, but at least they're dry inside.

"Here, take a flashlight with you," Lou says. "There's no light in the outhouse.

When I return to the café, I find Lou helping an older man get out of his wet clothes.

Shivering in his underwear, the man cries, "I carried her on my back, but . . . the water . . . Bea lost her grip . . . I searched in the water . . . but c-couldn't find her," he sobs.

"Your wife?" Lou asks.

The poor man nods and falls onto his knees. Remembering the frigid water and my sister's still face, I take his arm and help him onto his feet.

"Would you like a drink instead of tea?" Lou asks.

The man looks at him bewildered, pats his bare sides and says, "I have no money!"

"I didn't talk about money." Lou grabs a bottle from the shelf behind him. "I asked if you wanted a cup of tea or a drink?" He pours the man a gin.

"Help him find a place to hang his wet clothes, will you?" Lou says to me as he takes the empty glass from the man and refills it.

After he throws back his second drink, I take the man upstairs. Lou is right behind us with an armful of clothes.

"Make sure he gets some soup," Lou says.

I nod and return the boots to Henk.

"How is he?" I nod at Machiel, still on the floor in front of the stove.

"He's sleeping," Henk answers, "but you can check on him."

"I will after I hang these wet clothes and get soup for the man who just came in." I spread his wet clothes over a couple of wooden chairs and fill a bowl with soup.

I carry the bowl over to the table where the man has found a seat. He's shivering. "What's your name?" I ask.

"Crijn," he answers.

"I'm sorry about your wife, Crijn." I sit down beside him.

"She couldn't hang on anymore." His eyes fill with tears.

Soon, a man about Crijn's age sits down beside him.

I scan the room to see where Father is. When I don't see him, I return to Machiel and kneel down beside him. I touch his face. His skin still feels cool. For a moment I watch him breathe in an even rhythm, like the waves in a calm sea.

Reluctantly, I get up.

"I'll keep him warm tonight," Henk reassures me.

"Thank you." I can't believe it has only been a few hours since I met these two young men. It seems as if I've known them forever. I suppose tragedy brings people closer.

One by one, I check the members of my family. Neeltje sleeps with Oma. Sara sits on Mother's lap. Father holds Jacob, and Martin is nestled on the floor against my father's feet. Adriaan is curled up beneath the window, and Liesbeth and Rosa have found a spot under the table. Clasina is snug between them.

"I've asked around to see if anybody knows anything about Luuc's family," Rosa whispers, "but no one does."

I lay down beside her on the wooden floor, and Rosa offers me part of the blanket. *Luuc.* I have to think hard to put a face with that name.

"I wish we knew if his family is safe," Rosa continues.

"They are," I assure her. "Their farm is built on higher ground. Let's try to sleep. Who knows what tomorrow has in store for us. We can't stay here forever."

"Once the water recedes, do you think we'll go back home?" Rosa asks.

"The dikes need to be fixed first. Now that the tides can come in freely, the land will be flooded again and again."

"Where will we go?" She's close to tears.

I put my arm around her. "I don't know, but at least we have each other, and Oma."

I listen to the sounds around me. A chair shifts. Someone cries. I hear coughing and snoring, and still the wind howls and howls.

Despite the fact that my whole body aches and I'm chilled to the bone and exhausted, I can't fall asleep. In my mind, I hear the roaring, angry sea. Billowing waves crest again and again. I feel the boat rocking beneath me. As soon as I close my eyes, I see Clasina's body disappear into the dark, cold waves and Machiel dive after her.

I force myself to think of Luuc, but my thoughts are drawn to the young man in front of the stove and the kiss I still taste on my lips — *a kiss that holds a promise.* I want to pray, but the right words don't come. Tonight, my prayer is directed to the force of nature instead of to God:

Oh, mighty sea,
why did you take

everything from us?
Why did you
devour our land,
our home?
Why take
so many lives?

15

More Challenges

WITH A JOLT, I sit up, feel around with my hands, then remember that Clasina is safe. The pitch black night comes in through the windows, and I've no idea what time it is. Soft light from the turned-down oil lamps fills the room with shadowy figures.

I move the blanket and stand up.

"Where are you going?" Rosa panics.

"Outside. I'll be right back." I tuck Rosa in and tiptoe around tables, chairs with sleeping people and their belongings, and I stop at the stove.

Machiel and Henk are both lying on the floor. Carefully, I step over Henk and kneel down beside Machiel.

"Klara," he whispers. "I was hoping you'd come."

A warm feeling hugs me, and my heart sings. "Are you feeling better?"

"Now I am," he says softly. "Come closer. Give me some of your warmth."

"I can't stay," I whisper, while I stretch out beside him on the floor.

Machiel drapes his arm around me and it feels so good.

I hold his face in both hands. He has a straight nose, full lips and dark curly hair, but his eyes — dark and mysterious — are spellbinding.

I snuggle closer.

"When this hell is over," Machiel says softly, "I'll find you and I'll ask you to marry me."

"Marry." I catch my breath. "But . . . I . . ."

I'll probably never see Machiel again. He isn't from our island. He's a fisherman and most likely doesn't go to the same church. My parents will never allow . . . What am I thinking? Why am I thinking at all?

"You don't have to say yes tonight" — as if he can read my thoughts. "Some day."

"Someday . . ." I repeat.

All I want at this moment is to hold this man close. I don't even care that I know nothing about him. I can't explain, but I feel drawn to him as a moth to a flame.

You're romanticizing the fact that he rescued you, my inner voice reasons. "I need to go."

Instead, Machiel pulls me close and kisses me gently.

I return his kiss, more urgently.

"Goodnight, my angel." He strokes my hair. "Your warmth saved me."

Again, I find his lips. I can't get enough and for a few seconds I forget about the hell we've landed in. At this moment, I know exactly what Dora means about kissing and feeling like floating up to heaven. If only I could hold on to Machiel and this feeling forever. If only Machiel were Luuc.

"What took you so long?" Rosa asks. "You were with that boy, weren't you?"

"I just checked on him, and he's doing much better. Let's try to sleep."

I don't feel like talking. In all the misery, I only want to think of Machiel and his kiss even though I know it's wrong and we can never be together.

Little hands touch my face, waking me from a restless sleep. Clasina falls on top of me. "Klara, I feel better. But I need to pee." She pulls my arms. I wrap my arms around her, kiss and hug her, and hold her close.

Henk and Machiel are still sleeping, but I find Henk's boots under a table. Faint morning light comes in through the windows as I carry Clasina down the stairs.

"Good morning, ladies." Lou is already cutting slices of thick rye bread.

"I'll help you as soon as my sister's done." I point outside. The sight and smell of the bread makes me hungry.

"I can use some extra hands," Lou says when we re-enter the kitchen.

"I can help." Clasina sits proudly on a barstool.

I butter thick slices of bread, fold them double and cut them in half.

Clasina stacks them on a tray. "You know that I almost drowned," she tells Lou. "Machiel saved my life."

"I heard." Lou winks at her. "The flood has produced many heroes. One day we should write down their stories."

"I can't write, but Klara can." Clasina fills a second tray with sandwiches.

The back door opens and an old man wearing a red-knitted toque rushes inside. "I heard on the radio that the army is coming. Today, planes will drop off rubber boats, and soldiers will get us out of here!" he takes a deep breath. "All over the country they're fundraising to collect money, blankets, clothes, you name it. They call it 'wallets open dikes closed.'"

"It's good to know the rest of the country is thinking about us," I say.

"Coen, do you know how much land has been flooded?" Lou asks the excited man.

"Most of our islands, part of the province of South Holland, the province of North Brabant, even the province of North Holland and the island of Texel. But it's not just our country. England, Scotland, Belgium and the coast of France all have been affected." He pauses. "They estimate over a thousand people have drowned in the Netherlands and many more are missing."

I clasp my hand over my mouth. Over a thousand . . . the number overwhelms me.

Lou swears. "How much of our island is flooded?"

"We were hit the worst," Coen speaks fast. "The wife and I will run out of food and might have to leave, too. Unless they start dropping food like they did during the war."

"Where will the army take us?" I turn to Coen.

"They're getting the Ahoy Hallen in Rotterdam and the Market Hallen in Den Bosch ready for thousands of evacuees. They're talking about fifty thousand people who need to be evacuated!" Coen says it in a way that shows he can hardly believe it himself.

"Fifty thousand?" I repeat. A number impossible to fathom.

"I need to get back." Coen opens the back door.

"Keep us up to date with radio announcements, will you?" Lou requests. "Mine died." He pours hot water from the kettle into five teapots. "I'll take these upstairs."

I pick up Clasina and carry her upstairs first, stopping by the stove to take off Henk's boots.

"Where were you?" Father's voice startles us both.

"We made food for everybody," Clasina answers.

Father looks at me, his eyes filled with suspicion. His gaze travels from the young men beside the stove back to me.

Anger rises in me and in a harsh voice I say, "You need to thank those two. Clasina and I wouldn't be here —"

"I know!" he says loud enough for people to hear. He turns and stomps down the stairs.

Machiel and Henk get up. Machiel drapes his arm around me, and Henk lifts up Clasina. I bite my lip and refuse to cry.

"Your father has lost everything. That makes a man bitter." Machiel squeezes my arm.

"Come, Clasina. Help me feed all these hungry people." Henk grabs one of the trays with sandwiches that Lou just brought upstairs.

I take the other tray and walk over to my grandmother. "Oma, are you warm enough?"

"I'm very cold." Oma shivers.

"I'll get you and Mother closer to the stove."

When everyone in the room is fed, I sit down. Never has plain old rye bread tasted so good. Now that the morning light comes through the windows, I have a chance to look at all the people.

Besides my family of twelve, there's a young couple with a small baby, a toddler and two young children.

Then there's an elderly couple. The woman cries while she tries to hang some clothes over empty chairs. Two girls, who look like they could be twins, sit staring into nothing. Crijn still sits at the table with the other man. My eyes pause at Machiel, who's watching me. I want to treasure the moments I've shared with my fisherman, my hero.

Rosa asks me to help her change the little ones. We quickly change Neeltje and Sara into clean diapers and take them to Clasina, who is teaching them a new finger game. When I turn, Machiel and Henk are pulling on their oilskin coats, toques and gloves.

As I walk toward them, my mind floods with conflicting thoughts. I don't want them to leave, but who knows how many more desperate people need to be saved.

"We'll be going." Machiel touches my arm.

My throat feels thick with emotion, and I have difficulty speaking. "Be safe." I can't stop the tears while I hold onto his gaze. Will I ever see him again?

As if Machiel reads my mind he whispers, "I'll find you, I promise." He bends down and kisses me.

"What right do you have to kiss my daughter?" Father's voice stabs me in the back.

"I have no right," Machiel says in a calm voice. "But when this nightmare is over, I'll be back to ask you for permission to marry your daughter. I know this is not the time or the place."

"You're right about that." Father's voice is agitated. "You will never marry her. Since when do fishermen think they can marry farmers' daughters. Besides, she's been spoken for already! Stay away from her. I warn you! And you . . ." he grabs my arm. "Go see your mother. You are a disgrace! Your mother's daughter."

His words stun me like a slap in the face. I hold onto the table for support and watch Machiel go, and it feels like he's taking all the warmth of my body with him. A strong urge to run after him and tell him that I'm not going to marry anybody overwhelms me, but Father pushes me ahead of him, away from Machiel.

I slump down on a chair beside my mother, who must have watched the scene from a distance.

From the looks on people's faces, I realize everyone has witnessed this horrible drama. Mother takes my hand.

"Father said I'm just like you." I search my mother's tight face, but she doesn't reply. "I kissed a fisherman who saved my life. If that's my sin . . . I refuse to ask God for forgiveness."

"Klara. No! Don't turn against God. What you did" — Mother pauses — "was out of gratitude."

"And your sin? Did *you* kiss a stranger, like I did?"

But my mother's face is closed; her secret remains locked up. She gently touches my face and says, "Not now . . . someday."

Alone with my thoughts, I try to figure out what sin my mother has committed and how kissing Machiel is comparable. She must have kissed someone other than my father.

Sara's crying disturbs my pondering. After I change my sister, I glance at Father. *I'll stay away from him as much as is possible.*

He seems to be avoiding me, too. I've tarnished my family's reputation by kissing a fisherman while I'm betrothed to Luuc. I feel beaten, confused by my own feelings.

Lou keeps the stove going, and twice more I help him bring up sandwiches. The day drags on, and despite Coen's announcement, there's no sign of military help. Later that afternoon, more families arrive. All are cold and sad and without words.

In the early evening, a large group of evacuees comes in, creating more noise, smoke, wet clothes and taking up more space in the now crowded room. Their faces speak of loss and desperation.

My family moves closer to the corner as space becomes limited. Jacob and Martin cry and want to go home. The soup tastes watered down, but at least it's warm. Avoiding Father becomes impossible in these tight quarters. Every time I steal a glance at him he looks away.

I shudder when I think of another long night on the hard floor with only the one blanket for the four of us.

"Do you miss Luuc?" Rosa asks, as soon as we have found our hard bed for the night.

I know what Rosa witnessed this morning, so why does she ask? I'm sure everyone who was here this morning knows how I feel about Machiel. How I made a fool of myself. Everyone seems to think so, but I want to hang onto my strong affection for the fisherman. I realize it's wrong to feel this way, but I yearn to be back in Machiel's arms.

Mother is wrong. This fondness I have for Machiel is much more than gratitude. I can't explain it, but it warms my heart and gives it wings. That's why Rosa's question infuriates me.

"Do you miss Luuc?" I fire back.

"Why . . . why are you asking me?" Rosa answers in a tight voice. "You did something very stupid this morning. You should be thinking of Luuc instead of lowering yourself with that fisherman."

"Are you finished?" Anger surges through my mind, and I clench my fists to keep my self-control. "You need to listen to *your* heart," I say through gritted teeth. "It will tell you how *you* feel about Luuc." With that I turn my back to her, not wishing to hear her answer, but Rosa stays silent.

After my anger subsides, I ponder Machiel's words about the

flood being hell. I'd learned that hell is eternal fire, but to me and, I'm sure, to everyone here, it's the destructive water that's hell.

I have nothing to write on, but the words keep coming:

The night stretches out
like a lonely road
to nowhere.
The noise, the stench
overwhelm my senses.
Sadness, despair
choke my heart.
How will we get out of here?
Where will we go?

16
Another Long Day

"KLARA. I NEED TO GO DOWNSTAIRS!" Clasina's wake-up call rouses me from my sleep.

I lift her in my arms and carry her downstairs. We're surprised to find the floor dry and clean. A pair of boots waits for us at the back door. When we return, we help Lou make sandwiches for breakfast.

During our second long-day at the café, I try to keep myself busy by helping Lou, directing new evacuees, showing them where to dry their clothes and handing out food.

The boys play with other children, and Liesbeth has found a girl who shares her passion for the Dutch princesses.

I'm concerned that Oma is shrinking even more, and Mother's complexion has turned a worrisome white.

The little ones cry or sleep, and even Clasina bursts into tears for no reason.

I change and feed the little ones as if I were a machine. Though I'm grateful to the people of White Church for all their donations, my mind is numb. Every now and then I allow the rugged face of Machiel, my prince, to come to mind and warm my heart. I wish I could transport my mind to fairyland to meet my prince, but the misery I see around me prevents me from having these dreams.

Another long night fills me with dread. I listen to the even breathing of my sisters, but my mind finds no rest. As soon as I close my eyes, I experience the horrific ordeal of Clasina being ripped out of my arms and Machiel diving after her. It leaves me sweating, with a racing heartbeat and a pain in my chest.

Early the next morning I find Lou already making breakfast.

"Good morning," he says. "I'm counting on your help, you know."

"Listen. The wind is gone."

"It was the stillness that woke me," Lou replies.

The front door opens. Two military men march inside and look around. "They told us we'd find many evacuees here," one of them says.

"I'm glad you're here," Lou's smile welcomes the men at the door. "They're upstairs." He points.

Please take us somewhere. Somewhere safe, warm and with enough food.

"How many?" the older one asks.

"About a hundred," Lou answers. "I can't take any more. I'm running out of space and food. How will you transport all these people?"

"We'll take them by 'duck' to Harbour Town," the younger one answers.

I run upstairs and wake up the rest of the family. "Two military people are downstairs," I tell them. "They'll be taking evacuees to Harbour Town."

"Soldiers?" Martin jumps up.

"Did you see their guns?" Jacob pumps my arm.

"No guns, but they have some kind of a boat." I shiver. The thought of going back out in that cold angry water scares me. How safe is this boat? What will the situation be like in Harbour Town? The dikes breached there, too. We've heard the stories — entire neighbourhoods swept up and destroyed by a wall of water rushing through a hole in the dike; houses swallowed up and people drowned in their sleep.

"We better gather our belongings." Mother gets up and starts picking up clothes. Suddenly, she cringes, grabs hold of the table.

"Mother! What's wrong?" I stare at her white face.

"I just have cramps because my feet are so cold. It's passed already." She produces a faint smile.

"Are you sure?" My eyes move from my mother to my grandmother.

"I'll watch her." Oma pats Mother's arm.

While I worry about my mother's condition, I round up my sisters. "Lou needs help downstairs, and we might find out about the soldiers' plan." Liesbeth, Clasina and Rosa follow me to the main floor, where the two men in uniform are standing at the bar talking to Lou.

"We came to help," I say when Lou looks up.

"These loaves need to be sliced thin, and I only have a little butter left." He points to the twelve loaves lined up on the bar.

"How many people will fit in one of those ducks?" I hear Lou ask.

"Twelve soldiers in full gear," one of them answers. "But with kids we can add more bodies."

Lou turns toward me. "Klara! How many in your family?"

"Nine kids and three adults, and what in the world is a duck?" I ask.

The young soldier looks at me, his eyes twinkling. "Actually it's spelled D-U-K-W; it's a six-wheel-drive, armoured, amphibious truck that can transport people over land and water," he answers. "The Allied troops used them during the war to land on the beaches in Normandy and called them 'ducks.' The American army stationed in Germany has sent us several. Look outside." He walks to the door.

We follow him and when we look down the street, we see a big boat on wheels. The front end looks like an army truck.

"It looks funny, but it's better than the flat-bottomed boat we were on," Liesbeth comments.

"Looks safer than the rowboat," I add.

All morning we wait for something to happen, but it's well after noon when Lou comes upstairs to see Father.

We quickly gather our meagre belongings and work our way down the stairs. I'm the last one, with Clasina holding my hand.

"I don't want to go on a boat." Clasina tightens her grip.

"This boat is safe," I try to assure her. "It's like a big truck and we don't have to row. It has a strong engine."

An older couple joins us and the soldiers help everybody board the duck. The remaining evacuees come downstairs to have a look at this unusual vehicle.

"I'll miss your help." Lou winks at me.

"Thanks for being there for us," I answer.

The engine starts, and the truck drives down the road. We pass the church, where a second armoured vehicle is parked.

When the duck turns south, we see first-hand the destruction the storm and the flood have caused.

"The sea is too strong for men," Father says.

"The government should have upgraded the dikes after the war." The old man bristles with anger. "Now it'll cost much more to rebuild." He looks agitated as he surveys the carnage.

I'm surprised the way the duck eases through all the debris and floating cadavers.

My body feels numb, but I wish my brain would go numb, too. It keeps on worrying about where we will end up, where Machiel, Dora and others are, and when this horrible nightmare will end.

When the duck rocks on the waves, I feel Clasina's body tremble.

Two helicopters circle around. We watch as one of them drops a rubber dinghy close to a cluster of farm buildings on a small island in the middle of the sea.

I watch my mother. Her face has turned ashen.

I close my eyes and see Machiel. I feel his rough shaved skin caress mine. I can almost taste his lips, and a flicker of warmth touches my heart.

Soon the church and houses of Harbour Town draw nearer. When we reach the first street, the ride becomes bumpy as the duck now uses its wheels and transforms once more into a truck. There are so many stones, bricks, pieces of wood and other debris to get through. People in rubber boots, carrying shovels, brooms and buckets, try to clean up the enormous mess now that the water has retreated.

Men wearing protective clothing and masks are loading animal cadavers on a wagon pulled by horses.

"How are we going to find shelter?" Mother asks one of the soldiers.

"You'll have to register at the Red Cross post," the soldier answers. "It's in the church."

The truck slows down on Main Street. Cattle, pigs, sheep and horses crowd the street. While people move to the side for the approaching vehicle, the animals do not. The smell of manure and rotting cadavers makes me pinch my nose.

"Here's the Red Cross," one of the soldiers points. The duck stops at the church, and we disembark.

The lineup of evacuees pours into the street.

"Hold hands!" Father yells. "We need to stay together!"

We move up slowly. The little ones cry, including Clasina. I watch the boys struggle to hold it together.

Oma and Mother walk together, arm in arm. Suddenly, Mother stumbles and Father steps forward to support her and Oma. After what feels like an eternity, we finally enter the church. People in Red Cross uniforms have set up tables and write names in ledgers. A woman with a tired face takes our family names.

"How many?" she asks without looking up.

"Three adults, nine children," Father answers.

"I'm very sorry, but we have no place for you here," she says. "It's chaos. All the homes that were spared from the floodwaters are full. You'll have to go on the ferry." She glances around the room and waves at a young man wearing an armband with a red cross. "He will take you down to the harbour," she says.

"Where will the ferry take us?" Father's voice is strained with fatigue.

"To Bergen op Zoom," the woman answers.

"That's a two-hour boat ride," Father says. "Can we get food here, before we leave?"

"This town has no food left. Planes are dropping food packages, but so far most have landed in the water." She shakes her head. "Follow this young man. Next!"

I can't believe what she's telling us. I grab Clasina's hand and like a flock of sheep, we follow the Red Cross fellow through the streets.

We walk between houses, stumbling over debris because the main roads down to the wharf are still under water. At the quay, a long line of men, soldiers and civilians fill sandbags, trying to patch the enormous cavity in the dike. Wearing hip waders, they stand up to their knees in the water.

"It's Luuc! I see Luuc!" Rosa's cry sounds like a seagull spotting its prey. "Klara! I see him!"

Unbelievable. How can she spot Luuc from such a long line of workers when all these men look alike except for the ones in military uniforms?

"Luuc!" Rosa cries at the top of her lungs.

A head turns. Rosa waves. A man leaves the line of workers and slowly walks toward us, then faster, until he reaches our family.

"Dear God!" He looks at me in disbelief. "How did you recognize me?"

"Rosa spotted you," I say. Luuc's face is flushed from the hard work and the sharp wind.

"On Monday night, we got the news that you all had been saved. Do you know that there's only a one-and-a-half square kilometre of dry land in this whole town? And that's where all the people from outlying areas of Harbour Town, plus the evacuees from flooded areas, are waiting. It's madness."

We crowd around him, eager for news.

Luuc's voice is high-pitched with excitement. "We're only now getting some food dropped from airplanes. We get our news from amateur radio operators."

"How's your family?" Father asks.

"We're staying with the mayor. His house is in the dry zone." In the next breath, he says, "I can't believe my luck to see you." He grabs my hand. "Our farm was actually spared because it's built higher up, but Mother refused to stay there without electricity."

"Does the mayor have more room?" Father asks.

"Well, maybe for one." He winks at me.

"I need to help my family," I say quickly. "Rosa is very tired," I say. "Maybe she can stay."

Rosa's face turns bright red, and she looks away.

"The government and the army are trying to evacuate everybody in Harbour Town," Luuc says. "Prince Bernhard came down by helicopter this morning and urged the citizens to go to Rotterdam, but no one is willing to leave."

"No wonder," Father replies. "When the Germans flooded this area during the war, the people found their houses looted when they returned home."

"Do you have any news about Dora's family . . . or Miss Poortvliet . . . or the baker's family?" My heart beats fast. I need to know even though I'm afraid to hear the truth.

Luuc's expression grows dark. "Dora's family all made it, but they couldn't get to their grandmother." The excitement has left his voice, and his tone is sombre.

Oma shudders and tears fill her eyes. I take her arm. She's known Dora's grandmother all her life.

"Miss Poortvliet . . ." Luuc pauses. "The baker's family . . . Jopie's family, they were all surprised in their sleep by the water. When the dike breached, a wall of water just gushed through New Port."

Rosa gasps. "The . . . the whole family?" She wavers, turns pale and faints.

In one quick movement, Luuc catches her before she falls down.

"Can you carry her onto the ferry for us?" Father asks.

We walk in procession toward the ferry. Our thoughts are with the ones we lost, and we feel overwhelmed.

From the west, a large plane circles low over Harbour Town.

We stop and watch doors open in the belly of the plane. Parcels come tumbling down. Most of them land in the water of the Oosterschelde. A few hit the roofs of nearby houses.

"That's one of the American planes dropping off food parcels," a man with a wheelbarrow full of debris yells. "How can they not aim right? They knew where to drop their bombs a few years ago!"

Defeated, everyone groans as the plane flies away and disappears from view. I wish someone with a boat would drag the food out of the Oosterschelde, but there is no one with a boat for as far as I can see:

We wander aimlessly,
without direction.
Follow others,
going nowhere.
Depend on
rescuers'
kindness
to herd us
to a safe destiny.

17

Long Ferry Ride

THE FERRY IS MOORED at a much higher water level than normal. An improvised gangplank has been constructed with straw bales, doors and pieces of wood. We walk downstairs into the hold. All the benches and seats have been removed, and rows of stretchers and cots have been put in place.

I'm relieved when we find some vacant, but there aren't enough for everybody, and my family will have to share.

Luuc lowers Rosa onto one of the stretchers.

His face is serious when he turns to me and takes my hands. "There are so many losses and the destruction is . . . I don't know how to describe it, but if we can ever find a way to live here again, you and I will get married. I promise. Maybe next year in May. Something happy for you to dream about while dealing with this . . ." His voice falters.

"I . . . I . . ." My throat closes before I can say more. I should be happy that during all this misery he still wants to marry me. I desperately search but don't feel anything. The passion I have for Machiel is absent when I'm with Luuc.

"I need to go back. Soon it'll be too dark." He lets go of my hands, touches his cap to salute my father and disappears up the stairs.

Rosa cries, and I stroke her hair. The loss of Jopie and her family has struck her hard. The family lived in the poor area of town close to the spot where the dike breached. They had no chance. After a while, she pulls herself together and covers Martin and Jacob with her blanket.

Liesbeth tries desperately to settle Sara and Neeltje down for a sleep, but the girls want Mother and refuse to stay put.

Mother and Oma have each found a stretcher.

Father hands them a blanket. He watches my mother struggle to get comfortable on the uncomfortable cot.

"Are you going to be all right?" I ask my mother. I watch her putting on a brave front. She smiles, but I can see the worried, anxious expression she's trying to hide.

"I'm just not feeling well. It'll pass. I'm sure. Look after the little ones. I'll help you in a little while." She closes her eyes.

I feel totally inept. How can I look after the little ones when I have no food or diapers? I sigh and then straighten my shoulders. We've made it this far; we'll manage somehow. Let's hope the Red Cross has food for us on the ferry.

More people come down into the hold, but there are no more stretchers, and many just slump against the wall. The space quickly fills up with people wrapped in despair.

"The ferry is overflowing with evacuees, so what are we waiting for?" an older man on the cot beside mine says. "They can't possibly fit in any more people."

Wall sconces spread a dim light in the hold. Through the portholes, I can see the light fading. "Another night," I whisper. Night shadows cause my demons to grow into gigantic threats, foreshadowing the enormity of what still lies ahead of us."

Adriaan has a stretcher all to himself and lies with his eyes closed. Jacob and Martin share one; so do Rosa and Liesbeth. I share my stretcher with Clasina, Neeltje and Sarah. Father sits on the floor between Mother and Oma.

The hours drag on. When the little ones finally cry themselves to sleep, I cover them with a blanket. I listen to parts of conversations around me — a young woman says that she was in a tree for ten hours before a helicopter finally rescued her. She can't feel her legs because they've been in that ice-cold water too long. She will have to get to the hospital as soon as the ferry arrives in Bergen op Zoom. I wonder if she will lose her legs, and I shudder.

"We owe our lives to the fishermen from Yerseke, Stavenisse and West Bay," an older man says. "They came as soon as they heard about the flooding."

I can only agree when I think of our two fishermen, especially the one with the dark eyes who has put a spell on me. I shake my head. To think that Luuc, the rich farmer, and Machiel, the poor fisherman, both want to marry me.

With a jolt, I sit up, hearing the sound of an engine and feeling the ship move. I must have dozed off.

"Finally," the man beside me says. "It's five o'clock. What the hell did we wait for all night long?"

No one answers him because no one knows.

I walk over to Oma and notice that Father is gone.

My grandmother grabs my hand. "Your mother isn't well."

"Where's Father?"

"He went upstairs to ask for help," Oma answers. She looks anxious.

I kneel beside my mother and stroke her forehead.

"I tried very hard," Mother says softly, "but I can't stop it. This little one is coming."

My head drops and I silently pray: "Oh, please God, not here on this overcrowded ferry."

Smiling bravely at her, I ask, "What do we do?"

"Father is getting help." Mother looks exhausted.

"What can I do?" I feel so useless.

"Look after the children, Klara," she whispers. Her body convulses in another contraction, and she clasps my hand in a tight grip. My heart sinks.

"Dear God, please don't punish my mother for her so-called sins," I silently pray again.

"Make some room, people!" Father leads a man in uniform through the sea of stretchers.

"We need to carry your wife upstairs into the captain's cabin," the man orders.

Father looks at me. "Klara, the doctor asked if there are any nurses on this ship."

While Father and the doctor carry Mother on her stretcher up the stairs, I go around asking. The word spreads quickly and a young woman in her mid-twenties comes up to me.

"I'm Rie," she introduces herself. "I used to assist the midwife. I can help."

"My mother is upstairs in the captain's cabin."

"Klara!" Rosa stops me at the bottom of the stairs. "What's going on?" She grabs my arm.

"Mother's gone into labour."

"But it's too soon!" Rosa cries.

"Please, look after the little ones." I take a deep breath. I need to be strong for my mother, I tell myself as I walk to the upper deck.

In the captain's cabin there is a narrow bed on one side. In the corner stands a table and two chairs that are anchored to the floor. A small counter with a sink and a petroleum stove with a single burner are located on the opposite wall.

The men lower Mother onto the bed. She grabs onto Father's arm as another wave batters her body.

The doctor looks at his watch. "Tell the captain to radio for an ambulance." He looks at me.

I run out the door and find the captain in the wheelhouse.

"My mother has gone into labour and the doctor wants you to radio for an ambulance," I answer when he questions my entrance.

"I'll do that right away," the captain answers.

Ambulance. It suddenly hits me that Mother will go to the hospital! Nobody in my family has ever been in a hospital. Panic chokes me. I can't think of the consequences at this moment. All I want is for my mother and the baby to be all right. Out of breath, I return to the cabin, where Rie already has placed a pot with water on the stove.

"When did you eat last?" the doctor asks.

"We haven't had a real meal since last Saturday night," Father answers.

The doctor nods. "She's weak."

"The captain has radioed for an ambulance to meet the ferry," I say in a constricted voice.

Another contraction takes hold of Mother. It looks like her whole body is fighting.

"Check on your brothers and sisters." Father's voice is tense.

As I make my way back into the hold, I feel like I'm in the sequel to a nightmare. I know that many women die in childbirth, and my mother is in labour during extreme circumstances.

My siblings are awake, but I don't know what to tell them when I see their questioning eyes.

"How is Mother?" Adriaan asks.

"Mother will go to the hospital as soon as the ferry docks," I answer. "The captain has radioed for an ambulance."

"An ambulance?" No one had expected an ambulance.

"How sick is she?" Martin's eyes are red.

"Mother has been very cold," I begin. "Her belly aches very much, and the doctor wants her to go to the hospital."

"Is she going to die?" Jacob's eyes are big with worry. "Remember Bea, our cow, had a bellyache and she died." Tears fill his eyes.

I take his hand. "No, Jacob. Mother isn't going to die, because we found a doctor and a nurse on the ferry. They're looking after her. She's going to the hospital where she will get medicine."

I ask the woman on the stretcher beside me how long it will take to Bergen op Zoom.

"We should be there shortly," she answers.

Adriaan looks at me and points up the stairs. "Check on her," he pleads.

"I will." I touch his shoulder.

People make room for me when I scramble up the stairs. Out of breath, I pause outside the captain's cabin. Gently, I open door. The oil lamp on the table spreads a yellow light.

Mother's eyes are closed, her complexion a yellowy-white. Father and the doctor sit at the table. Rie stands at the sink washing up. In the corner, I notice a bundle of towels stained with blood.

"Father?" I turn and look at him.

"The . . . little boy didn't breathe. God took him." He stares into the lamp on the table, his face wet with tears.

"This child was due the end of April. He still had three months to grow." The doctor looks at me. "His lungs were not fully developed."

I feel a lump in my throat. I wasn't happy when I found out that Mother was expecting again, but now that the little boy who would have been my brother has died, a thick layer of sadness descends on me.

"Is Mother still going to the . . . hospital?" I ask.

The doctor nods.

"What shall I tell the children?"

Father looks at me for a long time, searching for words. "I don't know. Please pray with them that your mother is going to be all right." He puts his head down on his arms.

Fighting back tears, I head back down into the hold. My siblings are crowded around Oma.

"We're going to pray for Mother," I say.

"But how she is?" Liesbeth asks.

"Mother is very sick, and she needs to go to the hospital." I swallow the lump down. "That's why Father wants us to pray for her."

Even though the little ones cry, I fold my hands and pray in a pleading voice, "Dear God, please, please make sure our mother gets better. We can't lose her; we need her."

People around us stare, and I wonder how much they guess.

Oma's eyes urge me to come close.

"God took our little brother," I whisper.

She nods as if she expected this would happen. "He's with the angels and his little cousins. Your grandfather will keep an eye on him, too," she says softly.

A commotion at the stairs makes us all look up. A soldier with a megaphone is standing there. The ferry rocks from side to side and then stops.

"We've reached Bergen op Zoom," the soldier announces through the megaphone. "Everyone come up on deck. Bring all your belongings! If you don't have relatives who can take care of you, you'll be taken to the Market Hallen in Den Bosch! Make sure you register at the Red Cross first."

"What about Mother?" Adriaan panics.

"Father will stay with her," I assure him. "We need to be strong for her."

We gather the little ones and our belongings and follow the long line of flood victims, and I wonder where we will be herded next.

Fresh air, seagulls and more military personnel greet us at the quay. I notice a row of buses waiting for us, but first we need to register with the Red Cross.

My eyes wander to several boats docked beside the ferry. To my horror, I see coffins — rows of coffins — on the deck of a navy ship.

"They say more than twelve hundred have drowned so far," a man wearing a top hat says to me. "And how many bodies will they find once the water is gone?" he adds.

Twelve hundred or more . . .
so many families ravaged by the sea.
The waves,
hungry for lives and land,
have consumed our island,
our home,
animals,
everything we owned.

18
Telephone Calls

TWO AMBULANCES WITH flashing lights and blaring sirens drive up to the ferry. Paramedics jump out, grab stretchers from the back and hurry up the gangplank into the boat.

"Let's stay here!" I call out to my family, even though the soldiers try to herd everyone into a red brick building with a Red Cross banner over the door.

"You need to get moving!" one of them yells at me. "The buses are waiting!"

"We need to wait for my father!" I shout back.

In the confusion, Martin and Jacob disappear into the crowds. Adriaan hands Neeltje over to Rosa and sprints after them. It takes a few minutes before he returns with two crying boys.

"We didn't see you anymore, Klara," Jacob sobs.

"People pushed us," Martin cries.

"Stay with Oma!" I order. God, I don't want to lose anyone. The crowds choke me. My heart pounds wildly.

"Where is Father?" Clasina asks.

"He'll be here," I say, but I wonder why it's taking so long to bring Mother up. Is her condition worse?

Finally, I see two paramedics carrying a stretcher with the young woman who'd been in a tree for ten hours. Next, the stretcher with Mother comes down the gangplank. Father and Rie walk behind her.

"Wait!" I call. "We need to say goodbye to Mother!"

Our small procession halts beside the second ambulance. My brothers and sisters stare at Mother lying on the stretcher, but they're too shocked to speak. I notice how small she looks. Her face is drawn and pale. Holding Sara in my arms, I touch my mother's hand. "Don't worry about us. Get better, please."

"Klara, I . . ." Mother closes her eyes and presses her lips together.

Tears run down her face; my own vision blurs, and I move away.

The paramedics open the double doors at the back of the ambulance. Carefully, they move the stretcher with Mother inside. Father looks at us, then follows, his head down. The doors close. The two paramedics hop in the front. The lights are flashing and as the ambulance pushes through the crowds, it turns on its sirens.

"We better line up." Adriaan's words bring everyone back to the moment. "It will be a long time before it's our turn to register, and we're all so hungry."

Oma points at a woman in uniform. "I'll ask that Red Cross nurse over there if she can phone Neeltje for me, to let her know where we're going."

"Do you know her phone number?" Liesbeth asks.

"It's up here." Oma touches her head. "I have trouble remembering places and things, but I can remember phone numbers. I even know Hendrik's number, in America."

"You should telephone him and tell him that we're all right, except for Mother," I suggest.

"We're next," Adriaan announces as the people ahead of us move inside the building.

I notice a big banner hanging on the wall announcing WALLETS OPEN DIKES CLOSED, just like the old man in the café had mentioned.

"Where will we go next?" I ask after we've registered.

"You'll board bus number thirty-six. It will take you to Den Bosch, to the Brabant Hallen — the indoor cattle market," the nurse explains. "A committee has organized food and clothes for the flood victims, and there are cots to sleep on. Military personnel will help you get on the bus."

"Can my grandmother telephone her daughter in Roseville?" I ask.

"Telephones are in the office on the right. You might have to wait. It's busy in there."

"We can't pay," I tell her, feeling embarrassed.

"You don't need money," the nurse says. "You'll have to go through the operator."

"Can we telephone my uncle in America?" I feel encouraged.

"Just ask the operator, and she'll connect you," the nurse replies.

The office is a noisy place. Benches are placed along the outside walls underneath a row of square windows. People occupy several phone booths. We hear talking, yelling and crying as they speak to their loved ones.

A friendly looking woman takes us to one of the telephones.

"You call her," Oma says while she takes the children and finds a place to sit on a wooden bench along the wall.

After I've told Aunt Neeltje where we're going, I join my family on the bench. "Aunt Neeltje will visit us tomorrow at the Brabant Hallen in Den Bosch," I tell them.

"Where is her family?" Martin asks.

Oma swallows. "Aunt Neeltje's husband and her two little boys died ten years ago."

Martin gasps. I realize my younger siblings are not aware of Aunt Neeltje's tragic loss.

"I told the woman that you would call Hendrik in America. I'm not up to it, right now." Oma points at the volunteer who looks at me. "I gave her the number already."

I make my way to the telephone and wait while the woman dials the operator and tells her Uncle Hendrik's number.

"It's early in America," she says. "Six hours' difference with our time. It's four o'clock in the morning." She hands me the receiver.

I listen to the ringing tone. My heart pounds. I can't believe I'm phoning America.

"Hello," a deep voice on the other side of line says.

Startled, I respond. "Is this . . . Hendrik?"

The line crackles with static. Then the voice speaks urgently, "Who is this? Gilda? Is it you? Is something wrong with Mother?"

"No, I'm Klara, Gilda's daughter. The oldest," I explain. "We had a terrible flood on the first of February."

"It was in the news," Hendrik says. "How is everybody? How is my mother?"

"Oma is good. We're fine. We lost our farm and the animals. They drowned. We lost our dog, Max, too." The words come tumbling out of my mouth.

"That's . . . that's awful!"

The line crackles again, and I'm not sure if my uncle is saying something else.

"Tell Oma I'm coming in . . . in October!" Uncle Hendrik's voice is clear now. "I'll telephone Neeltje next week."

Static interferes once more.

"Uncle Hendrik, can you hear me?"

"Yes, I can hear you," he says in a hoarse voice.

"Will you visit us?"

"I'd like to meet you, Klara . . ." The line crackles some more, then the connection is lost.

Dazed, I look into the receiver. "I've lost him," I say when I notice the woman watching me.

"You were lucky to get through," she replies. "Most times you can't even have a conversation."

"Uncle Hendrik will come to visit in October," I say when I return to my family.

Oma's face lights up. She fingers her coral bead necklace. After taking a deep breath, she says, "We better find the bus." She gets up from the bench and heads for the door.

Like ducklings, we follow her outside. In my mind I recap the latest events:

I wanted to leave the island.
See the world.
But . . .
in a rowboat?
A duck?
A ferry?
A bus?

I did not imagine
to travel the world
this way.

19

Brabant Hallen, Den Bosch

ONCE OUTSIDE, I notice many people already lined up at each bus.

"This way!" a soldier with a clipboard in his hand motions us. "Bus number thirty-six is filling up fast, and the children have to sit three to a seat."

I make sure Adriaan sits with Martin and Jacob, that Rosa and Liesbeth sit with Neeltje. Oma holds Sara and I have Clasina on my lap.

None of us has been on a bus before, nor have we ever visited the mainland, but everyone is too tired and too hungry to enjoy the ride. It doesn't take long before the hum of the engine and the motion of the ride puts most of us to sleep. Even Oma nods off, and I feel her weight sag against me.

I look out the window and watch the landscape and the villages slide by. My thoughts return to the conversation with Uncle

Hendrik. It must have been hard for him to imagine the flooded land and the devastation on the island where he grew up. What puzzles me most is the fight between Father and Hendrik? Was it so bad that Hendrik had to leave for America? I have no answers and come to the conclusion that my family has more than one secret.

My worries about Mother keep me company while the bus drives past towns and farmer's fields. How unreal this all feels. Here we are on a bus, far away from New Port, even Schouwen-Duiveland, something I've longed to do, but not like this.

The hum of the engine and the rocking of the bus make my eyes want to close. I need to keep an eye on my family, but it becomes harder and harder to fight the battle to stay awake.

When the bus jerks to a stop, I straighten up. After rubbing my eyes, I look out the window. We've stopped in front of a large building. On the tower, I notice a sign in huge letters that reads BRABANT HALLEN. We have reached our destination — the indoor cattle market in Den Bosch. I don't even question the fact that we're staying at a cattle market. I'm just grateful that we may be able to eat soon.

Oma stirs and sits up.

I stand up with Clasina in my arms. She weighs heavy with sleep, and I have to shift her weight onto my shoulder.

My brothers and sisters stir and by the time we disembark with our few belongings, they're fully awake. We're ushered into the building to a large area with long tables and chairs already filled with many people.

The aroma of coffee, soup and bread mixed together is a pleasant welcome, along with the noise that echoes from the concrete walls in this huge building. A row of windows at the top brings in the light. Industrial light boxes hang from the beams.

I'm overwhelmed by the large number of people, the huge space and the noise, but I also feel for the first time that maybe here, in these halls, we'll be looked after, and a small weight lifts off my shoulders.

A soldier directs us to one of the long tables, and I can't believe the large number of displaced people, families just like ours. I hold Sara in my lap, but Neeltje sits all by herself beside Clasina. It looks like Neeltje has grown up in the last few days. As soon as we're seated, a small army of volunteers comes around asking if we want coffee, tea or milk. Large serving trays piled high with sandwiches are placed on each table. Bowls of warm soup are handed out.

"If you haven't had food for a couple of days, eat slowly," the women warn.

Soup and coffee have never tasted this good. My stomach hurts from receiving the unexpected nourishment, but I don't care. It feels so good to eat again. The boys attack the sandwich pile like a flock of hungry ravens. Cutlery clatters, chairs scrape the concrete floor, people talk and children cry, but it's better than all the previous places we've been. Even Oma's face looks less pale after she's finished eating. I wonder where we'll be sleeping with so many people.

After the meal, a volunteer tells us about the clothes that have been donated. "Donations came from all over the country, and we even received clothing from Germany, Belgium and France," she informs us. "We actually have too much. After you've washed up you can go into the next hall and make sure everyone in your family gets a clean wardrobe."

When I see the abundance of clothes and shoes, I'm overcome with gratitude. "Let's get cleaned up first," I order.

Armed with towels, facecloths, soap and diapers, we take the little ones to the washroom. The boys are sent to the men's room.

I look into Adriaan's eyes. "It's up to you to make sure they get clean." I point at Martin and Jacob.

The spacious women's room is tiled from floor to ceiling in black and white tiles. I feel like I'm in a palace.

"Look at the water closets!" Rosa cries. "You have to pull the chain to flush," she giggles.

Liesbeth and Clasina pull the chains and make all the toilets flush. We all laugh, and it feels so good.

Six sinks with hot and cold running water are located across from the water closets. Two change tables have been set up on the same wall.

"Let's give them a bath in the sinks," Oma suggests.

We strip the little girls and once Sara and Neeltje sit in the warm water, they smile and splash and giggle. Oma and I lather their little bodies until their skin turns pink. Even Clasina has a turn. She smiles and giggles just like Sara and Neeltje did.

I wish I were small enough to sit in the warm water in the sink and soak all the grime and dirt from my body.

By the time we all return to the hall, a volunteer with a big smile shows us where to find clothes for everybody. It takes a while before my siblings have chosen new clothes, including coats, shoes, hats and mittens. For the second time since our ordeal, I notice smiles on their faces when they proudly carry their new wardrobe.

The clothes I choose are so different from the traditional clothing on the island. I'm worried what Father will say if I wear something too colourful. I haven't covered my hair since I lost my lace cap, and it now looks like a huge nest. Rosa, Liesbeth and Clasina have lost their caps, too, but their straight hair isn't unruly like my curls. I smile when I remember how much Machiel liked my hair.

It seems so long since I met the kind young fisherman with the dark eyes.

When she sees that we have chosen our clothes, the helpful volunteer returns and guides us to an area where we have to sleep tonight. In a third hall, hundreds and hundreds of cots are made up with sheets, blankets and pillows. Close to an exit sign, we find ten cots, move them close together and put our clothes underneath.

"I'll try to telephone the hospital," I announce. I make my way to the office and explain our situation to a woman with a friendly face, sitting behind a desk.

"Our mother is in the hospital in Roseville," I tell her. "Can I telephone to find out how she's doing?"

"This is not a good time," the woman answers. "We're expecting another influx of evacuees. Four more buses will be arriving shortly. Come back tonight, after eight."

"Thank you." I get up and return to my family. "I can call tonight," I announce.

Later that afternoon, we're herded back into the dining hall. The population has doubled since our arrival, but we manage to find seats together. Volunteers bring bowls of thick pea soup, with chunks of sausage and bacon and slices of black rye bread with cheese. My family devours the delicious food. Barley cooked in berry juice, with raisins and cinnamon, finishes the meal, one of my family's favourite desserts.

The younger children are ready for bed, and even Adriaan struggles to keep his eyes open, but he and Liesbeth want to wait up for the news from the hospital.

"Are we going to sleep with all of them?" Clasina points at the hundreds of evacuees. "Did all their houses drown?"

"Yes, all these people lost everything, just like us," I reply.

Just after eight o'clock, I'm back at the office. The same woman still works the phone and fills out papers.

"I'm Bea," she says. "Do you have the number of the hospital?"

"No, I don't." My mouth feels dry.

Bea checks the telephone book. "There's only one hospital in Roseville." She dials the number and hands me the telephone.

"Can I speak to Jannes van Burgh?" I ask, when a voice at the other end of the line answers. "I'm his daughter. My Mother, Gilda van Burgh, was admitted this morning."

After what seems forever, I hear the receiver being picked up.

"Klara?" Father's voice sounds exhausted.

"How . . . how is Mother?"

"Your mother had surgery. . . . We have to wait and see. . . . She's lost a lot of blood. . . ."

My throat closes when I sense that my father is having a hard time holding it together.

"If she makes it through the night . . . she has a chance." His voice is barely audible.

The thought of Mother not making it through the night is unbearable. Father is silent at the other end of the receiver.

"What . . . shall I tell . . ." I can't finish the sentence. Tears choke me.

"I don't know," Father whispers. "How are you and the children? How's Oma?"

"Good. We all have clean clothes and good food, and we'll pray for Mother," I manage to say.

"Yes," he says.

I wait, but he offers no more words. "I'll call back tomorrow," I say before I hang up.

When I return to my family, my heart feels so heavy it slows down my feet.

Rosa, Adriaan, Liesbeth and Oma gather around me. Fear clouds their eyes.

"Mother's stomach was so bad the doctor had to operate," I tell them in a tight voice.

Oma touches my arm.

"She's lost a lot of blood. . . ." I catch my breath.

No one speaks.

"Mother is weak. If . . . if she makes it through the night, she'll be all right." I feel warm tears run down my face.

Oma cries softly. I throw my arms around her and rest my chin on the top of her head. Adriaan blows his nose. Rosa and Liesbeth embrace.

"Let's pray for Mother and ask God to make sure she gets better." I wipe my face on my sleeve. "Dear God in Heaven, please hear me when I cry to you for help. . . . Please heal our mother. . . . Take care of her . . . so she can take care of us. Amen."

While we pray, the big hall fills up with people who are all finding a cot for the night. But despite my exhaustion, I still can't settle down. My mind keeps churning. What if Mother . . . ? How can we ever go back to the farm if . . . ? How can we be a family without Mother? No, I scold myself. Don't even think that way.

I lie down and cover myself with the grey wool blanket. Even Machiel's face is far away tonight. His rescue, his kisses . . . was it just a few days ago . . . or was it a dream?

In the early morning hours when sleep finally claims me, the recurring images of Clasina and Machiel disappearing in the icy waters leave me drained and tired by the time I wake up. My first thought is Mother. Has she made it?

A small hand touches my face. "Klara, is Mother coming here from the 'hostibal' today?"

I pull Clasina close. "I'll phone Father after breakfast."

My sister puts her arms around my neck. "She'll be all right."

I smile. I wish I had Clasina's optimism. "You're right," I reply. "Hungry?"

People around us are getting up, scrambling to the washrooms and then to the hall where the food is being served.

"Let's see who's awake and we'll go for breakfast." Clasina and I dress in our new clothes. Beside our cots, Sara and Neeltje yawn and stretch, ready to get up. Martin and Jacob are glad they can go for breakfast, so they hurry to finish dressing.

Oma, Rosa, Liesbeth and Adriaan are still asleep. I decide to let them rest.

Taking the little ones and the boys, I find a place setting for everyone at one of the tables. Sara and Neeltje each gobble up two slices of bread with jam. I wipe their faces before they both slide off their chairs.

Suddenly Clasina calls, "Look, Sara is walking!"

My baby sister is walking from chair to chair around the long table, and she makes the people who sit on those chairs smile. Tears fill my eyes. Mother has to know. I get up. "Keep an eye on Sara," I tell the others and head for the office.

Bea, already at her desk, has help from a young woman with a long brown ponytail.

"Good morning," Bea says in a cheery voice.

"Good morning, Bea. Can I phone the hospital?"

After Bea connects me, I wait; the receiver trembles against my ear.

"Klara?" Father's voice sounds tired.

"Father . . . how . . ." My voice tightens to a whisper. "Tell Mother . . . Sara can walk."

"She . . . she will like that," he says. "She will like that very much."

Tears stream down my face. My heart fills. She's alive.

"I'll come tonight," he adds.

Bea gets up and wraps me in a big hug.

"My mother made it through the night," I tell her.

I return to the hall just as Sara is rounding the corner and wobbles over to the next chair. Adults and children are clapping and encouraging her. I've never seen a bigger smile on my baby sister's face. Under protest, I scoop Sara in my arms and carry her back to my family. Even the late sleepers have arrived at the dining hall.

"Mother made it through the night!" I announce with a smile.

"Will she come here?" they all ask.

"Not yet, but I told Father to tell Mother about Sara."

"They'll keep her in the hospital until she's strong enough to travel," Oma says.

"Will we see Father?" Adriaan asks.

"He'll come tonight." I watch a smile light up my brother's face.

One of the young volunteers comes to our table with a box of puzzles and board games. More children join in, and for the next while, the older children are occupied. Sara practises her walking with Neeltje and Clasina.

During the noon meal, Oma tells us that she will go home with Aunt Neeltje.

"But Oma, who will look after us?" Liesbeth stands up from the table. Martin and Jacob start crying.

Clasina pipes up. "Klara, Rosa and Adriaan will 'yook' after us and all the volunteers, right Klara?"

I agree. "You need some rest, Oma, and you won't get that here."

"But we'll miss you," Clasina adds. She jumps off her chair and hugs Oma. Martin and Jacob follow their little sister.

At two o'clock, Aunt Neeltje arrives by taxi. She tells us that this morning she visited Mother in the hospital. And even though Mother is very weak, she told me to give you her love.

"I wish I could take you all home," Aunt Neeltje says, when it's time for her and Oma to leave.

"Don't worry," I reply. "We'll all visit you soon."

"I hope you do," Aunt Neeltje says, before she and Oma hug all of us and say goodbye."

That evening, Father arrives. He seems to have aged by at least ten years, and he is so thin. Adriaan is the first to hug him, and my father ruffles his hair. The gesture reminds me how close we came to losing Adriaan that very first night of the flood. After father hugs the little ones and Clasina, Martin and Jacob, he shakes hands with Liesbeth and Rosa. I feel the tension when he looks at me.

"How is Mother?" I break the awkward moment.

"She's very weak, but she's determined to see you soon." He wipes his eyes with his handkerchief.

I watch how all my siblings crowd around him while Neeltje and Sara occupy his lap. He leads us in prayer, and we thank God for keeping Mother safe. "Heavenly Father, I prayed to you and you listened to my cries. You saved us when we had lost hope. We thank you, praise you for keeping Mother safe. Amen."

After Father has left again, Rosa and Liesbeth help me put the little ones to bed. Today, the volunteers handed out toothbrushes and toothpaste. Before Rosa and I take the girls into the bathroom, I tell Adriaan to make sure the boys don't squeeze too much toothpaste. Sara and Neeltje have never used toothbrushes and toothpaste before. "Don't eat the toothpaste," I warn, when I see Neeltje swallow a big lump of the white paste.

Sunday, the eighth of February is a day of national mourning. Remembrance services are held everywhere, not only in churches but also in schools and cafés. We listen to Queen Juliana's speech on the radio and learn that the death toll has risen to almost fourteen hundred. The queen's words fill me with a deep sadness. It feels like I need to mourn every one of those lost lives:

Who were they?
The lost ones
who couldn't stay safe,
who couldn't fight the water,
who couldn't stay afloat,
who struggled
till the end.

20
Waiting

THE DAYS STRING TOGETHER like the beads on Oma's coral necklace. Every morning, our expectations are raised, only to be dashed by late afternoon. Some families leave to stay with total strangers. The government offers money to citizens who will take in evacuees, but nobody has enough space in their homes to take in a family with nine children.

Father has come to stay with us at the Brabant Hallen. He visits the hospital every day, and one of my siblings accompanies him. Mother wishes to see the little ones first. We're relieved that she's improving, slowly, but she's still too weak to join us. Liesbeth, Martin and Jacob want to go home to see their friends and to go to school.

I find the days long. I'd like to volunteer, but Sara, Neeltje and Clasina hang on my skirts from the time they wake up till the time they go to sleep. My only news comes from the radio and the newspapers, which are delivered to the Brabant Hallen every day. I ask Bea if she knows where I can get books to read.

"What's your interest?" she asks.

"I love poetry."

"I'll see what I can find for you." She picks up the ringing phone.

Every night after the evening meal, we all sit together. Father takes his pipe from his coat pocket, followed by a bag of tobacco. We've watched him do this a hundred times. He slowly fills his pipe, tamps down the tobacco and lights it. It's so familiar. I inhale the aroma of the tobacco smoke and close my eyes. First, he tells us how Mother is feeling, and after that he reads from the Bible.

Three days later, Bea calls Father into the office to inform him that there's a house available near Roseville.

"Roseville!" I cry. "We will be close to Mother and the hospital, and we can visit Aunt Neeltje and Oma!"

"When will we go there?" Rosa asks Father. "How much does it cost?"

"Soon," he says. "It will be much better for us to live in a house, and the children can attend school. The government pays the rent, so you don't need to worry, Rosa."

"Why not to our own home?" Jacob asks. "Is it still flooded?"

"We're not allowed to go back yet," Father answers. "The authorities are worried about the spread of disease because all the dead animals haven't been cleaned up. The dikes need to be repaired and the water pumped out of the polder before the cleaning and rebuilding can begin."

"It's going to take forever," Martin grumbles. "How big is the polder?"

"Our farm is in the polder," Father explains, "but so are our neighbouring farms and all the land. A small dike borders all this land, and the water level is regulated by a pumping station."

We all agree that this will take time, and the sombre mood returns.

Before Father goes to the hospital to tell Mother the good news, he says, "Bea has something for you."

"I found you a poetry book." Bea pulls a thin book from her purse and hands it to me. "You may keep it," she says. "And here is a book with stories about gnomes to read to the children."

"But . . ." I have no words.

"Enjoy!" Bea continues writing down whatever she is busy with.

I look at the cover, tracing with my index finger the letters that form the title. The book is a collection of poems selected by one of my favourite poets, Jan Jacob Slauerhoff. I open the book and inhale the smell of words, ink and paper.

At bedtime, I read the story of a gnome named Pinkeltje. Even though this gnome is different from the one in the book Aunt Neeltje gave us, my younger siblings are eager to hear about Pinkeltje and his animal friends. Before I go to sleep, I read Slauerhoff's favourite poem, "Sea Fever," written by John Masefield. I can't help but whisper the lines on the page. "The urge to go to sea, to feel the ship move beneath my feet and to steer with the aid of the stars . . ." The words allow me to dream of sailing across the sea in a small boat. The waves gently rock our boat. Machiel's arms draped around me hold a promise. Stars guide us to the land of dreams.

One afternoon at the end of March, the office turns up the radio, and we listen to a special broadcast of the queen's visit to Harbour Town. Queen Juliana tries to convince the people to leave for fear of disease and lack of food, but the citizens refuse once more, as they're worried about looting. Next, she visits places where the repairs on dikes have started.

The newsreader gives an update on the latest dike closures, providing us with a little hope that dike closures could mean going back home.

In the days that follow, many families leave, but the Brabant Hallen still remain inundated with donations. Besides clothing, there are household items, bags and even furniture. I make sure our family has enough clothes, shoes and boots to stay warm and dry till spring. I even secure four suitcases.

Rosa, Liesbeth and I take turns helping other volunteers pack clothes and goods to be sent to third-world countries where there is also imminent need.

"On Monday, April fourth, a taxi will take us to the house," Father tells us on a Saturday night. "You'll attend the local school, except for Klara and Rosa. The girls will run the household and help Mother when she leaves the hospital."

That Monday morning, we pack our belongings in the suitcases and say goodbye to the families we've gotten to know during our stay at the Hallen. Bea hands me another small book of poetry and promises to stay in touch.

Right after the noon meal, a big black taxi arrives. Father and Adriaan sit in the passenger seat with Martin and Jacob on their laps. I join Rosa and Liesbeth in the backseat. We hold Sara, Neeltje and Clasina on our laps. Our belongings are stowed in the trunk.

Everyone chats and points at buildings, street signs and people on bicycles. Farms and villages scattered around the countryside pass by in a flash, and before long, we enter the town of Roseville.

As the taxi drives down Main Street, we look in awe at the

many different stores and their colourful window displays.

"Look," Rosa points. "Sweaters in every colour of the rainbow."

"Look at the dresses!" Liesbeth cries. "The mannequins are wearing pink, green and yellow and pale blue." She stretches her neck to look back as the taxi passes. "Dresses for princesses," she says in a dreamy voice.

I notice a bookstore. How I'd love to browse the shelves and find books about faraway places and different cultures.

"Don't get any ideas about frivolous clothes and fancy things." Father has turned his head.

"We won't, Father," Liesbeth answers. "We're only looking."

When the taxi leaves Main Street, we enter the outskirts of Roseville, and before it turns left we pass a school with a large yard. Now the pavement ends, and we continue down a gravel road with farms on either side. The car stops in front of a small red brick house with a square front yard and a fence that's in need of paint. Everyone tumbles out of the taxi.

Father opens the door and Martin and Jacob run inside the house, while the rest of us carry our belongings from the trunk.

"It's so small!" Martin is back. "We all have to sleep upstairs on the floor."

I'm surprised to find the house completely furnished. A black cast-iron stove stands in the front room. There's a long table with twelve chairs and two highchairs. The bedstead is built against the back wall, beside a large closet.

From the kitchen, a door leads to a small mudroom. The cellar is underneath the bedstead. Straight out the back door stands a wooden outhouse. The fence around the backyard borders a farmer's field.

"No more flushing water closets," says Rosa, disappointed.

I fill the kettle with water from the pump, and the boys explore the backyard until the rain sends them inside.

When everyone sits round the table drinking tea and eating spice cake, I sigh. It isn't home, but at least there are no crowds of sad people sharing this space with us.

"Tomorrow you'll go to school," Father says.

21
Starting Over

IN THE MORNING, Father walks with the children to the school in Roseville.

"We need to get a large sheet," I mention to Rosa when we're cleaning the breakfast dishes, "We can have some privacy if the boys sleep on one side and we on the other."

By the time our brothers and sisters return from school for the noon meal, Rosa and I have made potatoes with turnips, meatballs and gravy.

Adriaan tells us about his morning. "My class is full of evacuees. There are two girls from White Church and a boy from West Bay."

West Bay! My thoughts accelerate. Machiel is from West Bay.

"The teacher is also an evacuee," Liesbeth adds.

"Are there any girls your age?" I ask.

"One, but she doesn't talk." Liesbeth picks up a piece of carrot.

"When the teacher asked us where we were from, she started to cry."

"Her family probably all drowned," Martin says. "I would cry, too, if that had happened to me."

"When is Father coming back from the hostibal?" Clasina asks. "I'm not going back to school. A boy said I talk funny."

"You show me which boy said that, and I'll talk to him," Adriaan pipes up.

"Adriaan." I notice the hurt in my brother's eyes, which tells me that he's been teased about his limp. I don't want him to strike out and get into trouble on the first day.

"I'll talk to him. That's all." Adriaan gets up from the table and walks outside.

"Father can talk to the teacher tomorrow morning," I tell Clasina. "And you can stay home this afternoon."

"Can I see Mother?" Clasina pleads.

"You have to ask Father."

When the children leave for afternoon school, Neeltje and Sara take their nap. In the quiet of the house, my mind keeps returning to the child from West Bay — he might know Machiel!

"Here." Rosa throws a notepad and a ballpoint pen on the table. I can tell by her red face that she's mad.

"Who are you going to write?' I ask.

"I'm going to let Luuc know where we are and tell him that you refuse to write him!" Her voice is high pitched. "I bet you're still thinking of that fisherman!"

"I would have . . . but we just got here." Rosa's comment catches me off guard. I have to admit that I haven't even thought of Luuc. Rosa is right about Machiel.

"You had lots of time to write him when we were in the Hallen," she accuses me. "He must wonder where we are."

"You're right. I could've written, but I was too worried about Mother."

"So worried, you forgot the boy of your dreams? I mean the one you're going to marry?" She rolls her eyes.

"Rosa, stop! Have we not been through enough misery? Do you need to make it worse?"

"*You* are making it worse by not letting Luuc know." Her strident voice wakes up Neeltje, who starts crying. This wakes up Sara, and then Clasina joins her sisters.

"Now . . ." I pause. There's no point in defending myself.

The door opens and Father walks in. "What's going on? I could hear you screaming down the road. Rosa, why are you crying?"

"They're missing Mother!" I say quickly and pick up Sara.

Clasina throws her arms around my legs, and Neeltje runs to Father.

"Why is Clasina not at school?" he asks.

"A boy said I speak funny, and Klara said maybe you take me to see Mother in the hostibal."

"How is she?" I ask, avoiding his stare.

"She wants to leave the hospital," Father answers. "But if you all scream and cry, she's better off staying where she is."

"In a few days, we'll be adjusted to this place." I try to save the situation. "Mother needs to come home. We'll all feel better."

"Clasina, if you're ready, I'll take you to Mother," Father says after he finishes his meal.

"Can I come with you?" Rosa asks.

Father nods. "We'll catch the two o'clock bus."

As soon as the three of them are gone and the two little ones are changed, I decide to take them outside, but not before Neeltje convinces me she doesn't want to wear a diaper anymore. I have to agree — she's been asking to go to the bathroom ever since we stayed at the Hallen.

In the mudroom is an old stroller, which comes in handy. Sara laughs and shrieks while Neeltje helps me push her.

The weather is mild. Neeltje's little feet march along in her new boots. It doesn't take long before we reach the school. In this two-room school, the kindergarten class is housed in a makeshift wooden building at the back. A sandbox and a wooden climbing set can be seen from the front of the building.

"Let's wait for Adriaan, Liesbeth, Martin and Jacob," I tell the girls.

Neeltje repeats the names of her siblings, and Sara parrots her sister.

"School." Neeltje points at the red brick building.

At last, the double doors at the front burst open. First, the older children come running down the steps, followed by the younger ones.

As soon as I spot Adriaan, I push the stroller towards him, call-ing his name.

Surprised, he looks up.

"Who is the boy from West Bay?"

"Why?" he asks.

"Who is he?" I repeat the question.

Adriaan turns toward the bike rack at the end of the school-yard. "The boy with the black toque who's getting his bike now."

"Here," I say pointing at Neeltje and the stroller. "Watch the girls! I want to talk to him." Quickly I stride over to the boy, who's ready to mount his bicycle. "Hey!" I call out at him. "What's your name?"

The boy turns and looks at me with big eyes. "Machiel. Why?"

"Machiel!" I gasp. "I also know a Machiel from West Bay, but I don't know his last name, and I'd like to write him a letter because he saved my little sister from drowning." I'm out of breath. "I hoped you might know him."

"I have two cousins named Machiel," he says.

"He's a fisherman."

"My cousins are both fishermen."

My heart jumps. "How will I know?"

"How old is the Machiel you know?" he asks.

"I don't know. Maybe eighteen or nineteen."

"Yep, my cousins are eighteen and nineteen," he chuckles.

"What's their last name? What's the address?"

"Last name is van Rijn."

I search my brain for clues about how to find out about the right Machiel. "Does one of them have a friend named Henk?"

"My cousins have many friends."

"The address?" I urge, when I notice the boy is itching to get on his way.

"Harbour Street. I have to go." He mounts his bike and pedals away.

"Did you get your information?" Adriaan asks.

My face is on fire. "Please, don't tell."

"I won't," he replies. His smile says he likes the idea of keeping a secret.

Liesbeth is talking to a girl, and Martin and Jacob finally leave the building to join us.

"Why are you so late?" I ask.

"Martin doesn't know his timetables, and I stayed with him," Jacob answers.

Martin doesn't look at me. His face is blotchy, as if he's been crying.

"We'll work on them tonight after Bible reading," I say.

"No story?" Martin looks disappointed.

"A little story," I answer.

"Why did you come to school?' Liesbeth asks.

"Because the girls needed fresh air." I wink at Adriaan and he smiles again.

On the way back, Adriaan carries Neeltje on his shoulders. "Thanks, Neeltje," he says and makes a face. "My neck is suddenly getting warm. Is Neeltje not wearing a diaper?"

Neeltje looks horrified, so I pat her leg and tell her not to worry. "We all had accidents at your age," I assure her. Then I promise Adriaan I will wash his jacket as soon as we get home.

Martin and Jacob fight about who will push the stroller and argue that it isn't fair that Clasina and Rosa went to see Mother in the hospital.

After everybody has tea with milk and a slice of buttered rye bread, the boys play outside. Liesbeth keeps Sara and Neeltje occupied by rolling a ball back and forth. While everyone is busy, I take out the writing pad and pen and sit down at the table.

My first letter is to Luuc. I might as well get that one over with to get Rosa off my back. I tell him where we are and how we're doing. I close with the hope that he and his family are well. Then I sign the letter with my name. I leave the letter to Luuc for Rosa to see and rip the last page from the notepad for my letter to Machiel.

I check on my siblings before I write Machiel's letter and thank him again for risking his life to save Clasina and for taking us to safety:

To Machiel,

I hope you haven't gotten ill after jumping in that ice-cold water. We stayed at the Brabant Hallen with hundreds of other evacuees but we are glad that my family has been given a temporary house close to Roseville. My younger siblings are at school, and I found out that your cousin Machiel is in my brother's class. Your cousin told me that he has two older cousins both named Machiel. I hope my letter is addressed to the right cousin and, if not, please pass this letter on to cousin Machiel.

I've been praying to God to keep you safe. I'll never forget you and think of you all the time. Please don't answer my letter. It will cause trouble in my family.

Forever grateful,
Klara

I quickly fold the second letter, stick it in an envelope and write his name and address on the front.

A sound in the hallway makes me stick the letter in my undershirt.

The door opens and Clasina runs toward me. "Mother is good. She'll come home soon. She was soooo happy to see us." She spreads out her arms to show me how happy our mother was.

To hide my tears, I hug Clasina. I suddenly realize how much I miss my mother.

Rosa watches me with suspicion. "Why is the notepad still on the table?"

"I was writing Luuc," I answer. "You were right when you said I needed to write him, so I did." *Why do I defend myself?* "Go read it," I urge.

Rosa hesitates but can't resist and grabs the notepad.

"This isn't a love letter," she says with a frown.

"This is not the time for love letters." I say, even though I know she's right. Then I can't help myself and add pointedly, "Maybe you should write him a love letter. You know exactly what you want to say to him!"

I turn around and check on the little ones.

"What's the matter with you two!" Father says in an agitated voice. "Why are you fighting about Luuc?" His eyes travel from Rosa to me. "It has all been decided. God willing, Luuc and Klara will marry next May. I don't want to hear any more about it! The subject is closed. Understood?" He grabs the newspaper and sits in his chair.

I fold the letter and stuff it into an envelope and write the address on the front. I place the envelope on the mantel, ready for the mailman tomorrow. Rosa's eyes shoot daggers at me, but I bite back my words.

During the evening meal, the tension in the kitchen presses like an invisible weight on us. Bible reading takes forever, and Father's droning voice washes over me while I try to figure out how I'm going to get Machiel's letter into the mail unseen. By the time my father closes the Bible, I have an idea.

"Can I visit Oma tomorrow?"

"When do you want to go?" he says without looking at me.

Surprised, I say, "When you get home from the hospital."

Father nods. "You'll need money for the bus. Do you know how to get to Aunt Neeltje's?"

"I have to change buses at the station and take the bus to Nightingale Street," I answer, hardly containing myself.

As promised, I help Martin with his timetables, but after many attempts, he still doesn't retain the numbers.

"Tell your teacher we'll practice every night." I pat his head. "You'll have a test every morning after breakfast," I add.

Martin looks horrified.

"What about the little story?" Jacob asks.

"If you get your pyjamas on quickly and jump into your beds, I'll tell you a little story."

Everyone snuggles around me on the bed upstairs. Even Liesbeth, who pretends she's too old for stories, joins us.

"Tonight Paulus the Forest Gnome needs to help Raven. Raven had an accident while flying —"

"I yike your stories better than Father's Bible stories." Clasina puts her arm around me.

The boys smile and nod, as if it's our little secret.

"The Bible stories teach us important lessons," I say.

"Paulus the Forest Gnome teaches us that we need to help others," Clasina replies.

I laugh and put my arms around her. "You're right!"

That night, I dream that I'm on a bus. Machiel sits on the other side of the aisle from me, but every other seat is filled with young men who all look like Machiel. When I turn my head, all the Machiels smile at me. I panic. Which one is the real Machiel?

"You cried in your sleep," Rosa says the next morning during breakfast.

I hold my breath. I remember the bad dream about Machiel. I pray I didn't call his name.

"What were you scared of?" Rosa asks.

"I dreamed Clasina fell into the water. . . . I was afraid to lose her."

"That's why you called Machiel?"

My face burns. "I don't remember much of the dream. I must have called him to rescue Clasina." I cut my rye bread and don't look up. I feel Rosa's eyes like sharp knives boring into my soul, forcing me to admit to . . . what exactly is it she wants me to admit?

Machiel's letter is tucked safely in my undershirt. I even slept with it, for fear that she would find it.

During the morning, Rosa watches me like a hawk. Never before have I felt my sister's animosity. The only way I can explain her behaviour is that she's jealous.

When Mother was spared, I promised God I wouldn't question his ways and would marry Luuc if that is my destiny. *So why were you so quick to get Machiel's address?* I know there's no way I can ever marry Machiel, but I also know that I will never, ever forget him.

22

Volunteers Needed

"HERE'S THE MONEY for the bus." Father hands me a ten-guilder bill as soon as he comes home from the hospital.

I pull on my boots, coat and hat before I hurry out the door. The cold and blasting wind takes my mind right back to the flood. In spite of my winter coat, I shiver as I walk to the bus stop close to the school.

The bus comes around the corner just as I reach the bus shelter. I find an empty seat near the back. This time, I enjoy looking at the sights of Roseville until we reach downtown, where I need to change buses. How I wish I had time to walk down Main Street to admire the window displays in all the stores.

A poster on the wall in the bus station shows Red Cross workers carrying children toward two white ambulances. In the background is a submerged farm and three people in a boat. Underneath the picture the caption reads, "Only with Your Support Is

Red Cross Relief Possible!" I stare at the poster until the bus honks, announcing its arrival.

After many stops, the bus turns onto Nightingale Street, where the row houses, with tidy little gardens, all look the same. In front of a large brick building, I get off the bus and open the glass door to the entrance hall. A granite staircase takes me to the third floor, and I ring the doorbell. Surprised, Aunt Neeltje welcomes me inside.

"How is Oma?" I hand my aunt my coat.

"She's knitting socks." Aunt Neeltje points to a chair near a large picture window, which makes the small room light and bright.

"Klara, I am so glad to see you." Oma holds out her hands and thousands of little wrinkles lift up her face into a warm smile.

I kneel in front of the chair and grab her hands. "I've missed you, Oma. We all have."

Oma doesn't speak. Her bottom lip trembles.

"We've been phoning the hospital every night," Aunt Neeltje says. "We're glad your mother will be discharged soon. Come sit at the table."

While Aunt Neeltje pours tea, I look around the small room. I have never visited my aunt before. There is a round table with four chairs. A white tablecloth embroidered with red and pink roses covers the table. A small bookcase holds books and two photographs in silver frames. One picture is of a smiling young man holding a baby and a little boy on his knee. The other one is of two little boys sitting on a swing. My uncle and two little cousins we never got to meet.

Oma joins us at the table. "How is the house?"

"It's very small for our big family, but the older kids are going to school and that makes it easier for Rosa and me to look after Sara and Neeltje during the day."

My aunt tells me about her volunteer work with the church. "I help place evacuees with guest families. There's so much work to do because often the guest families don't work out."

"How are you and Rosa managing?" Oma asks.

"We're not getting along," I confess. "Today I saw a poster at the bus station. The Red Cross needs volunteers." I take a deep breath. "I've been thinking about it on the way here. I'd like to help our community on the island."

"You need to discuss it with your parents before you make that decision," Oma replies.

"I don't think Father will let me go."

"I worry about the chaos and devastation you'll find." Oma looks away.

"The temporary house is too small for our family. There's no Spinach Academy for Rosa in Roseville and not enough work for both of us."

I stir the spoon around and around in my cup. We drink our tea in silence, all three contemplating what the future will hold for us. When the clock chimes, I reluctantly get up. "I need to catch the bus." I hug Aunt Neeltje and kiss Oma.

"Take this." Oma pulls her wallet from the pocket of her apron. "Two ten-guilder bills should help you when you're going to volunteer."

"No, Oma, you'll need that money," I protest. "I can't take it."

"Take it," my aunt says. "Use it in case of an emergency. If you change your mind or don't use it, you can give it back."

I tuck the bills safely in my pocket.

"I saved some pictures from the newspaper for Liesbeth." Aunt Neeltje hands me an envelope.

I smile when I think of my sister's reaction. "She'll love these, Aunt Neeltje. Thank you."

Oma hands me my coat and then holds the envelope while I button it. With one last hug for both of them, I hurry out the door.

At the bus station, my eyes return to the poster. I buy a stamp for Machiel's letter and push it through the slot in the mailbox. During the last leg of the trip, I close my eyes and allow my thoughts to wander to the fisherman who can make my heart sing.

Everyone meets me at the door calling out at the same time. "How's Oma? Will she visit us? How big is Aunt Neeltje's place?"

"Oma is knitting socks for everyone," I begin.

Sara snuggles on Liesbeth's lap and Neeltje settles with Rosa.

"Oma knit socks," Neeltje says. We all laugh. Neeltje has never said so many words in a sentence before. She usually points at people and things.

"Oh, I hate knitting," Liesbeth says.

"Here." I hand her the envelope.

Liesbeth's face beams when she discovers the photos of the royal family. "I'll start a new scrapbook and share it with Oma."

"Where's Father?" I ask.

"He went to the farm down the road to phone the hospital," Adriaan answers. "He's trying to get a taxi to bring Mother home."

"This is not our home!" Rosa bursts out. "Don't call it that."

Adriaan shrugs his shoulders.

The back door opens, and Father enters the kitchen. He places a can with milk on the counter, hangs up his coat and cap and walks into the front room. Surprised, he looks at all his children sitting at the table.

We all look at him with great expectation.

A hint of a smile touches Father's face when he says, "Monday morning at ten, I'll pick her up. That is . . ." — he looks around the table, his face, stern — "if you can behave and make sure Mother doesn't get too tired. She's still weak."

"We will, Father," we all promise.

He turns to me. "How're Oma and Neeltje?"

"Oma was knitting socks," I answer.

"That's a good sign," he says before he grabs the newspaper, but in the next breath he adds, "Do something to your hair before you go to church on Sunday!"

If I felt somewhat uplifted this afternoon, Father has now killed my warm feelings.

"I can do your hair," Liesbeth whispers. "I saw a movie star in this magazine."

"Why don't you cut it short?" Rosa interrupts. "Your hair is always in a big tangle."

"My hair is too curly to be short; I'll look like a mop you clean the floor with. Remember the photograph that was taken in kindergarten?"

"You yooked yike a mop?" Clasina bursts out laughing.

"I need to wash my hair first." I head to the kitchen, put on the kettle, find shampoo and a towel. I wet my hair with cold water from the pump and lather in the shampoo.

Liesbeth rinses my hair with the warm water from the kettle. "You have too much hair," she cries. "It's hard to get all the suds out."

After my tangles are towel dried, we return to the front room.

"Sit down," Liesbeth orders and gets the hairbrush, bobby pins and elastics.

"Don't make me look like a princess," I warn. "That hairstyle won't match my outfit or my personality."

We spend the rest of the afternoon giggling and playing hair-dresser. After my hair has been coiffured into a new style with big rolls of hair framing my face, Clasina's long hair is fashioned into a braided ponytail.

Friday and Saturday are spent cleaning the little house from top to bottom and catching up with laundry and ironing.

Saturday evening brings back our bathing ritual, and Rosa helps me prepare the Sunday meal. This way, the rest of the family can go to church in the morning while I cook the noon meal. I'll attend the afternoon service because I have a plan.

Every time Rosa looks at me, I can feel her anger. She is trying to control her outbursts, but they're just simmering below the sur-face, ready to erupt at any time.

After the Sunday noon meal, I attend afternoon service by my-self in the hope of finding out more about the volunteers on the Red Cross poster. Thankfully, Rosa attended church this morn-ing; she'd just remind me that Luuc is the only person I need to take care of.

Two elderly women are busily chatting as we walk into the church. When the women sit down, I join them in the pew. My eyes catch the stained glass windows and the large organ. I can't wait to hear the organ music filling the church.

"You must be from the islands," the one beside me states.

I tell her about the temporary house and how lucky my family is that we haven't lost anyone during the flood but that our animals all have drowned, and our farm buildings are heavily damaged.

"It will be a long time before you can go back and rebuild," she says.

"That's why I'd like to do volunteer work. I've seen the Red Cross poster," I say eagerly.

"You can sign up in the vestry, the building behind the church."

"Thank you," I say before I focus my attention on the heavy oak pulpit, where the minister raises his arms to be closer to God — or to make him look bigger.

"'We will give thanks to the LORD, for he is good.'" His voice echoes loudly and clearly.

"We welcome all victims of the flood." His eyes briefly rest on me, and I nod at him.

"It is God himself who sent the spring tide," he preaches, now in an accusing voice.

What! I can't believe he's saying this. Does he know how much people have suffered? How many have died? I love God, but I can't believe he is punishing us — judging everybody.

"God's verdict came over us. His breath breached the dikes and flooded the land. It is his punishment for all our sins!" The minister is now shouting.

Sins! My breath catches. What sins? Is he talking about Mother's sins, too? Again, I question why God needed to punish so many innocent people and animals. Even the organ music and the hymns we sing can't take away the bitter feeling, the disappointment the sermon leaves me with. Does everybody but me believe that this horrible flood is actually a punishment for all our sins? I don't understand.

After church, I hurry to the building with the Red Cross banner. Inside, the walls are decorated with the same Red Cross posters that I've seen at the bus station.

"How can I help you?" a young woman at the desk asks.

"I'd like to volunteer," I answer. "Can I help out in my hometown, New Port on Schouwen-Duiveland?"

"You can," she answers. "We have groups of young women from

all over the country helping with the cleanup. Would you like to join them?" She looks at the notes in her book. "The first 'silt and soap' group left for your island this past Thursday."

"When will the next group leave?" I ask.

After I fill out the papers, I'm told to be at the church by Wednesday at eight in the morning. I will need a tetanus shot before I can go.

"Wear rubber boots and coveralls and bring several changes of clean clothing." The young woman hands me a list with items I need to bring.

All the way home, I hope and pray that Father and Mother will let me go.

23
Last Straw

WHEN MONDAY MORNING arrives, the little house shines. We all want Mother to be pleased, even though this is not our home. At ten-thirty, a taxi halts in front of the house. Rosa jumps up and opens the door.

Thin and pale, Mother walks into the house. She hugs Rosa, the little ones and me.

After her eyes survey the small front room with the second-hand furniture, she walks into the kitchen. "I guess this is better than staying at the Brabant Hallen with hundreds of other evacuees," she says. "I'm grateful to the people who gave us this house to stay in."

We all share the same thought; it isn't home, but it will be fine for now.

After we drink coffee, Father gives me some of the money the government pays us once a week, and we make a grocery list. Rosa insists that she needs to accompany me to help carry the shopping bags.

"When do you expect a letter from Luuc?" she asks as soon as we are outside.

"I assume the mail is slow on the island."

"You must miss him." Rosa continues.

"What about you?" I fire back. "Can't you let it go? You seem to be obsessed with Luuc!"

Rosa's face turns crimson, and it isn't from the wind. "I just feel that you don't appreciate him." She marches ahead, the empty shopping bags swinging from her hand. "He's the best catch. You'll never be poor. You won't have to work so hard on his farm. His family can afford maids to do the farm chores. Most girls envy you."

"You must be one of those girls!" I bite back.

"And what if I am?" Rosa taunts.

"Then I feel sorry for you." I kick a stone.

"You know what I think?" She turns and holds her hand up to stop me.

"I think you're in love with that rough-looking fisherman. How can you? Girls like us don't marry fishermen. You'll be poor and live in a tiny house. During heavy storms you'll be sick with worry. And what if he drowns? You'll have nothing and end up in the poorhouse."

"Are you finished?" Bristling, I push my sister's hand aside and stride past her.

"You don't want to listen, but you know it's true!" Rosa runs after me. We stop in front of the butcher's shop.

I turn and face her again. "You don't know what you're talking about. A mean, jealous cat! That's what you are!"

"You can't handle the truth!" She opens the door to the butcher shop and stomps in ahead of me. We are the only customers and get served right away.

"You are not from around here," the butcher, a man in his fifties with a round face, says.

"We're from Schouwen-Duiveland," I answer.

"I heard that island was hit hardest." He shakes his head and asks what we would like. I order sausages, ground beef to make meatballs and a kilo of beef rump. He wraps the meat in brown paper and takes the money I hand him.

"I'm glad you survived," he says with a smile. "Come back soon." We thank him and promise to return.

After visiting the greengrocer for potatoes, carrots and cabbage, and the baker for bread, we lug the heavy shopping bags back to the house in silence. My thoughts are too angry to start a conversation, but the anger strengthens my belief that I've made the right decision to become a volunteer. I have to get away from Rosa's incessant questions. Helping to restore our farm will make me feel useful and allow me to sort out my conflicting emotions about my future as Luuc's wife.

That night, after the little ones are in bed, I muster all my courage and announce, "I've signed up to join the army of volunteers to help clean up the island."

Adriaan looks at me, admiration radiating from his eyes.

"You are so brave," Liesbeth whispers.

"The bus leaves Wednesday morning at eight o'clock." I look at Father and then at Mother.

My father takes his pipe out of his mouth. "There's no way you're going to the island to clean up."

"But listen," Mother says, to my surprise. "The sooner our house is clean and livable; the sooner we can go home." Her eyes hold mine. "It will be a terrible job, Klara. Do you think you're strong enough to face . . . the destruction, the mess, the loss?"

"Yes!" I reply quickly.

"Can you handle the filth . . . the cadavers?" Father searches my face.

"It will be difficult, but I want to do this," I answer. "We all want to go back home, even if it will never be the same as before."

"Then you have our permission," Father says.

Mother's face lights up, and her eyes fill with tears.

I avoid Rosa's gaze; happy she doesn't respond. Luuc is not who I want to think about at this moment.

24
Silt and Soap Crew

THE BUS WAITS at the church. I board and find the seats filled with young women and girls like me. They all chatter and some of the dialects sound foreign to me.

"Sit beside me," a girl with a gap between her front teeth, says. "I'm Aaltje."

I push my bag into the overhead storage. "I'm Klara." I hold out my hand, and we shake before I sit down.

Soon, I find out that Aaltje comes from the eastern part of the Netherlands, from the province of Overijssel.

"We decided as a group of friends to come and help out," Aaltje says when the bus leaves Roseville and drives onto the highway in the direction of Bergen op Zoom.

"Its so great that you're helping, too." I smile at her and look out the window. For a moment I close my eyes and relive the last few days leading up to my departure. The tension in the little house had become so unbearable that Wednesday morning couldn't come soon enough. Rosa couldn't stand being close to me, so I changed our sleeping arrangements. Liesbeth agreed to sleep with Rosa, and I spent the last few nights trying to sleep between a kicking Neeltje and a restless Clasina.

This morning, when I kissed the little ones goodbye, Clasina clung to me. The boys wanted to know exactly how long it would take me to clean up our farm.

"I'm helping out in New Port," I told them.

Liesbeth hugged me hard, and so did Mother. Father shook my hand, but Rosa hardly said goodbye.

"What's wrong?" Aaltje asks.

I blow my nose in my hanky and tuck it back in my pocket. "It was hard to leave my family this morning." My eyes fill with tears. "We lost everything during the flood. That's why I signed up."

"How terrible," Aaltje says. "I can't even imagine what it must be like for you and your family . . . and I've no idea what to expect. One night, my friends and I went to the theatre to watch a movie. Before the movie started they showed a Polygoon newsreel. It was all about the flood. That's when I saw the devastation. The worst for me was the many dead cows piled up along the road. I love our cows and the little calves."

"We lost all our animals, including, Max, our dog."

Aaltje shakes her head. "I'm so sorry."

By the time the bus reaches the ferry, I've become acquainted with Aaltje and her family, and we realize that we've much in common. Seventeen-year-old Aaltje also lives on a farm and is third in a family of eight children. She has a boyfriend and hopes to marry next spring, on her eighteenth birthday.

The rain slaps our faces when we carry our bags out to the

ferry. The group of about thirty girls crowds into the hold, where the smell of fresh brewed coffee lures us. The cots and stretchers have been removed and replaced by the regular benches. I'm introduced to other girls from Aaltje's town.

After two hours, we arrive in Harbour Town, which looks much different from a few weeks ago. The ferry is now able to moor properly. The dike has been closed temporarily with sandbags, which hold the water back for now. From Harbour Town, we're loaded onto another bus.

During the ride we're jostled about as the driver tries to manoeuvre around gaping holes and places where the road has completely vanished. Just before New Port, we're transferred to three flatbed wagons pulled by teams of horses.

When the rain comes down harder, we cover ourselves with oilcloth sheets. The streets of New Port are completely gone, and I flinch when I notice the piles and piles of rubble where houses once stood. A handful of men are loading a wagon with debris. I recognize the area where Jopie's family lived, but there's no sign of their small clapboard house or any other house on their street. I have to swallow hard when I think of lively Jopie, with her dark eyes and big smile. Her sisters and brothers all looked like their older sister, but they're gone, too.

Further down, a man and two boys search through the rubble, and I see others with wheelbarrows, horse-drawn wagons, tractors and old trucks, all clearing debris.

I crane my neck to see if I can find Oma's street, but before we've come close to Juliana Street, the horses turn into School Street. The street sign is gone, but the houses on both sides are still standing. They have been spared because they stand on higher ground outside the flood area.

In front of the two-room school building the wagons come to a halt. "This is the school I went to," I tell Aaltje.

"Being here must bring back many memories from when you were little," Aaltje answers. "It seems eons ago, a different lifetime," I respond.

Inside, we're welcomed by another group of women.

"This classroom was for grades one, two and three." I say, standing among the rows of cots that fill the room. "The other room was for grades four to six."

Aaltje finds two cots side by side in the last row near the window. "Let's take these two."

White sheets hang from the top of the windows to give us some privacy from the road. I point to the large poster depicting a primer with pictures and words underneath. "In grade one, I sat beside Dora," I tell Aaltje, "and even today, we're best friends. We used this primer to learn to read. Our teacher, Miss Kievit, was very strict."

"We used the same primer," Aaltje adds. "My grade one teacher was so mean, she spanked us for no reason."

We stuff our bags and other belongings underneath the cots and hurry into the other room. At one side, long tables hold several petroleum stoves with big pots from which come the pleasant aroma of soup. A map of the Netherlands and one of Europe still hang from the ceiling. The blackboards cover the wall behind the tables with the stoves. A large portrait of Queen Juliana in full regalia adorns the wall leading to the hallway.

While standing in line, I scan the faces to see if I know any of the women who helped cook the food. It isn't until I get to the end of the line that I recognize Nurse Jannie. She's helped my family every time a baby was born.

"Klara, what are you doing here?" Surprised, she almost drops the ladle. "You have to tell me all about your family and where they are."

"We're all fine," I answer, "but have you heard from Dora's family? Where are they?"

"They're okay. We'll catch up later." She fills the next bowl with soup.

After we've settled in, we're each given a pail with cleaning supplies, a shovel and a broom.

Beth, a sturdily built woman in her forties with a boyish face, is in charge of the work crews. "You'll need to wear your coveralls and rubber boots," she instructs us firmly. I realize quickly that no one messes with Beth.

"Before we can start cleaning, we'll be shoveling mud and sand. The houses that are still standing are covered in a layer of silt, and I warn you about the smell."

Back in the sleeping area, we change into our coveralls. I pull back my curls and tie a large handkerchief around my hair. Grabbing my pail, Aaltje and I follow the others outside. The rain has let up and we march down the road to the first house in a row of houses that had been flooded. The water has retreated, and these buildings are deemed salvageable.

Beth divides us into groups of five: three young women from the new crew with two who arrived last week. Aaltje makes sure she stays close to me.

I remember Jaap and Maaike, the elderly couple who lived in this house. Jaap fixed wooden shoes, and Maaike's crocheted bedspreads were famous all over the island. I wonder where the couple is now.

Beth is right. The stench makes us gag as soon as we open the door and walk into the hallway. Stains as high as my shoulders on the walls show where the water level had been.

"We'll throw what's left of the furniture into the wagon out front," Beth announces. "With the front and back doors open we can tolerate the smell."

We form a line out the front door so we can pass along the items.

After the front room has been cleared of broken furniture, the task of scooping up broken china and other items begins. Because I'm closest to the door I carry buckets heavy with debris outside and empty them into the wagon. Since the buckets are heaviest before they're emptied into the wagon, Beth relieves me and sends me further inside the house.

Books turn into mush as soon as I lift them off the floor. The enormity of the job hits me when I find an album with family photographs — there isn't one picture that can be saved. Discouraged, I drop the album into my bucket. My thoughts wander to our farm. I think of all the items that were so dear and are now lost. At that moment, I make up my mind that I want to clean out our farmhouse. I'll ask Nurse Jannie and Beth tonight.

We work all afternoon until the light fades and our backs hurt from lifting and bending. Back in the dining room, a crew of young men stop talking and eye our group with interest. Cigarette smoke forms a cloud above their heads, and the smell of disinfectant mingles with tobacco.

"The 'corpse and cadaver crew' joins us for all the meals," Beth explains. "You girls know your place!" she reminds us in a stern voice.

Corpse and cadaver crew! The images that come to mind make my stomach heave . . . animal bodies but also humans. I scan the tables to see if I recognize any of the men. There aren't any locals as far as I can tell.

Later, Nurse Jannie finds a few minutes to come and sit with me. "Dora's family is staying with Mrs. Timmer's cousin in Rotterdam, except for her father. Mr. Timmer was asked by the Red Cross to identify the bodies of the victims that have been recovered because he knows almost everybody in the area. It's a macabre task." Her lip trembles. "The bodies are horribly decomposed because of the salty seawater."

"Where are . . . the bodies?" I ask, fighting back nausea.

"All lined up in the vestry."

I try to remember all the people I know who have drowned. I swallow hard before I muster up the courage to say, "I'd like to clean our farmhouse."

"No, that'll be too traumatic for you." Nurse Jannie shakes her head. "Someone else needs to clean your home."

"I'm strong. I can handle it." I sit up tall.

"I'll discuss it with the Red Cross people. Leave it with me." She gets up from her chair.

I'm sure they won't let me, and the disappointment adds to my tiredness. I get up from my chair, ready to find my cot.

25

Secret Meeting

THE DOOR OPENS and two more members of the corpse and cadaver crew enter.

"Any food left!" the first one calls.

My heart misses a beat before it starts to sing. That voice . . . Machiel's. Now what? I try to think fast. My palms sweat. My face burns. Beth has made it clear that I'm not to mingle with the male crew members. I force myself to pretend that I haven't seen him and continue to cross the hallway to the sleeping area.

A hand on my shoulder stops me.

"I would recognize your hair no matter how hard you try to hide it," says the voice I've longed to hear.

"Machiel, what are you doing here?" I instantly know that's a stupid question.

"I should ask you the same," he says with a twinkle in his eyes.

"I . . . we can't . . . we shouldn't talk," I stutter.

"You mean we shouldn't be seen talking to each other," he corrects me.

"You better go," I whisper.

"I will, my angel." He touches my cheek, turns and walks into the dining room.

I stumble to my cot as if I were drunk. I can't believe that he's here. I'm happy, scared, confused, but my heart is overjoyed. I pray softly. "Please forgive me, God, that I feel so much pleasure seeing Machiel."

"What's wrong?" Aaltje follows me. "You look upset." She rummages through her bag until she finds pyjamas and her toothbrush. "I'm beat. I'm going to sleep."

"I'll do the same," I say. "This is my town, and I find it very hard to see all this . . . carnage."

"It must be awful," Aaltje says.

Most of the other girls decide to turn in early as well. For the women who travelled from far away, it has been an extremely long day. I hear Beth's firm voice from the hallway. "There's no gawking into the women's sleeping quarters! You know the rules. After the evening meal you go back to your own sleeping barracks at the warehouse down at the wharf!"

Grumbling male voices pass right outside the window. I wonder if Machiel is staying at the warehouse down at the wharf. I guess he is — where else would he stay? Finally, I hear the men wander down the street. My heartbeat slows and finds its natural rhythm.

Exhaustion makes me sleep, but a few times my heart wakes me. It won't stop singing.

I need to stop thinking about him. I must never be seen with

Machiel. It's easy for Luuc to find out in this small town, and I shudder, remembering an incident two years ago.

A boy from another town was seeing Johanna, a girl from my school. The local boys didn't like the fact that an outsider was courting a local girl. As was the norm, the boys beat him up and he never returned, leaving the girl with an unwanted pregnancy. She became an outcast and was forced to leave the island. I haven't heard any rumours about what happened to her, but it's not something I ever want to experience. I often think of Johanna. She lived with her mother, who was widowed when Johanna was just a baby; her father died at sea during a storm.

Over the next few days we get into a routine. Some days we clean houses all day, and other days my group cleans houses in the morning and has kitchen duty in the afternoon. The big meal in the evening is important for the men who are away all day recovering bodies and cadavers in the polders.

Machiel and I don't talk, but our eyes speak our feelings. When I fill Machiel's bowl, my hand trembles to the "accidental" touch of his hand.

One night, when the men are leaving, Machiel's hand brushes mine, and I feel a note pushed into my palm. I quickly close my fingers over it and head to my cot.

Sitting down, I read the scribbles jotted on a scrap of newspaper. *Every night at eleven, I walk to the lighthouse. Meet me if you can. Make sure no one sees you.*

I feel flustered. How am I going to get out of the school unseen? I do want to talk to him so badly. No, admit it . . . I want to hold him, kiss him.

But I'm going to marry Luuc. . . . Talking to Machiel once, just once, that won't be a sin . . . or will it? I realize it's a betrayal of my family, his family and what's considered right in our community, but I'm betraying my heart if I *don't* talk to Machiel.

Aaltje plops down on her cot. "I'm going to write a long letter to my Arie," she says. "I need a little distraction from this hellhole. I don't know how long I'm going to last." She pulls a notepad and pen from her bag. "Sorry, I'm not very social when I'm writing," she adds, "or I'll make mistakes."

"I have lots of thinking to do myself," I tell her.

The lights go out at ten. I wait till I hear most of the women breathing in an even rhythm. Pretending to visit the outhouse, I take my boots and coat and tiptoe outside. The light of a flashlight shines from underneath the door of the outhouse, and I leap behind the shed. From here, I can keep an eye on the wooden building without being seen.

The door opens and Beth comes out. Her flashlight points at the shed, and I duck down on my knees. Mud stains my pyjama pants, and I feel the cold penetrate the light fabric.

As soon as I hear Beth close the school door behind her, I walk down to the road. The quay isn't too far, but I need to watch where I'm going in the dark. Without a flashlight, it's hard to see. Electricity has only partly been restored so there is no light from any windows.

The smell of the salt air makes me feel at home, no matter how devastated that home is right now. My boots make squishing sounds in the mud, but there is no other sound. Even so, I stop and listen every now and then. All I hear is the gentle music of a calm sea, not at all like the angry monster from the night of February first.

The path to the lighthouse is rough and uneven, but my eyes have adjusted to the darkness. I watch the light on top sweep the land three times before it turns to the sea. Out of breath, I finally reach my destination. . . . No sign of Machiel. What if he's changed his mind?

Touching the wall of the lighthouse, I walk around to the other side. My heart drums fast in anticipation. I can hear it, feel it in my chest.

Footsteps sound behind me. I turn. In the next moment, Machiel reaches for me and gathers me in his arms.

Without a word, my lips find his mouth, and I lose myself in a gentle kiss. All I want is for time to stop, for the earth to stop turning so this kiss will last.

Out of breath, Machiel slowly pulls away. His fingers trace my lips, my eyes and nose. His lips sprinkle soft kisses all over my face, my hair and neck.

I caress his hair, his face and his ears and pray that this moment never ends.

"My angel," Machiel whispers. "We are so perfect together, but —" he pauses — "I don't know why I told your father I would come back and ask to marry you." A sigh escapes his lips.

"I'm a poor fisherman. I've nothing to offer you. We are five brothers in my family, and I'm the third. My two older brothers have families and there isn't enough money in the fishing industry right now for all five of us to make a living. And we need to look after our parents."

He takes off my headscarf and pulls my hair down, trailing the curls with his fingers. "The other one, the one your father said you will marry, has a big farm, money . . . and is well respected." His voice sounds defeated.

"How . . . where, how do you know him? Please, tell me, is he here in New Port?" Tears fill my eyes. "Everybody expects me to marry Luuc. But . . . my heart . . . belongs to you." I pull his head down till his forehead rests on mine. "It always will," I whisper.

"Our hearts will always remember," Machiel adds, caressing my cheek.

Holding onto this moment, we listen to the gentle roll of the waves on the rocks. In the distance, we hear the engine of a small fishing boat. The beam of the lighthouse sweeps across the water in an alternating rhythm reflected in the dark water.

"I've been to your farm, Klara . . . removing cadavers," Machiel shatters the enchanting moment.

"How . . . bad is it?" I'm afraid to breathe.

"There's a lot of cleaning still to be done . . . and you need to rebuild part of the house and the barn."

I slowly exhale. "I've asked if I could help clean our farm, but Nurse Jannie thinks it's too traumatic for me. I told her I'm strong."

"It will be a terrible task," he says softly. "A crew of men has started clearing away rubble. Luuc is one of the volunteers, and he is in charge." Machiel strokes my forehead.

"Why is he at our farm?" I swallow hard. "Who put him in charge?"

"He wants to impress you — or your father. I've met him a few times." Machiel traces my eyebrows. "He likes to order others around."

"He wants people to obey him. He . . . he needs to be in control. I know from experience." As soon as I say this, I feel the tension in Machiel's body. "Did . . . does he know who you are?"

"He doesn't know my name. He wouldn't know. I'm just another person who takes away the bodies of drowned animals." He takes my hand, and we walk to the water.

"Why are you cleaning up dead animals and . . . drowned people's bodies?"

"This work has to be done, but it's not easy." He sighs. "The animals . . . I'm getting used to, but finding people . . ." He swallows.

"Oh, Machiel." I pull him close.

"We can't meet again. I'm afraid to be found out," I say.

"I know," Machiel replies. "You'll be an outcast. Your father will —"

"It's Luuc and his friends I'm worried about. They'll find you and beat you up." I shiver with that thought and press myself against his body. Machiel pulls me even closer, and I cling to him.

"Did you get my letter?" I whisper.

"No, I didn't, but there are many Machiels in my family."

"I know." I chuckle. "I got your address from your cousin Machiel who was at school in Roseville. I wonder if his house had flooded."

"West Bay wasn't affected by the flood, but my one aunt and uncle who live outside town lost their house. They went to Roseville to stay with my aunt's parents."

We stand in silence. I want to savour this moment, standing together and talking like a normal couple. If only this were true, I could be happy for the rest of my life.

Machiel breaks into my thoughts. "You need to go. I'll walk you down to School Street."

Without speaking, we walk back to the quay and down the road. After one last kiss, I return to the school. The building is quiet when I slip back beneath my covers. Only then do I realize how cold my body is and how warm my face and heart feel.

26
Our Farm

BY THE END OF the second week, I have permission to go to our farm with a crew.

"The cadavers have been removed," Nurse Jannie says, "and a group of men is clearing away the rubble."

Aaltje, Beth and two other girls are in my crew. We grab our buckets, cleaning supplies and lunch pails and hop onto a horse-drawn wagon. The sun warms our faces on this early March morning.

The driver is a man from outside Harbour Town who owns the two horses that miraculously survived the flood. "Both animals managed to climb on top of a wagon and stay there until they were rescued," he tells us.

I wish our horses had climbed onto a wagon . . . and Max . . . and . . . *Oh, it's no use*, I reprimand myself, as tears choke my thoughts.

My stomach feels queasy, not just from the bumpy ride but from the prospect of seeing my home. Memories of the time spent on the second floor with my family, when the water created havoc downstairs, come flooding back. Images of the swollen bodies of our animals float by, as in a bad film. Max — will anybody have found Max?

Our pastures have turned into muddy fields, and the ditches are filled with seawater. How will these fields ever again turn into green meadows sprinkled with wildflowers and grazing livestock?

There's nothing left of the house Piet and his family once occupied. A big lump fills my throat, and tears threaten to take over, but I need to be strong.

When the wagon enters the farmyard, I rub my eyes. This place certainly doesn't look like our homestead. Father always insisted on a tidy yard, where everything had its place, and now . . . rubble, piles of wood, rusted machinery, milk cans and bricks from the collapsed machine shed are scattered everywhere.

Where the big barn doors once hung is now a gaping hole. A handful of men shovel dirt out of the barn.

A man in coveralls and wearing a black cap strides towards us. "This is no place for women! Why did you bring them here?"

I recognize that deep baritone voice. Machiel was right. Luuc is in command here. I shiver. I had hoped he would be finished by now.

As soon as he catches sight of me, his face darkens. "Klara! Who in their right mind sent you here!"

I grab my bucket off the wagon and plunk it on the ground. Next, I fling the supplies into the bucket and bristle. "I want to clean our home so we can move back."

Luuc stares at me, moves his arms as if he is going to grab me, but quickly recovers. He points to the wagon. "My future wife is not working in this . . . disgusting filth. Go back on that wagon! All of you!" He waves at the others.

I stand with my crew beside the wagon, bucket in hand.

"I wasn't told that someone is in charge here." Beth strides towards Luuc. She slams down her cleaning gear. With her hands on her hips, she says, "My task is to clean up the farmhouse with my crew. As far as I'm concerned, I'm only following orders given by the authorities and not by some boy with a big mouth!"

Luuc takes a few steps back.

I move beside Beth, plant my feet firmly on the ground. "This is my family's home, Luuc!" My voice doesn't waver.

Beth picks up her bucket. "Now if you'll let us through, the girls and I have a big job to do, and we're not here to waste time."

"What about Klara?" Luuc looks from Beth to me.

"It was my idea." I look at him directly.

"You and the men stay in the barn," Beth points at Luuc, "and the girls and I will tackle the living quarters." She turns to us. "Let's follow Klara!"

Thank you, Beth. Despite the fact that Luuc's behaviour infuriates me, I almost smile.

As we enter the house through the mudroom, I gasp at the rotten smell. Covering my nose with my sleeve doesn't make any difference. The contents from the cellar were deposited on the main floor by the moving water, and there's glass everywhere from the blown-out windows and the broken jars of preserved vegetables. Green and black mould cover areas of the room where most of the food collected.

We step over soggy rotting food remnants covered in a mixture of sour milk and broken eggs. Buckets, pots and pans, wooden shoes, clothing and toys are scattered everywhere, and the stench is sickening.

From the top of the stairs, Beth and I can see that the cellar is filled with a slimy scum. Beth pinches her nose and makes a gagging sound. "Good God!" she chokes. "No one can work in this stinking place without throwing up. We'll check out the rest of the house, and then we'll need to empty that cellar first." She turns away and heads for the kitchen, where we're met by more of the same.

I pause, taking in what once was such a cozy room. The stove is covered in rust. Furniture is scattered all over, most of it broken. The antique lamp that spread a warm light in the evenings lies in pieces on the floor, the white glass bowl shattered in a million bits. Rusting cutlery, broken plates, cups, saucers and bowls are everywhere. The rolltop desk has lost its drawers, and the rolltop is bubbled and bleached from the salt water. The grandfather clock, the radio and the pictures on the wall are all in pieces scattered on the floor. The paint is peeling, and the wallpaper has soaked off the walls.

I can't breathe. This . . . this was my home.

"Let's check the upstairs," Beth says. "If it looks all right, then we move everything upstairs that is somewhat salvageable. Whenever you're ready." Beth squeezes my shoulder.

I hear the girls walking up the stairs. I'm unable to move. I feel overwhelmed by the odour of mould and by memories. I force myself to the front room, where I encounter more chaos. The china cabinet is still upright, but the glass doors have been smashed and its contents strewn on the floor. The photo albums my mother had so carefully put together are covered with a layer of silt. The salt has eaten away the photographs, and the paper feels like porridge. Numb, I push the albums into the corner.

The waterlogged wallpaper in the front room hangs in tatters. Most of the paper has been soaked right off, just like in the kitchen. The four armchairs in striped fabric don't look like they can be salvaged. The legs of our round coffee table are rotted. There's glass and pieces of ceramic from the table lamps scattered on the floor. The carpet is a mushy, stinking mess. I don't even want to look inside the two bedsteads. It looks like a giant dismantled the doors and threw them on the beds.

Suddenly I run out of the room, remembering the jewellery box and safe that I left on the shelf behind Adriaan's bed. I need to go upstairs. With a giant leap, I land on the fourth thread. The first three are gone, leaving a gaping hole in the floor. The rest of the treads are soft and mouldy.

Upstairs, the gaping hole underneath the skylight reminds me of those dreadful days. Looking outside, I relive the moment when we were rescued by Machiel and Henk. The yard is still littered with debris. Inside, birds have made their nests on the exposed slats underneath the window. I pick up branches and mud off the floor and notice that the dirt-covered linoleum is cracked. Even though the floor is dry, the wood underneath the linoleum might be rotted. Everything else is the way we left it on that afternoon more than two months ago. The oil burner, cups, cutlery and empty buckets.

I need to feel there is something familiar. I walk straight into my room, where only the pillows remain on the bed. Here, the linoleum floor is dirty and shows cracks as well. Otherwise, the room is as I left it. My sanctuary was saved, my sacred little room that was so dear to me from before everything was lost in that storm. It means a small part of me from before is still here — the poetry collection, the notebooks with my poems in the bottom drawer of my dresser, Oma's cross-stitch picture above my bed, all small reminders of my life before the flood. I sit down on the bed. If I close my door and shut my eyes, I can pretend the flood never happened. After a few minutes, I get up and trace the cornflowers on the wallpaper with my finger. Near the floor, the paper is peeling off the wall. The legs of my washstand are damaged from the water, so are the legs of my bed and night table.

Then I remember the jewellery box. I open the door and return to the boys' part of the attic. The shelf above Adriaan's bed is empty, except for the sailboats and pieces of driftwood. The jewellery box and the metal box with our money and important papers are gone! Thieves must have looted our place as soon as the water retreated. I feel violated. In the midst of this chaos, how could someone come in and rob us of the few precious items that remained? I pick up Adriaan's sailboats from the shelf and put them on the dresser in my room. Blinded by tears, I stumble down the stairs. The women have already started the cleanup. Beth has asked the men for hip waders, and when she comes back, she descends into the cellar with two buckets.

As soon as Beth shovels the slime into the bucket and fills it to the top, she hands it to Aaltje who, in turn, hands the bucket to Sietske. Next, I'm in line and pass the bucket on to Ria, who opens the door in the mudroom and empties the mess outside. We all gag and complain, for it takes us almost four hours before most of the stinking mess from the cellar has been dumped outside.

By noon, we're ready to eat our sandwiches and drink tea from thermos cans. The men have set up a handwashing station in the barn. A tank with clean water has been delivered by horse and wagon from the milk factory.

Beth and the girls have found a place to sit on the front stoop, but I don't feel like taking part in their conversations. I'm grateful that they let me sit alone outside the kitchen on an upturned bucket, surveying what was once our yard. There's no sign of the flowerbeds or the vegetable garden. The sad looking apple trees are still standing, but they have already died. The seawater has killed the roots. The same fate will hit the row of pollard willows at the end of the yard.

A dull ache fills my heart. I realize that I always took my home for granted and now that most of it has been destroyed, I miss it more than I would have ever imagined. I drink the tea from the thermos can but leave my sandwiches untouched.

After our break, we empty the kitchen of broken furniture and other debris. Then we begin the enormous task of removing the layers of mud and sand. We use shovels to scrape up the stinky goop and put it into pails before we carry them outside.

Aaltje glances at me from time to time. I'm glad she's not talking to me because this whole experience is too huge for words. I can hardly fathom what I'm doing, let alone talk about it.

At five o'clock, Beth calls it a day. "Let's see if we can find our ride back."

Our driver has been helping the men clean out the stable and is happy to leave. I don't look for Luuc, but he's right there when I climb onto the wagon.

"I'll be at the school at eight tonight," he says. "Meet me outside. We need to talk."

Suddenly, my body shivers; I don't like his tone, and I don't want to talk to him. Beth watches Luuc, and her disapproving eyes meet mine before she turns and climbs onto the wagon.

"He's handsome," Aaltje says on the ride back. I smile because I know she's trying to cheer me up, but I don't respond. My mind is too focused on what Luuc will say and do.

We wash up and change while the smells from the dining room waft into our makeshift dormitory.

"We'll have pork chops tonight," one of the girls calls out.

My stomach feels tight. I'm not hungry, but I put a little food on my plate to avoid questions about why I'm not eating. A few minutes later, the men from the cadaver crew find their seats. I feel Machiel's presence right behind me, but I'm afraid to turn and look at him.

The pork chops with gravy, potatoes and turnips disappear quickly, and I have to admit I was hungry after all. The cooking crew has even made a custard pudding for dessert.

After the meal, I lie down on my cot, dreading my meeting with Luuc.

27

Unexpected Rescue

AT EIGHT O'CLOCK, I reluctantly get up and grab my coat.

Beth meets me in the hallway. "I'm not known for making exceptions, but in your case . . ."

I don't know how to respond, and without a word, I open the door and walk outside. Darkness has settled over the town, but here and there, lights are on. A few stores have been cleaned out and are open but with limited supplies.

Machiel and a few other men are standing a little way from the school, talking. I notice the glowing tips of their cigarettes.

When I look in their direction, I can feel his eyes on me, and I return the gaze.

Luuc startles me when he arrives out of nowhere and jumps off his bicycle. "Let's go for a walk." He grabs my hand and leads me down to the wharf.

Without speaking, I walk beside him while Machiel's eyes caress my back.

"Why did you not wait till everything was cleaned up?" Luuc starts. "I can't stand it that you're working in the dirt."

"It's not the dirt, Luuc. It's all the things we've lost that make it hard," I say.

"Tell your family that I found your mother's jewellery box and a metal case. I brought them home, thought they were important."

Relief washes over me. "I'm so glad you found them. I thought they'd been stolen. I'll write my parents and let them know."

"You wrote that your family moved to a house in Roseville. How is it?" Luuc asks.

"It's very small, and everybody is homesick. What about your family? Do you not need to help out on your farm?"

"We're doing well," he answers. "Once we got a generator and had electricity, my mother agreed to go back to the farm. My brothers are old enough to help, and we still have two farmhands. I was glad to leave the mayor's house because his wife — she thinks she's the queen."

When I don't reply, Luuc kisses me. Gentle at first, but soon his kisses become demanding, rough.

"I've missed you, Klara," he says softly. "I was worried that after the fight we had before the flood you'd still be mad at me, but I can tell you're not." He pulls me behind a small brick building and throws his arms around me.

I try to move away, but he presses me against the wall, trapping me. His lips find mine, but I find it impossible to kiss him back.

Luuc pulls away. "I thought you would throw yourself at me after missing me for weeks."

I feel as if I've turned into stone.

"I can't believe you're so cold." He searches my blank face as if expecting to find the answers to my odd behaviour there.

"It's everything that has happened. You don't know it all." I think of Mother and the baby she's lost.

"And I need to know about Dora and what happened to Piet's family. . . ." I stammer, trying to distract him. "Their house is gone."

Luuc pauses, then says casually, "They're gone."

Shocked, I try to swallow my tears, but they won't stop flowing.

Luuc kisses them away, gently this time. "I've heard rumours," he whispers.

"Rumours?" Something in his tone makes me tense and my mind whirls. The incident at the café with Machiel flashes through my mind. Father had made such a spectacle. I'm certain that scene has spread all over the island. Or has Rosa written him a letter . . .

Moving closer, his hands grip my shoulders too tightly, and I wince. "I heard my bride was unfaithful and kissed a fisherman. How low can you go? Only a working-class woman from the gutter would do something so disgusting."

Slapped by his words, I have no response. No comeback. No explanation he would want to hear.

"I'll punish you for cheating on me!" His voice is angry, and I feel the first tendrils of fear.

Luuc's mouth is on mine; his body presses me hard against the wall. With one hand he unbuttons my coat, then begins tearing at my sweater.

I can't breathe. I feel sick. In one swift move, I twist my body away, kick his shin and when my hand claws free, I slap his face.

Stunned, he steps back. "What the hell do you think you're doing!" he screams, and now his voice makes him sound like a madman. "I'll teach you a lesson!"

Luuc's hand comes down hard, sending a stinging blow to my cheek.

I lose my balance and stagger away from him, but he pulls me back.

"I'm not finished," he growls. His hand has my wrist in an iron grip.

"When we're married, I'll do anything I like to you, anytime I like, and you will take it, just as a proper wife should."

When I stay silent, he moves closer. His tobacco breath brushes my face, and his eyes become tiny slits. "And don't expect me to be faithful. There are plenty of willing girls in the area ready to throw themselves at me."

I try to grasp the threats he's uttering, but I've never thought about him not being faithful.

Suddenly, it's as if another dike breaches, but this one is inside me. All my pent-up anger rushes in, flooding me with a fury I have never felt before. I wrench my wrist out of his grip. "Are you finished?"

"No! Did you even consider my reputation when you kissed him . . . my family's reputation? Gossip is flying, and my parents are not pleased with you!"

Anger and adrenalin help me find the words. "It's all about your reputation," I blurt out. "You don't care about me!"

Luuc takes a step back and scrutinizes my face.

Why me? I wish there were another farmer's daughter he could marry and that his family would approve of.

"Were the fisherman's kisses better than mine?" He ridicules me in a high-pitched voice. "Did you like it when he touched you?"

Am I the first girl who has refused his advances? I'm not giving him the satisfaction of a reaction.

He moves closer again, and I feel his anger. He grabs my arms and presses his body against mine. "I should just take what's mine!"

"No!" my scream is silenced by his mouth.

"What's going on?" a loud voice yells. "Are you forcing yourself on one of the girls from the cleanup crew? You big shithead! The girls are here to help!"

Taken off guard, Luuc pulls away and lets go of my arms.

I stumble to find my balance. My body is shaking. When I look up, I see eyes as dark as the ocean before a storm. It's Machiel. My Machiel. With a roar, he bears down on Luuc. His fists strike out so fast that Luuc doesn't have time to duck. Blood sprays from his nose and mouth. "That's for treating her . . . like dirt . . . like she's nothing to you!"

I look at Luuc's bloody face. The prestigious farmer — the man with authority — has turned into a snivelling little boy. My mind is filled with contempt, fear and anger, but I can't voice it.

His anger spent, Machiel shoves Luuc down the street. "Get lost!"

Luuc pulls his handkerchief from his pocket and wipes his bloodied face. He pinches his nose. The blood runs a trail down his coat and into the mud.

"She's my bride," he snarls through clenched teeth.

"She deserves better," Machiel growls back.

"You think a fisherman can offer her more?" Luuc taunts.

"She should never marry a man who thinks he's better because of his father's big farm."

I stand frozen on the spot and try to think what just happened, and then Machiel's arms are around me, holding my trembling body steady.

"If you ever force yourself on her again, I'll kill you!" Machiel's arms tighten around me protectively. "Don't show your ugly face again, or you'll be dead! I will warn the women at the school to watch out for you!"

With a loathing glance at me, Luuc turns and retreats into the darkness.

Suddenly the tears come — angry tears and tears of disgust.

Machiel strokes my hair and holds me until my shaking body calms.

"I hate the way he treats you." He kisses my eyes, my hair, my burning cheek until our lips meet.

"If . . . if I marry him, it's . . ." I snuggle closer. "I have to accept that he . ." I can't finish the thought. "I'm scared, Machiel. Now that Luuc knows who you are, he will find you." My arms tighten around him. "He will take revenge!"

Machiel doesn't respond, and I rest my head against his chest. We stand quietly until his voice breaks our silent world. "Tomorrow, we're moving on to another area. He won't find me, but you need to be strong. Don't be alone with him. I don't know what he'll do next."

"I want to go with you!"

"You can't, and you know that."

"I know I'm unreasonable. . . ."

"You need to be strong," Machiel repeats.

The kiss is too short. We walk down the road with our arms around each other, but the road back to the school isn't long enough.

Just before School Street, Machiel stops. He touches my face. "I'll find a way to see you. I just don't know how or when."

"Can I write you?" I cling to him.

"I'm . . . not good at writing back. I never did well at school."

"I don't care. You're my hero. You've saved me twice."

"I'm no hero, but I hope you don't need saving when I'm not around."

One last kiss, and Machiel is gone.

Slowly, I walk into the school.

Beth meets me in the hallway. She looks at my bruised face, and her expression turns to anger. She points her finger at me. "I realize that young man is your future husband, but I strongly suggest that you rethink your choice of the man you want to spend your life with. As long as I'm in charge here, no more outings for you after dinner!" With a brisk turn, she leaves me standing and stomps down the hallway.

I totally agree with Beth. If I had a choice, I'd never lay eyes on Luuc again. Just the thought of him makes me cringe, and my stomach heave. That night and in the nights that follow, sleep won't come. Luuc's attack haunts me and makes me feel dirty.

28
Trying to Adjust

BY THE END OF APRIL, we finish the cleaning of our farm. At first, we use salt water from the cistern to scrub the goop out, but later, the dairy factory provides us with a large tank, and three times a week clean water arrives.

The next job is to make the house comfortable again.

After the painter has replaced the windows, he starts painting and wallpapering every room downstairs. Dora's father and his men build new doors and a new outhouse in the barn.

As the electricity is being restored, more stores open, and slowly some citizens return to New Port. It's time to return to my family and to bring them home. I haven't seen them for almost six weeks, and I miss them terribly. At the end of the last day of cleaning, I tell Beth that I'll walk back to the school. "I need to check something, Beth."

When her eyes question me, I shake my head. "No boys this time," I say.

Slowly, I walk in the direction of the dike. Here and there are fragments of what was once our seawall, our protection. Basalt blocks are strewn over the fields as if they were pebbles. When I get close, I can see that my small piece of sanctuary has been untouched:

Stepping over mud cakes,
crawling over basalt blocks
until,
I find my secluded place.
The spot
where dreams of faraway shores
were born,
where I imagined
the people, the places
I'd visit one day.
With my eyes closed,
I listen to
waves lapping
gently onto the rocks,
singing my song.
Wind brushes my face,
the salt tickles my tongue.
Sea birds greet me.
I find peace.

The trip back to Roseville is uneventful.

Clasina is beside herself when I walk in the door. "You were gone too long," she cries.

I watch Sara walk without help, and Neeltje can't stop telling me about the goat in the backyard. "We got her from the farmer next door," she says.

"You look much better." I hug my mother, who has shed the traditional dress. I touch her short hair.

"But you've lost weight," Mother says in return.

"Just a little hard work," I reply and then turn to Martin.

"How are the times tables?"

"Hard," he answers, "but Liesbeth helps me."

"And I'm helping him, too," Jacob adds.

I ruffle his hair, "Good for you."

"Do you want to see my new scrapbook?" Liesbeth opens the drawer in the table, and I sit down beside her.

She opens the book. "Look at this one." She points at the photo of Queen Juliana dressed in raincoat and rubber boots with a scarf tied around her hair. She carries a bucket. "Can you believe she'd do that?"

"It means she cares about her people," I answer.

"Tell us about the farm," Father joins us at the table.

"The farm will be okay," I start. "After the crew cleaned the living quarters, Dora's father and his men have started rebuilding. They started in the front room, building the bedsteads and closets."

"That's good news." Father looks at me with hope in his eyes.

It's good to be back. I feel warm inside when my eyes travel around the table. Even Rosa seems happy to see me.

"I have a job," she announces. "I'm helping the Red Cross make textile packages for the families who've lost everything."

"I can help, too," I add. I don't want to sit around doing nothing.

"Tell us about New Port." Rosa's eyes light up.

"I don't know where to begin." I drink my tea. "What struck me was the large number of volunteers who helped with the cleanup and the repairs on roads and houses." I don't mention the corpse and cadaver crew, nor do I mention Luuc. Even though I haven't heard from him since his attack, I'm worried sick what'll happen next time we meet.

"You cleaned every day?" Father asks.

"Yep." And now I dread the question that will follow.

"What about Sundays? You didn't work on the Day of the Lord!"

"We all did, Father. There is no church or service to attend," I meet his gaze. "I did read my Bible," I add and that wasn't a total lie. A few times I had read from the Bible when I wasn't too exhausted after the long days.

"Everything has changed," Father says more to himself. "After the war, people lost respect for the church, and after the flood they lost respect for traditions and moral standards. The influence of the mainland has even transformed your mother." His gaze turns to her short hair.

I can see in his face how hard these changes are for him to accept.

"I'll have a look at the farm and get things organized for us to move back." Father gets up. "I've heard they want to consolidate the farmland, and I'd like to be involved in those decisions."

"What does *consolidate* mean?" Adriaan asks.

"You know how the Smid farm owns land behind our farm. Well, that's just one example, but the government has decided that this is a good opportunity to rezone the farmland."

"Would we get the land from the Smids," Adriaan asks," because it's closer to our farm?"

"That would be a possibility," Father replies. "The Smids would get a parcel of land from us that is equal in size."

"Trading land to make it easier for everybody?" Adriaan looks at Father.

"But it will not all work out evenly for some farmers, that's why I want to be there." He takes his pipe and tobacco pouch. "Is the land around our farm mostly dried up, Klara?"

"Yes, but it's not the same as before the flood," I warn. "In many areas water is still being pumped out of ditches and the polders. The water in the wells and cisterns is not drinkable. Fresh drinking water will be delivered in tanks. The pastures won't be ready for grazing cattle for many years — because of the salt water in the ground, nothing will grow. The house will need more work to make it feel like home."

"We'll work hard," Mother states, determination shining from her eyes. "Even if the house is not completely finished, even if we don't have cattle, we can make it work and live on the farm."

I smile and nod. "How's Oma?" I ask.

"She and Aunt Neeltje visited last Sunday," my mother answers. "She misses New Port and is anxious about her house."

"Oma's house and the houses on her street have all been torn down. They'll be rebuilt with prefabricated homes donated by Norway."

That night, in bed, Rosa whispers, "Did you see Luuc?"

"Yes. He was busy organizing people during the cleanup."

"He must've been so happy to see you?"

"Did you write him a letter?"

"Why . . . how?" Rosa is lost for words.

"I was wondering because you talked about writing him before I left, and he was well informed about the incident at the café with Machiel."

When I don't get an answer, I know enough. Just the thought of

Luuc fills me with rage, and before I try to sleep, I pray softly. "Dear God, you have saved Mother. . . . I am grateful with all my heart. . . . But I'm scared and confused about Luuc. . . . I don't know what to do. . . . Please guide me to make the right decision. Amen."

In the days that follow, I join Rosa at the Red Cross. We fill each textile package with eight single sheets or six double sheets, six pillowcases, eight single blankets or four double, six tea towels, six large towels, face cloths and three tablecloths.

At the beginning of April, the radio announced the delivery of the first textile package to a family in one of the flooded towns. The big news at our house is Father's departure for Harbour Town on the ferry. He will evaluate the situation in New Port and find out if and when our farm is livable.

I fall into a routine, helping Mother in the morning with the little ones, then off to work for the Red Cross. I keep my distance from Rosa, and I'm saddened by the fact that the sister I had fun with all my life now resents me.

May brings warm spring weather. The newspapers are filled with updates on dike repairs and people returning to their homes. We wait anxiously for Father's return and news about the farm.

The number of evacuees at the school has declined significantly. The boys miss their friends, and Liesbeth seems lonelier than ever.

"Let's visit Oma and Aunt Neeltje," I suggest to her one Saturday afternoon. Liesbeth jumps up and runs to ask Mother, who smiles and nods.

We take the two o'clock bus to Aunt Neeltje's flat, and Oma beams when we walk in the door.

While my aunt makes tea, Oma asks me about my volunteer

work on the island; then she asks Liesbeth how her scrapbook is coming. "I cut out some glossy pictures of the queen and the princesses from a fancy woman's magazine."

Oma spreads the photographs out on the table, and Liesbeth's eyes light up.

"You should read this, Klara." Oma produces a light blue airmail letter from her apron pocket and hands it to me "It's from Hendrik."

I fold the soft tissue paper open.

In his letter, Uncle Hendrik asks about Oma's health. Next he wants to know about the closing of the dikes and the rebuilding of our farm:

How are Gilda, Jannes and the children?

I look up at Oma and smile. It's strange to hear my parents referred to by their first names. To me they're just Mother and Father. I return to the letter and realize that Oma never told him about Mother being in the hospital:

I enjoyed talking to Klara and would like to meet her and the rest of the children when I come to visit.

"I hope to meet him, too." I look up at Oma again. "I liked his voice when I was talking to him on the phone."

I continue reading about how Uncle Hendrik works on a large dairy farm as a manager and is responsible for three hundred cows. He mentions that the owner of the farm is getting old and isn't able to handle all the work, so Uncle Hendrik has taken on many responsibilities to keep the farm running smoothly:

I have the best job in the world because there're at least ten horses and four ponies on the farm, and I ride my favourite mare every night after work if the weather allows for it.

When I come to visit in October, I hope to find you all in good health.

"Does he not have a family?" I ask.

"If he does, he's never mentioned them," Oma says.

The afternoon passes by quickly and before we know it, Liesbeth and I are back on the bus, with a bag full of socks and pictures of the royal family.

During the bus ride, I ponder Uncle Hendrik's letter. My thoughts travel to America, and I envision the large herd of cattle grazing in huge pastures.

Saturday night brings the ritual of family bathing and listening to the radio.

Suddenly we hear the front door — Father's back.

29

Back to the Island

EVERYONE GATHERS around Father. We're all anxious to hear how things are at home, on the farm. Mother gets him a cup of tea, and we watch him fill his pipe.

"It's not going to be easy. We have to start from scratch."

"That's what I expected." Mother slices the kettle cake.

I watch the tension in Father's face.

"Some of the ditches are still filled with water, and plans for the rezoning of the farmland are not quite complete."

"How's the house?" Mother asks.

"Mr. Timmer has finished building new sleeping alcoves and a closet in the front room." Father puffs on his pipe. "He was assembling the kitchen cabinets when I left."

"How long before we can go home?" Adriaan asks.

"Maybe August."

That's still a long time in this crowded little house, I think.

"But what's most upsetting," Father says, "is that we trusted our daughter when she went to clean up . . . but she's put us to shame."

I jump from my chair. What's he talking about?

"I spoke with Luuc." Father looks directly at me. "He's not very happy with you. First of all, he heard about the scene with the fisherman in the café in White Church. Then you were not very forthcoming with your future husband! What do you have to say for yourself?"

All eyes are on me.

My stomach feels sick. I'm choosing my words carefully. "I was upset," I say softly. "Luuc was right. I didn't show any affection for him. He had just told me about Piet's family."

Mother's eyes moisten.

Rosa squirms on her chair, clutching her hands.

"He also told me about the rumours and that someone had written him a letter about the 'scene with the fisherman.'" I turn to Rosa and look straight at her, but she avoids my gaze and flees from the room.

"I promised Luuc I'd deal with our daughter and that he will not be disappointed when he marries you. Right, Klara! I'm counting on it. You are not going to disappoint us!" With that statement, he gets up from the table and walks outside, slamming the door behind him.

Father's words make me ill, and I can't speak; neither do Mother, Adriaan and Liesbeth.

I rest my head on my arms on the table.

"Father's bark is worse than his bite." I feel Mother's hand on my shoulder.

If only I could talk to her about Luuc, but her face is as closed as a locked door for which the key has been thrown away.

Without a word, I get up and go upstairs, undress and find my side of the bed. By the time Rosa and Liesbeth come up, I pretend to be asleep, but my mind keeps turning in circles all through the night. Father's words, Luuc's threats. Father's words, Luuc's threats.

July brings sunny days and rainy days. My younger siblings have finished school for the summer. For four whole weeks, everyone is home, and the little house is filled with tense, stressed and bored children.

Volunteer work comes to an end when most evacuees return to their own towns and villages.

I read in the newspaper that the ministry will start the repairs on some major openings in the dikes. After the sandbag fixes, the dikes need to be upgraded so that they will become a trusted defence system against future spring tides.

I find it interesting to read that during the invasion in Normandy, in 1944, the Allied troops used caissons — large concrete cases — to construct harbours in the ocean. These caissons are now being used to fill the openings in the dikes.

By August the closure of several major openings is complete.

When word comes that every family that lost their belongings in the flood will be given the basic contents of a household, Mother perks up. "I want to go back," she says after the radio announcement. "I don't care how much work needs to be done. I'm ready to take it on."

"With God's help and government funding, we will rebuild our farm," Father adds.

"I'll roll up my sleeves and help," Adriaan says.

We all agree with Adriaan.

After we finish our meal, my father says, "Thank you, Father, that you have kept us all safe. We will work hard to make our house into a home and ourselves worthy of your blessing."

This time, I agree with Father's words.

"Please forgive Gilda and Klara for their sins. Amen."

Mother's sins! My sins! Here we go again. Mother's sins have been forgiven, because God didn't take her. And what about my sins? If kissing a fisherman is such a great sin, why did God send Machiel to save Clasina? It's all so complicated, and I wish I could talk to someone to help shed some light. But it's Mother's sin I can't get out of my mind. Oma knows, and she's keeping it from me.

"Now you know how God feels about your reckless behaviour," Rosa snarls while we're doing the dishes.

"No, I don't. But do you know how God feels about liars?" I bite back.

My only hope is for Dora to understand my dilemma. Will she be back home when we move to the farm? Will Dora empathize? I can't answer that question either.

During the next couple of weeks, arrangements are finalized for my family to return to our farm. By the middle of August, we fill two taxis with children and belongings and leave the little brick house on the outskirts of Roseville. The goat will stay with the farmer for the time being.

We stop for a short visit with Aunt Neeltje and Oma. Father promises that as soon as we're somewhat organized, Aunt Neeltje can bring Oma to the farm.

The ferry ride is much more pleasant this time. We ride on top in the open air. The seagulls accompany us all the way to Harbour

Town, to the delight of Neeltje and Sara. They both screech like seagulls and make us all laugh.

Parts of the town are still in ruins, but the roads have been repaired and the taxis that are waiting for us when we arrive have no problems taking us home. Again, we're all humbled by the kindness of others when we discover that volunteers have furnished our home and stocked the pantry and some shelves in the cellar with canned food.

Dora's father has made sure the living quarters are ready for us. When I enter the kitchen, I find a note on the new table. *Tomorrow night, I'll come for a visit. D.*

Those words make me so happy. The following evening, when the household chores are done and the little ones tucked in, I anxiously wait outside.

The fields, still barren this August, at least are dry, but the ditches are filled with brackish water, and it will take years before the salt is gone and the green pastures return.

I squint my eyes when I notice a figure on a bicycle coming down the farm lane. Waving my arms, I start running toward my best friend.

Dora's bike clatters on the ground as she jumps off and embraces me. We look at each other and burst into tears. Where to begin, so much has happened to us since the flood?

"Look at you," Dora says. "You're not wearing your lace cap, and your hair is fashionable. It looks like you've finally experienced the mainland."

I burst out laughing. "There was just one small problem. I had to do it as an evacuee!"

Dora laughs. "Us, too," and she hugs me close. "My mother's cousin, Betty, is nice, but she lives in a flat on the sixth floor. It was crowded."

I wipe the tears off my face. "I'm so sorry about your Oma. It's hard to believe that we lost Miss Poortvliet and Jopie's whole family and all the others."

"Nothing will ever be the same as before the flood." Dora dries her eyes, too. "When we were in Rotterdam, I realized how much I missed our island, our town, our home and . . . you. We were so lucky that our house and the shop had minimal damage, but Oma . . ."

"I'm so sad about your Oma. She was always interested in our life." I wipe my wet face. "And yes, I missed you terribly. How about Bas? Did you get to see him while you were in Rotterdam?"

"No, he had to help his father restore plumbing here on the island. We wrote letters, but Bas's letters were not very exciting. What about you and Luuc?" she asks.

"What will we do next?" I try to avoid her question.

"I'm getting married," Dora states.

"You're what?"

"I'm not going to wait." Suddenly she takes hold of my shoulders and looks me in the eyes. "And you, my dear, dear friend, better do the same because you need to clear your name."

I step back as if I've been hit in the face. "What . . . what do you mean by that?"

"There are rumours, Klara and they better not be true. I hope with all my heart that they are *not* true."

I take a deep breath and slowly I say, "Tell me about the rumours so I know what I'm up against."

"That you kissed a fisherman from West Bay." Dora points her finger at me. "Tell me it's not true, or I'll be so disappointed."

"That's all you can think about? So much has happened . . . and all you . . ." That feeling of frustration and anger is beginning to choke me. "I . . . I see that you believe these rumours but . . . if you're my best friend . . . why don't you want to hear my side? Don't judge me before you know the whole story" — I don't wait for Dora's answer — "but if I lose my best friend, I have nobody!"

I wheel around and run home, my fists clenched. Behind the barn, I hit the wall until my hands are bleeding. The stump beside the barn becomes my seat. I cry and cry until I've no more tears left.

The cold words Dora hurled at me make me realize that I have no support. I can't share what I feel for Machiel. I can't tell her that Luuc attacked me. Even my best friend wouldn't understand. She lives by what's expected from a girl. She follows the rules. I can't.

I realize what I should have recognized all along. The love I feel for Machiel is true, is real. What I'm going to do with this new knowledge, I don't know. But my worst challenge is how to deal with Luuc. I cannot and will not be his wife, ever!

Since our telephone hasn't been connected, Father announces that Luuc will visit Sunday nights instead of Saturday.

Sunday night will be here too soon.

My family gradually settles into some of our routines from before the flood, but we all miss the animals terribly.

Father and Adriaan get their hair cut on Saturday night, as soon as the barber sets up shop in his front room.

We listen to a radio play while the bathtub is set up in its usual spot.

I knit quietly, my mind numb from worrying and lack of sleep. I wish Oma were here to talk to. My eyes meet Mother's, and they hold hers for a moment.

Rosa keeps looking at me and is about to open her mouth when my mother intervenes.

"Pour us all some tea, Rosa, and cut the cake we baked this afternoon."

Just after nine, we jump off our chairs when we hear a dog bark.

Liesbeth opens the door and there's Adriaan. A big dog on a leash pulls him inside the kitchen.

"This is Herta," he grins, and he and Father come inside. "There was a man at the barber's who said the dog belonged to his parents, who both perished in the flood. He was looking for a new home for their dog." He speaks without taking a breath. "I asked Father, and he said I could have her if I look after her." Adriaan looks at Father, who nods. He lets go of the leash, and the German shepherd sniffs and greets everyone with great excitement. There's no doubt about her welcome.

"And the barber said we could get two cats for Clasina if we want them."

"Clasina will like that, and the cats will keep us mouse-free." Mother rubs Herta behind the ears.

"And the big news is that Father is going to Friesland to get a cow," Adriaan's face beams.

"Tell us, Father," Liesbeth cries.

Father picks up his pipe and sits down. His eyes shine. "We'll have a stable full of cows before the winter."

"But how will we feed them?" Mother asks. "And what about the drinking water?"

"That's all taken care of." Father smiles at her. "The government will provide us with cattle feed. They have set up contracts with several co-ops. Farmers from all over the country are donating cows to give us a start. The dairy factory will deliver water when they pick up the milk."

"People are so generous." Mother blows her nose. "How will you get all the way up north to Friesland? That's a long way from here, and we've lost our car."

"I can borrow a motorcycle from one of the dike watchers. He bought it from a Canadian soldier after the war."

"A motorcycle!" Mother says.

"That's so amazing!" Adriaan can't contain his excitement. "Imagine, Father riding a motorcycle? It's a . . . a miracle!"

"But all the way to Friesland to get a cow?" Mother shakes her head in disbelief.

"Not just the one cow, but I'll have to stay a few nights," Father continues. "I'm going to visit five other farmers. The government is also giving me money to buy cattle in Friesland. In September, they'll organize the transportation of all these cows. Remember, twenty thousand cattle drowned."

That night, I find it hard to find sleep. I pray to God about what to do. Once more I ask if he will guide me, show me what to do or give me a sign.

When I wake up in the morning, I find no sign and no solution.

Even the next day during the service, I look for a sign, but all I feel is the judgement of the entire congregation pressing down on me. Watching my sisters, I don't see any signs of confusion. Gossip travels fast, and people like to believe rumours, even Dora. It makes me so sad to think that I have lost my best friend. I'm glad that she and her mother aren't attending the service this afternoon. I wouldn't know what to say to her. A sigh escapes me and Rosa pokes my arm, her eyes asking what's wrong with me. Kissing Machiel was so wrong but felt so good — why, oh why is this such a sin? Please, God, help me.

A young man in his twenties plays the organ. As we sing the hymns, my thoughts wander to Miss Poortvliet. I miss her.

In his sermon, the minister quotes from Colossians 4:2. "'Continue steadfastly in prayer, watching in it with thanksgiving.'" Sadly, he doesn't mention guidance.

I find it hard to pay attention to the sermon as my thoughts are already drifting to tonight:

During my walk home,
I watch the clouds sail by,
listen to humming insects,
the cries of gulls,
the gentle music of the waves
rippling in the distance.
The air is warm,
I shiver with anticipation.

30

Luuc's Promise

I TRY TO KEEP BUSY with the little ones after the evening meal.

"I'll get them ready for bed," Rosa says. "You get ready for Luuc."

Slowly I walk up to my room and sit on the bed. I hold my head in my hands. A tightness fills my chest as I relive that dreadful night in Harbour Town when Luuc promised what he would do to me once we're married.

"Klara! Luuc's here!" Rosa's voice interrupts my memories of that nightmare. A chill runs down my spine as I descend the stairs.

"You haven't even fixed your hair!" my sister scolds.

I push my curls back and fasten them with pins. I hang my apron on the hook.

"I made tea," Mother says when I enter the kitchen. "Luuc and your father can talk about the progress of the rezoning of farm-land."

Luuc already sits at the table. He's lit his pipe just like Father.

I take a seat at the opposite end.

"You can sit beside him," Rosa urges while she pours the tea.

"You've lost weight." Luuc's eyes travel over my body as if examining a cow.

"She isn't eating," my father says. "I don't know what got into her, but ever since she came back from that volunteer job, she's lost her appetite."

"That was no place for Klara," Luuc says. "She worked in the dirt for days. I didn't agree with my future bride volunteering. But your daughter is stubborn." He winks at me. "I'll have my hands full once we're married."

I don't look at him or my father. I'd like to scream that it wasn't from cleaning the dirt that I've lost my appetite.

As soon as Luuc finishes his tea, he gets up. "Let's go for a walk, Klara. We need to discuss our future."

When I rise from my chair, I meet Mother's eyes. A flood of emotions fills me. Does Mother understand how I feel?

I follow Luuc out the door into the barn. Martin and Jacob are building a fort out of scraps the carpenter has left behind.

"Where are you going?" Jacob asks.

"We're going for walk," Luuc answers.

"The fort looks great," I manage to say. "I hope you'll invite me when it's ready?"

"We will," the boys answer, "but you'll have to learn our secret code."

"Let's go." Luuc grabs my hand and pulls me outside.

Instantly, my body turns rigid with memory. Fear constricts my breathing. My legs move mechanically. I clench and unclench the fist of my right hand.

A flock of sparrows flits ahead of us as we walk through the parched fields away from the farm.

He tucks my arm under his. A light breeze comes up from the sea, and I tighten my shawl. A lone seagull cries.

"Are you proud that your fisherman beat me up that night in Harbour Town?" Luuc stops and turns to face me.

I forget to breathe.

He glares at me, waiting for my reaction.

I meet his eyes while I try to stay calm. "You shouldn't have attacked me!"

"You deserved a beating that night!" Luuc says."

"So did you!" I add as my fear turns into anger.

"Oh, you think we're even, but that's not how it works. You don't cheat on your husband, you obey him!"

"You're not my husband!" I spit back.

"Don't worry, I discussed it with your father, and he agreed that you need to be reined in. He gave his blessing for a fall wedding." On those words, he grabs my shoulders.

"This . . . fall?" I say in a choking voice. It feels like the world is collapsing around me.

"Only two more months, my dear Klara, and you'll be mine." He pulls me close. His lips claim mine; his hands roam and unbutton the front of my dress.

With all my might, I push him away.

Surprised, Luuc pulls back. "You didn't learn anything," he says out of breath. "I'm stronger, remember, and your fisherman isn't here to rescue you." Then he bursts out laughing. "You're unbelievable! Every girl in this area would do anything to marry me, and you . . . the chosen one . . . reject me because of a simple-minded fisherman! He has nothing to offer you. The fishing industry is struggling, and you, my beautiful Klara, will end up in the poorhouse. Your family won't take you back after you've lowered yourself into their class."

I just stare at him while a seething rage consumes me. Calling Machiel a simple-minded fisherman has pushed me over the line. At that moment, I become aware that I would prefer the life of a spinster, with all the ridicule that comes with that position, than to live with Luuc and dance to his drum. I feel disgusted with him. I turn abruptly and run back to the farm.

In the west, the sky shows a palette of pink and red banners to forecast another warm day tomorrow.

I hear Luuc's steps behind me. When he catches up with me, to my surprise he doesn't touch me. Instead he lights his pipe and inhales deeply.

"Klara," he says in a much less authoritarian tone, "let's start over and make plans for our wedding. Let's pick a date."

I move away. *You can pick as many dates as you want,* I think.

"I'll discuss it with my parents. And Klara, it'll be the biggest wedding in the area, and people will talk about it for years to come."

When I don't respond, he remarks, "Aren't you happy now? Make sure you put on some weight, because I want to grab onto something during my wedding night, and it better not be skin and bones."

A bad taste fills my mouth, and I feel the impulse to spit at him but turn my head instead.

"I'll see you next Sunday night," he says. "I've learned that you're not that eager to be touched, so I'll patiently wait till our wedding night." He stops at the gate to the farm, takes my face in his hands and kisses my lips. Before I can take another breath, he drops his arms, finds his bicycle and pedals off in the direction of New Port.

I watch him go. I stay at the gate until my breathing calms down. My decision to become a spinster is final, but getting out of my marriage with Luuc is going to be my biggest obstacle.

September brings cool, wet days. Classes resume at the school in New Port for Adriaan, Liesbeth, Martin, Jacob and Clasina. The cots have been cleared out and the desks put back in rows just like before the flood, except several desks are empty. It's a sad reminder of the students who didn't return.

The Spinach Academy in Harbour Town is still housing stranded evacuees, so Rosa is staying home for now.

The peddler, who is busier than ever, comes to the farm. His large trunk is filled with fabric, and Mother chooses a large piece of velvet in a rusty colour for new curtains.

Rosa is set up in the front room with the sewing machine. Every morning, she stomps to the front room, letting us know that she doesn't like her new job as seamstress at all.

When Father comes home from his journey to Friesland, we all laugh at this stranger wearing a long brown leather coat and cap and worn leather boots. The goggles make him look like a creature from another planet.

We crowd around him as soon as he finds his place in the armchair, fills his pipe and puffs out ringlets of smoke.

"The first farm I visited had forty dairy cows and the farmer gave me a four-year-old."

"Did you stay at that farm?" Adriaan asks.

Father nods. "The farmer and his wife had an eleven-year-old boy and a four-year-old daughter."

"Just like me," Clasina pipes up. "What was her name?"

"Her name was Martha," Father says. "She was just like you and asked many questions."

"At various farms, I bought fourteen cows and with the six donated cows from the farmers, that makes twenty. We'll buy more next spring. I've also purchased a flock of sheep."

"Sheep?" Martin asks. "We never had sheep before."

"Sheep are excellent grazers. They'll keep the new grass short so it will come in thicker."

"When will we get the sheep?" Jacob asks.

"Next spring," Father answers.

"And the government paid for all our livestock?" Mothers eyes mist over. "It's not a loan that we have to pay back?"

"No," Father reassures her, "but it will be a good feeling when we don't need to rely on government funding and we can take care of our own bills."

We all look forward to having animals again. A farm without livestock is like a ship without sails.

To Adriaan's delight, Father announces the purchase of a tractor.

In the following week, our telephone line is repaired. The new telephone hangs on the wall beside the coffee grinder. Mother calls Aunt Neeltje to tell her that we're ready for Oma to come live with us.

Father and Adriaan have further divided the upstairs and built a third room for Rosa and Liesbeth. The girls get a double bed, a dresser, a closet and a washstand. I help wallpaper their room in a rose petal design. Both sisters decide on a burgundy velvet curtain for their skylight.

Grandmother can sleep downstairs in the bedstead with Clasina and Neeltje. Sara will stay in the trundle under my parents' bedstead for now.

"Oma will come next Wednesday with Aunt Neeltje," Mother says when she hangs up. "Remember the letter Oma received from Hendrik, when we still lived in Rosedale?" Mother adds. "Oma just told me that Uncle Hendrik will arrive on the first of October, and he'll stay for a month." She turns and busies herself with pots and pans to get the noon meal ready, but her flushed face doesn't escape me.

When I look at Father, he shows no emotion, and I find that strange.

"He can come to your wedding!" Rosa says. "It'll be so exciting to have our uncle from America attend the wedding."

I leave the kitchen, taking Neeltje, Sara and Clasina with me outside.

"Are you excited for your wedding?" Clasina asks as soon as we're walking down the lane. Sara and Neeltje start picking grass-like spikes — flowers for Mother.

"I'm not excited," Clasina answers her own question. "You won't live with us anymore, and I'll miss you."

My eyes well up. I cough, trying to disguise how deeply Clasina's words touch me. "I'll miss you, too," I say instead.

"Choir practice starts again tonight," Rosa announces when we return from our walk. "Dora just called, and she hopes we'll be there. The young man who plays the organ during church service will be our new choirmaster."

"Can I go?" Liesbeth asks.

Mother nods her approval.

"I'm not feeling well," I tell them after the evening meal. "You'll have to go without me."

"You hardly touched your food," Father's voice sounds concerned. "You need to eat."

"What about Luuc?" Rosa asks.

"It's only choir practice," I say abruptly, cutting her off.

31

Reputations

"THAT WORKS OUT WELL," Mother says. "Klara and I need to discuss her wedding dress."

My heart sinks, and I feel the noose around my neck tighten.

"Liesbeth and Rosa will put the little ones to bed. Klara, you come with me to the front room."

Mother leaves the kitchen and with heavy heart, I follow her.

The front room has new carpet, wallpaper and furniture, but it doesn't feel the same as before the flood.

Mother pulls out a chair for me before she sits down. "Luuc's mother telephoned to tell me that she doesn't want Luuc's bride walking down the aisle in a cheap homemade dress. She's ordered a gown for you from one of the upscale stores on the mainland."

Heat rises in my face. My hands feel sweaty. I need to tell Mother about my decision. I can't postpone it any longer.

"I'm sad to see that you don't look like a happy bride." My mother pats my hand.

"Why do I need to get married so suddenly? Why not wait till I'm eighteen?"

"You have yourself to blame, Klara. Your behaviour with that fisherman is unacceptable. People are talking, and our reputation is at stake."

"Were you happy when you married Father?" I ask.

Mother doesn't look at me, but red blotches are appearing on her neck and face.

"Marriage is not the fairy tale they make you believe when you read the glossy magazines."

"You weren't happy, but you want me to be happy. You married Father, but your heart belonged to someone else." My hand touches my heart.

"Klara! Don't —" Mother gets up and walks over to the window.

"Tell me. You promised!" I get off the chair, too, and stand beside her.

But Mother stays silent.

"I can't marry Luuc. We have nothing in common, and I don't really get along with him." I pause. I know I can never tell her about the attack and that Machiel saved me from getting hurt. She wouldn't believe me. "I've tried hard to think that I could marry him and learn to love him over time, but I can't. I even asked God, but I didn't get an answer or a sign. I've decided not to marry him."

Mother turns to face me. "It's not up to you to make that decision." Her words are sharp. "Father and I decide your future. You have no choice in the matter. It will be best for your reputation and ours that you marry Luuc."

"Reputation ... reputation! What about my feelings?" I can't believe what she is saying. "You know how I feel, don't you?" I plead with her.

"What we feel is not important, Klara. I did the right thing for my family, for the church and my community when I married Jannes."

"Mother . . . how could you . . . how can you?" I cover my face with my hands.

"Did they not teach you at school to accept what's been handed to you and to be grateful? You could do worse, you know."

I walk to the door, but before I open it she stops me, "You will go through with the wedding. Next week, you and I will visit Luuc's mother for a fitting. In time, you will know that this is the best decision."

"That's how you feel? You've never had any regrets?"

"I told you, life isn't a fairy tale."

I leave the room and run out the door. I don't stop running until I reach the dike and climb on top. I walk down the other side to the water and look out over the salt marshes and the sea until I find my special place. In the far distance, ships dot the horizon. The slope is dirty, but I sit down anyway. New spikes of coarse green peek up through the brackish clay. Hugging my knees, I look at the waves lapping gently at the smooth surface of basalt. I wish my thoughts were as smooth as the waves tonight, but they're stormy, rough and wild like a hurricane.

I watch two gulls dive into the water catching their meal. A blue heron scans the coastline for its food, and three oystercatchers run back and forth on the rocks. I wish I were a bird. Life would be much easier.

Dear God, why did you make me a girl? I do not fit the mould. I feel trapped. I have nowhere to go. If only a ship would take me or if

I were a bird, I could fly away. A fishing boat? "No," I say out loud, "I can never be with Machiel." I cross my hands over my chest. "But Machiel will have a place in my heart forever." I stand up and call out to the birds, "Please, get me out of here. Let me join you when you soar over rivers and oceans, forests and cities. I want to be like you and be free."

As dusk blankets the land and the sea, I spot tiny lights bobbing up and down in the distance. I feel like one of those moving lights — a ship without a compass, going nowhere.

The waves meet the shore, lapping peacefully. I listen. It's as if they're calling me — no, begging me — to join them. I shiver, and the urge to become one with the water pulls me closer. My feet touch the line where the sea meets the rocks. I stare into the darkness, trying to imagine what it will be like to let the sea take me in her arms, gently rocking me until I become one with the waves. Time pauses. My mind is empty. All I do is listen to the pleading call of the tranquil, rolling waves as they wait patiently. My heart yearns, my mind wavers. . . .

What am I thinking? I pull my feet out of the water. My thoughts are bristling white caps, wild and angry, resentful. Reckless . . . like my risky relationship with Machiel. I take several deep breaths to clear my muddled mind, and shout at the waves, "I will never give in! I will never marry Luuc! I know my parents will insist I marry him, but I will not, and that is final!"

Only the waves can hear these words. But I need to hear them. I fought to stay alive during the flood, when so many lives were taken by the sea and now . . . like the never-ending tide, I need to persevere. I can't give up. . . . I can't give in. . . . I can't be seduced by the waves that want me to become one with them.

But if not into the sea, then where will I go? I can't just leave the

island and my family? I have no money and . . . I hold my head
with both hands and rock my body. "Oh, God!" I sob. "Please forgive me for my reckless thoughts. Please guide me. Please, please
show me what to do!"

When at last I get up, I slowly retrace my footsteps back to the
farm. All I can come up with is what I'll do for now — obey my
parents and play the part. But I'll never marry Luuc. How I'll stop
it, I have no idea. I need a plan because time is running out fast.

All is quiet at the farm. My family has retired for the night. In
the dark, I find my way to my sanctuary. I leave the curtain open,
crawl into bed and stare at the night sky through the skylight. A
few stars blink at me, but they offer no solution. I wait for my
mind to stop and for sleep to take me away.

On Wednesday afternoon, Aunt Neeltje brings Oma to the farm.
Having my grandmother back gives me comfort, but will Oma
listen to me? She lives by the rules of the church, the community
and the ancient traditions of our island. It seems to me that the
adults all feel the same about the role of women. It's about honour,
reputation and our place in society. But I don't fit the template. I
can't live by these rules, and as a result I've never felt so alone.

All my siblings are excited to have our grandmother live with
us, and Oma's face beams. Only when she looks at me do the
worry lines return.

On a sunny Thursday afternoon, Mother and I, both wearing our
Sunday dresses, ride our bicycles to visit the van Borselen's farm.
Mrs. van Borselen has invited us for tea so we can go over the
wedding arrangements and have a dress fitting.

I've never been to Luuc's farm, although I've passed by it many times and seen the grand-looking farmhouse. Two concrete pillars stand on either side of the double oak door, like sentinels on guard. Mother rings the copper bell.

Luuc's mother opens the door. Her hair is coiffed in an elegant roll at the back of her head. She's wearing a navy blue dress with a white lace collar and cuffs. Her necklace is made with six strings of coral fastened at the front with a golden clasp.

I immediately become aware of how common our dresses look. Our plain hairstyles don't show any class or elegance.

We enter a huge vestibule. The oak doors to the various rooms have ornamental trimmings. A majestic-looking staircase leads to the second floor.

"Dina will bring the tea to the front room," Mrs. van Borselen says. She leads us into a large room with tall windows and plush chairs.

After Dina, a girl I know from school, pours the tea in dainty china cups, Mrs. van Borselen clears her throat. "I need to tell you that I'm not pleased with my son's choice." Her eyes scrutinize me with a cold appraising look. "My husband and I agree that with no suitable girl available in this area . . . Klara will do. We are extremely disappointed that her behaviour has already stained our name and reputation." Her face and neck turn crimson as she speaks.

I don't understand either why Luuc insists on marrying me. Is it because I'm not willing to dance to his music? Is his pride hurt, his ego bruised because I prefer the fisherman? I feel a strong urge to tell her not to worry but hold back.

Mother fidgets in her chair, spilling tea in the saucer.

"The wedding date has been set for Thursday, the twenty-eighth of October. We've rented the hotel in Harbour Town for the reception and a meal. The owner is already renovating and upgrading the large hall for this wedding." Her eyes move from Mother to me, but when neither one of us responds, she continues. "I'm sure you'll understand why we won't have you organize this event."

While Mrs. van Borselen rambles on about the minister, the food and the orchestra that will be playing during the reception, I pretend that this is not my wedding she's discussing.

"It will be a grand affair, and we expect you won't disappoint us as our daughter-in-law." Mrs. van Borselen pauses when there's no reply. "Under my guidance, you will learn the rules of the upper class."

Under my guidance . . . I want to throw up.

"Now you need to try on the dress to see if it needs altering." Mrs. van Borselen's commanding voice startles me.

"Go on," Mother urges when I don't move.

Reluctantly, I follow Luuc's mother down the hallway into a large bedroom with a four-poster bed and a polished dressing table with a tall mirror. On a hanger in a wooden wardrobe carved with birds and intricate leaf patterns hangs a cream-coloured dress with puffy sleeves, a pleated bodice and a full skirt.

I've never seen a more beautiful dress.

Mrs. van Borselen takes the dress off the hanger and passes it to me. "I'll see you in the front room," she says and leaves.

I finger the soft material and reluctantly take off my Sunday dress.

The fabric feels smooth over my bare arms. I button the row of tiny pearl, buttons at the front. The door to my cage is closing. As tempting as it might be, I refuse to look at myself in the mirror.

How can I get away before I open the door to the front room?

"Just what I expected." Luuc's mother rests one hand on her

large bosom. "You need to fatten up if you want to bear any children," she says. "The dress needs to be taken in at the top. I'm glad I chose the one with the full skirt so it will cover your skinny hips."

"Klara has lost weight ever since she came back from volunteering," Mother says.

"Well, that was embarrassing and degrading. No place for the future van Borselen bride," Mrs. van Borselen says derisively, "and you've had enough time to regain the weight so there's no excuse." She takes a box with sewing pins from a sideboard and starts to pin the dress. She's so close, I can smell her cologne. "Stand still," she orders, when I start swaying.

"You're not expecting are you? Your face is pale." She puts the last pin in place, jabbing my arm in the process. "You can take it off and get changed."

32
The Visit

ON THE WAY HOME, my mother doesn't say a word, but after we place the bicycles in the shed, Mother puts her hand on my arm. "The only difference is when I got married . . . I was expecting." She leaves me standing there.

Stunned, I digest my mother's words. Mother was pregnant before she got married, but they got married. . . . So why was that a sin? I shake my head and walk towards the house.

As one day follows another, I do my chores automatically. I'm not hungry and barely touch food. My nights are long and restless. I can't look at Father and feel that he's avoiding me, too. I still can't believe he is willing to sacrifice my whole life to save our family's reputation.

I see concern in my grandmother's eyes and wonder if Oma is worried about my lack of appetite — or Mother's secret.

"Are you excited for Uncle Hendrik's visit?" I ask Oma one night when we're together in the kitchen, knitting socks.

"I can hardly wait," she says. "But it will be strange to see him again." The needles stop clicking as Oma stares into the past. "It has been so long. I still remember, as if it was yesterday, when he told me he had no future here. Now I know . . . with Jannes taking over the farm . . . Hendrik was right. Two families probably couldn't make a living."

"I hope they'll get along when Uncle Hendrik comes for a visit?" I add.

"I believe they will." Oma blows her nose. "They're grown up. They should know better."

The phone rings early Saturday morning, and Mother answers. "Yes, Neeltje. . . . That'll be all right. . . . We'll have tea ready." She looks at me, her face blushing. "This afternoon . . . for tea," she murmurs and disappears into the front room.

Father finishes his coffee and follows my mother. Oma clears the coffee cups and takes them to the sink. Adriaan announces he's going to the barn. Clasina and I dress the little ones in the hallway before we take them outside.

The door to the front room is open. Father stands in the door, his back turned to us. "You better tell Hendrik the truth. He has the right to know," I hear him say. He turns, looks up and our eyes meet. I'm shocked by the sad expression in his face . . . and then a thought slowly creeps into my mind. Before I can follow it, Clasina asks, "Who is Uncle Hendrik?"

"He's Father's brother. We'll meet him this afternoon," I reply with a sense of foreboding. What truth does Mother have to tell Uncle Hendrik? Is it linked to the fight between him and Father?

I have a feeling I know the answer to these questions, but the truth is almost too huge for me to consider.

By two that afternoon, we're ready for the visitors. The tea is steeping in the pot on the tea light. The cups and saucers, sugar and milk wait on a tray, and the plate with sliced spice cake sits on the table.

The children are outside, but Mother, Oma, Rosa and I are in the kitchen where the tension hangs around us like a heavy cloak. Mother continuously wrings her hands.

"They're here!" Adriaan opens the door to announce the arrival of the visitors.

Oma gets up. In two strides, a tall man with red curly hair hugs her in his arms . . . and finally I know the family secret.

"Sit down, Neeltje," Mother urges her sister-in-law and busies herself by pouring tea, but her hand trembles so much that I take over.

Oma dabs her eyes with a white handkerchief.

Uncle Hendrik blows his nose before he sits down.

"It's good to have you visit us." Father's words surprise me, but they sound genuine.

Hendrik nods. His eyes travel around the table and rest on Mother for a brief moment. I notice the strain between them before he moves on. Finally, his eyes catch mine. "Ever since I spoke to you on the telephone in February, I've been looking forward to meeting you in person, Klara."

Instead of answering, my hand automatically touches my hair.

As soon as everyone has tea and cake, questions for Uncle Hendrik fly across the table.

"How long was the boat ride from America to Rotterdam?" Adriaan wants to know.

"We moored in Southampton, England, where people got off the ship and others came on board. That took two extra days — altogether nine days."

"Is the ocean really big, and how high were the waves?" Martin hangs on Uncle Hendrik's every word. Jacob wants to know about the many cows and if Uncle Hendrik knows all their names. "Why did you never visit us before?" Rosa's question hangs in the air, as Uncle Hendrik doesn't respond.

Mother busies herself with the teapot.

After an uncomfortable silence, Father says, "There was no time for Uncle Hendrik to travel. He had too many cows to look after." The boys agree with Father, and the awkward moment seems to pass.

After more tea and cake, Aunt Neeltje and Hendrik leave in the rental car. I escape to the dike in search of solitude in my special place. My mind is too full. Uncle Hendrik. My Father. America. The words jump around in my head. I can't understand how my Mother . . . I can't believe nobody . . . you think my hair would have given me away a long time ago. . . . My thoughts ride around in circles. I miss the evening meal, and when the light fades, I slowly walk back to the farm but stay in the empty barn for a while to avoid facing my family. Finding a spot on the bench, I imagine the cows back in their stalls and think how simple their lives are. I remember the sounds of chewing and swishing tails and feet rustling in the fresh straw. I can smell their bodies, see their gentle eyes. How content cows are, how simple their existence when they are well cared for. Unlike my life, which has become even more complicated this afternoon.

When, at last, I return to the kitchen, I find only my parents. Everyone else has turned in for the night.

Mother pours me a cup of tea and looks at Father, who nods.

"Hendrik knows he's not your uncle," she says.

"Nobody in our family except for Oma and Aunt Neeltje know that Hendrik is your father," Father adds. "Nobody in town knows about this situation, and not to tarnish our reputation even more we'd like to keep it that way."

"We continue to pretend . . . ?" I can't believe what Father is saying. "Why did you keep this from me?" My eyes wander from my mother to my father, pleading for answers. "I can't believe that nobody in town suspected anything."

"That's because everybody assumed Jannes was the father," Mother explains, her face as red as the summer peonies. "When I became pregnant, I had already been promised to Father."

"Your mother made a mistake." Father looks at Mother.

"Why did you turn on Mother the night of the flood?"

"I kept repeating to myself that this was punishment for keeping a secret, for never admitting, not even to God, that you were not my daughter."

"But . . . but God knows . . . knew," I add.

"I still believe God was punishing us for our sins." Father faces me. "I'll never forgive myself for the things I said."

"You were devastated . . . the destruction . . . the loss of the animals." Mother wipes her eyes. "God punished me for my sin," Mother whispers. "He took my little boy."

"You are right. God punished me and you when we lost our little boy. But the worst part was when we almost lost you, Gilda." His voice is filled with emotion.

We sit in silence after Father's confession.

"But God couldn't possibly punish every person, every animal for Mother's . . . mistake?" I swallow hard.

"Maybe you're right. Maybe you're right." Father rubs his forehead and stares ahead.

I didn't get all the answers, but I got more than I bargained for.

In my room, I take my notebook and pencil. With a heavy sigh I plunk down on my bed. The words jump around on the paper:

I'm not Father's daughter.
I'm not my siblings' sister.
I'm not the girl
I was yesterday.
I don't know my real Father.
He doesn't know me.
Why didn't anybody tell me?
Why didn't anybody figure this out?
Do I have to live with this lie?
Pretending . . . ?

33
Machiel

"HOW WAS THE visit with your American uncle?" Luuc asks on Sunday night. The evenings are much cooler as we walk along the path west of the farm. He tucks my arm under his.

"It was good to meet him." I'm glad to talk about something other than the wedding. "He told us much about America and how big the land is. The farm he manages has three hundred cattle."

"Maybe we can visit him in the future," Luuc says.

I don't respond. My mind keeps churning around how to approach Hendrik.

"Or are you still fancying that fisherman?" He turns to face me.

I refuse to take the bait and stay silent.

As if Luuc feels he's gone too far, he says, "I know I've been a bit rough with you in the past, but I promise we'll have a good life together, Klara." He kisses my lips gently, but I twist my head away from him.

Luuc swears, but in the next breath he says, "My mother needs you to come for another fitting." He swings me around and we head back to the farm. "You're still not much fun, Klara, and I hope that'll change soon. When we're married you can't deny me my rights." His face shows a mixture of anger and disappointment.

I can't believe he thinks that I'll forget what he did to me.

Back at the barn, he jumps on his bicycle and pedals away in a fury.

As I watch him, I realize I can't keep up this façade any longer.

When Mother sends me to Harbour Town to pick up soap and brushes at the general store, I mail a letter to Machiel.

In the next few days, excitement takes hold of our family when a cattle truck delivers thirty cows to our farm. The stalls in the barn are filled with fresh smelling straw, and the hay that's been bought from the mainland is stacked up to the rafters. We can start selling milk to the creamery and don't have to live on handouts from the government any longer.

With the animals back, I find myself busy again with farm chores. I clean the milk pails while listening to the waves and thinking about my plan for the future. I've asked Machiel to meet me in Harbour Town, at the lighthouse, on Saturday afternoon.

When Saturday arrives, I offer to get some supplies from the general store in Harbour Town. It doesn't take my mother long to come up with a list of items for the kitchen that are unavailable in New Port.

"I'll come with you," Rosa offers.

"No." My face burns. "I want to stop in at Dora's." It isn't a real lie because I've been thinking about visiting her. Rosa eyes me with suspicion.

The sky threatens rain, and the road to Harbour Town is busy with horse-drawn wagons, cars and cyclists.

I decide to shop first for the items on Mother's list. My saddlebags bulge with soaps, polish for silver and copperware and a strainer. After I fasten the buckles of the saddlebags, I head in the direction of the lighthouse.

I lean my bike against the side of the tower. My heart beats in anticipation when I make my way to the west side of the building, the same place we met this past spring.

No Machiel.

Did he not receive my letter? Has he changed his mind? Maybe he is out fishing, or . . . he's given up on me, knowing that I can never be with him.

I wait. Every minute feels like an hour. I sit down on one of the rocks and gaze out over the water. The waves spray the rocks and my mind wanders, longing for distant shores.

"Klara!" his voice startles me.

He drops down beside me, and I feel his arms around me.

I start kissing him, and when I finally pull back, I see the same longing in his eyes that I've felt ever since our last kiss.

"I'm planning to go to America," I blurt out.

Machiel gasps. "What do you mean?"

"*If* Uncle Hendrik will take me . . . I can't marry Luuc. I've decided not to marry at all if you and I can never be together. . . . When Uncle Hendrik came to visit from America, I discovered he's my real father."

"Wait . . . what?" Machiel tries to interrupt.

But I can't wait. I want him to hear me out before I lose my courage.

"I'll ask Hendrik if he can take me to America. It's the only way to get out of my marriage to Luuc. If I stay, my parents will force me to marry him. I'm trapped. I need to get away from here." I catch my breath and close my eyes.

"Klara . . . I don't know what to say."

"You don't need to say anything. You've already told me there are too many people in your family and not enough fish to feed everyone. Now you can come to America with me. We can start a life together."

Machiel's eyes move to the sea. "But what will I do in America? I'm not a farmer." He closes his eyes.

I watch him as he sits with his thoughts turned inward. My hand wants to brush the dark stubble on his face, ask him what he's thinking right now, but I restrain myself, waiting for his response.

After minutes pass, I'm ready to burst. I grasp his face and pull him close. "Machiel, please. Say something," I plead.

When he doesn't respond, I get up and find a spot to sit away from him on a rock. Tears blur my vision, and the last ray of hope for a future with Machiel sinks. I feel like a pebble skimming the surface of the water for a few seconds — then falling to the bottom of the sea. As I stare at the horizon, I imagine he'll just vanish, go back to his fishing boat and his family in West Bay.

The church bells chime three times, and I scramble to my feet. I need to head back to do my chores.

Machiel rises at the same time. He hugs me close. "Klara." He struggles to find the right words. "You and I belong together like the fish and the sea. You will always be my angel. I wish I could come to America with you. But . . . I don't know what kind of work I can do there. I can't speak English, and I have no money to get there. The times for fishermen aren't very good. It will take me a long time to save enough."

Disappointment blocks my response.

"I'll try, Klara," he says as if grasping at straws. "I don't know what to do right now or what to tell you." He pulls me close and the kiss that follows holds promises, but are they too fragile for a future together?

I cycle home under a dark sky. My heart is filled with doubt regarding my future with Machiel.

Now I have to find the courage to call Hendrik and ask him to take me to America.

But what if he doesn't like the idea of having a daughter?
What if he doesn't like the idea of being a father?
What if he doesn't agree to take me with him?
What if . . . ?
What if . . . ?
What if . . . ?

34
Trapped

"IT TOOK YOU LONG enough to get those items." Rosa carries the milk pails outside to the pump. Her face looks flushed, and she blinks her eyes several times.

I notice my sister's restlessness. "What did you do all afternoon?" I ask in a calm voice.

Without a response, Rosa turns and disappears inside.

It'll be good once she knows that I'm not marrying Luuc, I think, as the water from the pump rushes into the bucket. Tomorrow morning when my family goes to church, I'll call Aunt Neeltje and ask Hendrik. Tomorrow night, I'll tell Luuc. I feel a little calmer now that I have a plan.

"I'd like to visit Uncle Hendrik when I'm older," Adriaan announces during the evening meal. "I'd like to see the big farm he talked about."

A knock on the door interrupts the conversation.

Luuc opens the kitchen door. "I apologize for interrupting your evening meal, but I need to speak to Klara now."

He appears agitated, and I look at Mother who nods to go ahead. My mind races wildly when I follow him into the barn.

"It's raining," he says in an angry voice.

"We can sit here." I point to the wooden bench at the end of the stalls. I sit down and try to slow my breathing. I need to stay calm. I smell the warm bodies of the new cows, but I don't think they will protect me.

Luuc fidgets, takes a piece of straw and starts to chew on it. "I heard you met someone in Harbour Town this afternoon."

"What . . . how?" I jump up and face him, anger rising in me. "Who told you?"

"Oh, so you admit it," he sneers. "You know exactly who I'm talking about. He won't bother you again. I took care of him."

"You what?" My blood boils. "What did you do to him?" I bend down and grab the lapels of his coat, "Tell me what you did to him! How badly is he hurt?"

"Whoa . . . I like the way you look at me when you're mad. I wish I could stir you like that more often."

"Answer me!" I scream. "I need to know!"

"Don't get all wound up. It was just a little warning. A little payback for what was done to me in the spring. He has a bloody nose, gained some bruises, that's all. He'll know to stay away from my future wife because next time he won't be so lucky!"

I let go of his coat and slap his face.

Startled, Luuc stands up and grabs my shoulders.

I look straight at him. "You'll have to find yourself a new bride because I'm not marrying you." I wrestle myself free from his grip, turn and run back toward the mudroom.

"What will you do? Become an old maid? You know how the community thinks about old maids? How will you support yourself? Handouts from your parents? Living off charity from the church? You'll come to your senses before that!" he shouts.

I don't stop running until I'm back in the kitchen.

The sudden silence makes me look at my family. I take a deep breath. "I told Luuc he has to find another bride." My eyes rest on Rosa.

"You did what?" Father knocks his chair over when he gets up. His eyes fill with anger. "You *will* marry Luuc!"

His words hang in the air, then hit me.

"No, I will not!" I turn around, close the door and run upstairs. I don't know how long I sit on my bed until the door opens.

Clasina climbs onto the bed beside me and throws her arms around my neck. "You're not marrying Luuc? What about your dress?"

"No, I'm not marrying Luuc, and I don't know what will happen to the wedding dress." I hug her close.

After a final squeeze, my sister lets go and leaves my room.

Overwhelmed, I don't notice when the door opens again.

Rosa, her eyes red, her face all blotchy, sits down beside me. "I feel rotten," she says.

"So how did Luuc know that I went to Harbour Town this afternoon?" I ask.

"I . . . I called him. . . . I didn't know you'd call off the wedding." Fresh tears stream down her face.

"Did you not hear Father? According to him, I have no choice!" I clench my fists. "But what makes me furious is that I have you to thank for Machiel being beaten up. What kind of a sister are you? I know how jealous you are, but why should Machiel pay for your childish behaviour! I can't even find out if he's badly hurt. He's not from this island, he has no telephone, and I have no boat. And you know, Rosa, if you really want to have Luuc, he's all yours. But I'll tell you one thing — he's not the nice young man everyone thinks he is. Now, leave me alone!" I stand up and open the door.

"Don't do anything stupid." Rosa looks at me, fear in her eyes.

"Get out!" I repeat.

When she doesn't move, I go down to the kitchen, ready to face the music.

The phone rings, and all eyes turn.

Even Neeltje and Sara stop babbling.

Mother answers. "Van Burgh . . . Good evening, Mrs. van Borselen. . . . Yes, I agree with you, Klara is a strong-willed girl. . . . Once she's made up her mind, it's difficult to talk her out of it. . . . No, don't worry. She *will* marry Luuc. Nothing has changed." Her eyes bore into mine.

All night, I struggle with my thoughts. This wasn't my plan. The noose around my neck is choking me. My parents will never change their minds, and I'll never ever change mine. I'm behaving against all the rules of society by refusing to marry him. My family and the whole community will ostracize me.

By the time my alarm clock rings, I've made up my mind. I'll leave the island and visit Hendrik at Aunt Neeltje's this afternoon, after church. The money that I was going to return to Oma will be enough for the ferry to Bergen op Zoom and the bus to my aunt's.

"Why don't you visit Dora after service this afternoon?" Mother suggests during the Sunday meal. "Maybe your friend can talk some sense into you."

Perfect, I think. After the church service, I'll visit Dora and then disappear.

"I'll come with you to church," Rosa says.

With Father's approval, we take our bicycles and pedal into town.

Rosa is not part of my plan either, which means I can't pack anything. But I'm so fuelled by anger and hurt that nothing will deter me. I'll get rid of Rosa when I visit Dora.

The vestry fills up quickly, and many heads turn when Rosa and I sit down behind Dora and her mother. I can feel the eyes of the parishioners on me. For a second, I cringe under the weight of their judgement. Slowly this feeling ignites my anger.

Dora turns around. "Will you come for tea after? We need to talk."

"Yes," I say. I'm glad she's asking. I don't want to leave her without an explanation.

The hymns and psalms fill the room, and I sing with a passion that's energized by adrenalin. I feel giddy, almost free. I'm in control. *As long as Hendrik agrees to take you,* my inner voice warns.

The minister from out of town preaches about hope and working together. "God blessed Noah and his sons, and said to them, 'Be fruitful, multiply and replenish the earth.'" I like the new minister's voice when he is reading. "'I will establish my covenant with you: All flesh will not be cut off any more by the waters of the flood. There will never again be a flood to destroy the earth.'" These words comfort me. Near the end, he asks the congregation to pray for all the families who decided not to return to the islands but to immigrate to other countries.

"Thanks for coming with me to church," I tell Rosa before she turns onto the road home.

My sister's face turns pink, but she leaves without a word.

As soon as Mrs. Timmer, Dora and I reach their house, I ask, "Will you go for a walk with me so we can talk."

"Just leave your bike here," Dora answers.

We link arms and walk along the dike.

"I can't stay long," I sound out of breath.

"Chores?" Dora asks.

I turn to face her. "Are you still my best friend?"

"Yes, for ever and ever, remember?" Dora sounds relieved. "The other night when you ran away from me, I thought I'd lost you."

"I was hurt . . . angry that you didn't want to listen to my side of the story. I can tell you now that you were right. The rumours were true. I kissed a fisherman. His name is Machiel. He's from West Bay, and he saved Clasina from drowning when he and his friend rescued us in a little rowboat."

Dora's mouth opens. She clasps my arm. "I didn't hear that part."

"That's what I thought." I squeeze her arm. "Luuc and I had a fight about Machiel and . . . I realize I don't love Luuc . . . I don't even like him . . . I won't marry him."

"But Klara, you have to marry Luuc."

"I know that's expected of me. I remember what we learned at school, but I love Machiel with all my heart."

"You can't marry a fisherman."

"I wish I could. When I'm with Machiel . . . he makes me feel loved, special, all those things from fairy tales, but I know . . ." I squeeze Dora's arm. I can't tell her about the attack.

"Don't ask me why it's impossible to marry Luuc." I have never in my life heard about a girl who was listened to, who was believed. If I tell Dora, will she believe me? She adores Luuc. Will my accusations about Luuc forcing himself on me add to the rumours that are already flying around? Luuc's family is one of the most prominent in the area, and who am I? A girl — not even from the same class. I take a deep breath.

"My parents are forcing me. And . . . I feel trapped, caged, imprisoned just thinking about being Luuc's —"

"I find it hard to believe that you refuse to marry Luuc. I don't understand. . . ." Dora interrupts me and shakes her head in disbelief. "I thought your marriage to Luuc would be a fairy tale?"

"Oh, Dora." I wrap my arms around her. "You don't need to understand, but the marriage would be no fairy tale for me. Can . . . can you keep a secret?" I watch how Dora searches my face in desperation. Slowly, she nods.

"Promise?" I add.

"Your secret is safe." She places her hand on her heart.

"I want you to know, and to believe, that Luuc is not the nice young man everybody thinks he is. He is controlling and demanding. He has a big ego. He is not used to . . . not getting what he wants. He . . . was very rough with me, not loving at all. But please keep this a secret. Please." I hope this will help her understand, even though I've left out the attack.

"You know him better than any one of us." Dora steps back and scrutinizes my face. "I believe you. That's awful. I can't believe he's such a . . . disappointment."

Relieved, I continue. "I'm leaving today. I'm asking Uncle Hendrik if he'll take me to America."

"To America? But . . . that's so far away. Are you sure your uncle will take you?"

"No, but it's my only chance to get out of this impossible situation."

"But Klara . . . how can you?"

"Tell me. What are my options? You saw how people in church looked at me?"

"I know, but how . . . I don't want you to leave. I'll miss my best friend. Have you thought this through?" She wipes her eyes.

I nod.

After a long pause, she finally responds. "If you succeed . . . you'll be doing something no girl has ever done before. You're breaking down all the barriers in this community." Dora grabs both my hands and looks at me, her eyes glistening.

"I don't care about the barriers. I just want to be happy."

She shakes her head. "Your life here would be impossible," she agrees. "Everyone would shun you."

"Maybe one day, a girl in similar circumstances will remember me and find the courage to follow her heart when there is no other choice."

Dora hugs me close. "I wish you all the best in America and please, please write!"

"I need to catch the ferry," I say urgently. "If my parents ask you where I am, please tell them you don't know."

"I promise." Dora's eyes spill over.

Back at her house, I grab my bike. "And remember, I always wanted to travel." I wave once and before I know it, I'm on the road to Harbour Town. A brisk western wind makes me push hard against nature's force, and with every turn of the pedal, I challenge the future that lies ahead.

I arrive at the wooden kiosk in the harbour at three-thirty. I check the schedule and smile with relief. The next ferry to Bergen op Zoom leaves in a half hour — not enough time for my family to discover that I'm gone.

"Return ticket?" the ticket master asks.

"One way," I respond.

35
Hendrik

I FIND A WINDOW seat inside the ferry. There aren't many passengers at this time of day. I don't worry that I'll have to share my seat with someone who wants to start a conversation. When the vessel slowly leaves the harbour, it suddenly hits me hard that I might never return home, never see my family again, never walk the dike again. Never sit in my special place, with my feet in the water, watching the birds catch their dinner, listening to the music of the waves and gazing at the ships in the distance.

I scan the coastline of my island as the boat turns east on the Oosterschelde. I feel torn between leaving my home and visiting those distant shores I've yearned for and dreamed of. My feeling of being in control slowly slips away. In my anger, I haven't really thought about the consequences of my plan. But what else could I have done? I can't live the way I was taught at school — being Luuc's submissive wife, serving him and bearing many children.

I get frustrated when I think of how Mother refuses to understand my feelings. My only explanation for her behaviour is that she must have pushed her feelings for Hendrik far, far away. She was too busy having babies and saving her reputation and her family's name.

The closer we get to the mainland and the further from home, the more my confidence sinks and my doubt grows about Hendrik's response to my request. He doesn't even know me. He might not want the daughter who has appeared out of the blue.

After the ferry moors, I buy my ticket and take the bus to Aunt Neeltje's. With sweaty palms and pounding heart, I ring the doorbell. Hendrik opens the door.

"Klara! What a surprise! Is something wrong?"

Aunt Neeltje is right behind him. "Come inside. You should've telephoned. No luggage?"

I shake my head. Suddenly, I lose my courage and stumble inside.

My aunt takes my coat. "Do your parents know that you're here?"

"No."

"You had a fight?" Hendrik asks.

"About Luuc," I manage in a tight voice. "I'm not marrying him, but Father insists. It's their reputation. Everyone expects me to marry him. It's everyone's reputation." The words rush out. "I can't do it. I can't do what my mother did."

"Whoa! Stop! Sit down." Uncle Hendrik pulls out a chair. "Let's start from the beginning."

"No," Aunt Neeltje interrupts. "First, you're going to call your parents. They must be sick with worry."

Reluctantly, I dial the number.

"Rosa van Burgh," the voice answers.

"Tell Mother I'm in Roseville," I say and hang up.

"Sit down," my aunt urges. "Have you eaten?"

I shake my head.

"You ran away from your family and your wedding." Hendrik clears his throat. "What are you planning to do next?"

Before I can answer the question, the telephone rings. Aunt Neeltje answers and summons me to take the call.

"Mother . . . I told Rosa where I am. . . . I *was* thinking, I didn't lose my head. . . . You and Father don't want to listen to me. . . . I know it's your reputation . . . everyone's reputation. . . . Accept . . . how I feel." The last words end in a sob. And I hang up the phone.

I close my eyes and take a deep breath to muster my courage. "I've asked God to help me . . . to guide me or give me a sign." The words finally come to me. "I've tried hard to convince myself that I could marry Luuc, but I can't do it." I take a sip from the tea Aunt Neeltje has put in front of me and watch Hendrik closely. He definitely looks like Father, but his eyes light up when he talks, and his hair is as wild and out of control as mine.

"I can't do what my mother did . . . not for the family." I try to make my point. "Not for their reputation, for the church and the community. I'm . . . not marrying Luuc," I repeat.

Aunt Neeltje's face pales.

"Is . . . is there work for me . . . for a girl like me in America?" I watch Hendrik's expression change from concern to discomfort.

"Do you realize what you're planning, Klara?" asks Hendrik. "America is far away, and you won't be able to see your family, at least not for a long time."

"That is a lot to ask from Hendrik," my aunt points out.

My throat closes. "I'll work hard. If I can't go to America, where will I go?"

"I don't know." Hendrik rubs his forehead. "It's so sudden. I'm still trying to come to terms with the fact that I have a daughter."

"I only found out last week that you are my father," I whisper.

"I'm angry and sad that I didn't know you when you were little, when you learned to walk . . . said your first words." He looks at his hands. "And I regret that we don't have time to get to know each other now." He takes a sip of his tea. "It's impossible for me to stay much longer."

Hendrik stares at the window. Sharp lines in his forehead reveal his struggling thoughts. "People will talk about you," he says softly. "Have you thought about the consequences if you don't marry Luuc?"

"That's why I need to leave. If I stay and don't marry Luuc, I'll be humiliated and ridiculed in town by everyone, and so will his family and mine."

A gnawing feeling tells me that Hendrik doesn't want to take me to America, or that he doesn't want a daughter. I feel like I'm standing on the edge of the cliff and there's no way back.

"I'll ask my neighbour if I can stay with her for the night. You don't need me. The two of you will have to sort out this difficult problem." My aunt gets up and grabs her things from her bedroom. "Here's a nightgown. You can sleep on the cot in the living room, and Hendrik, you can sleep in my room."

She leaves us alone.

Hendrik sits deep in thought.

I've so many questions that I'm afraid to ask. I eye him nervously. His hands show the strain of hard labour, and he wears no wedding ring. "You never married?" I ask to fill the loaded air with small talk.

Hendrik smiles sadly. "Every time I met a nice girl, I made the mistake of comparing her to your mother. I couldn't do it. Gilda was the love of my life."

I fidget, finding it hard to sit still.

Hendrik looks up. "Klara, have you really thought this through? Believe me, it's not easy to leave everything you love behind."

"I know. But where else can I go? I can't go back."

"I need to think," Hendrik replies, "and I find it difficult to think straight right now because I was in a similar situation."

I get up from the table and sit down on the chair near the window. The cot has been folded and stands on its side against the dresser.

"There's someone else, isn't there?" Hendrik sits down in the chair opposite mine.

"Yes, but I can't marry him either. He's a fisherman and has no future on the island, but I love him very much." I stare ahead, feeling my last bits of hope for the future crumble like a piece of stale bread. "I'll make more tea." I get up.

In the tidy little kitchen, I find what I need. As I wait for the water to boil, I peek into the living room. Hendrik sits holding his head in both hands.

Startled, he looks up when I place his tea on the table in front of him. "Tell me about this fisherman?"

My face grows warm. "During the flood, he and his friend rescued Oma, Mother, Neeltje and Sara. Later, they came back for Clasina and me."

"Where were the others?"

"They had been picked up by two men with a flat-bottomed boat, but there wasn't room for all of us." My chest tightens. "Machiel and Henk had a little rowboat. It was difficult for them to steer through all the rubble in that small boat" — I pause. I don't want the tears to start now.

"What happened?" Hendrik asks.

"At some point, the boat jumped and when I lost my balance,

Clasina flew off my lap and landed in the freezing water." I shiver when I relive the moment. "Machiel . . . he took off his coat and boots and dove in. When I had almost given up, he found her. I was so afraid they would both die of hypothermia." I wipe my face with the back of my hand.

"He's a courageous young man," Hendrik states. "Are you sure that your feelings for him aren't just gratitude?"

"I feel so much more than gratitude," I answer. "How I feel when I'm with Machiel is so different from what I feel for Luuc. I've come to resent Luuc." I stare at the clouds passing by the window. "Machiel feels the same. I . . . I've asked him if he'd come to America with me."

"What did he say?" Hendrik stirs his tea.

"Machiel doesn't know how to farm."

For the first time that evening, I notice a faint smile touching Hendrik's face.

"Would there be work for him?" I ask without looking at Hendrik, even though I think that Machiel only knows about fishing and saving people.

"America is the land of opportunity, and there is more work than there are people."

"But . . . for a fisherman?" A whisper of hope enters my heart.

"Lake Michigan is as big as the sea and full of fish," Hendrik's eyes twinkle just for a moment before his expression becomes serious again. "I don't know what to do or what to say to you right now." He gets up. "I need to sleep on it. There is much to think about, and as I told you, I can't think straight right now."

I don't sleep at all on the small cot in the living room. I toss and turn, my mind full of doubt and hope, hope and doubt. Will Hendrik take me? Will he not? I remember the game I used to play with Rosa in the summer when we were younger. We'd pull the petals of the meadow daisies one by one, singing, "He loves me, he loves me not."

Suddenly, it hits me. With a start I sit up. *God has given me a sign. He sent Hendrik!*

36
Decision

THE CLOCK ON the mantel shows five-thirty in the morning when Hendrik walks out of the bedroom.

I'm awake already, or maybe I never slept.

"We need to talk," he says. "I'll make tea while you get dressed."

When I return from the bathroom, the table is set. There is sliced rye bread, butter, cheese and jam. The tea steeps in the pot on the tea light.

"I've been thinking about you, your situation and your plans for the future for most of the night." Hendrik butters a slice of bread.

"I didn't sleep either," I confess.

"Did you change your mind?"

"No, but I realize that it must be hard for you to accept me as a daughter."

"It's still so hard to believe that I *have* a daughter." Hendrik studies my face, but it doesn't make me feel uncomfortable.

"I asked God to give me sign when I felt cornered. I thought God wasn't listening, but this morning I realized that God has given me a sign — he sent you."

Hendrik's forehead creases. "The Lord does work in mysterious ways." He smiles at me. "Then it was meant to be that we met."

Hendrik's words encourage me. "I don't want you to feel that you have to look after me, but if you can get me started in America — if there's enough work, then I can take care of myself."

"You can start by working on the farm. Jack, my boss, recently lost his housekeeper when she went to live with her ailing sister."

"But . . . I don't know how to speak English. Would Jack agree to that?"

"You can take classes," Hendrik says. "You'll pick up the language quickly when you work with other people."

Classes! I can hardly breathe. The tightness in my chest all those sleepless nights during the past months slowly dissolves. I take a new, deep breath. My heartbeat picks up speed. Is it going to work? Am I getting away? "I'm so relieved," I say in a choked voice. I don't know what else to say.

"Let's eat." Hendrik's voice is filled with emotion.

My stomach rumbles, and it hits me that I feel ravenous. Since Luuc's attack, my body has refused food; now that Hendrik will take me to America, it screams to be fed.

"I'll be leaving at the end of the month, and if you've made up your mind, then we need to get you a visa and a ticket on the boat to America."

I have to place my hand over my heart for fear it will burst. "Thank you," I whisper.

We eat our breakfast in silence. After I drink my tea, a new thought strikes me. "Can I write Machiel, tell him about Lake Michigan and all the fish? Can I give him your address?"

Hendrik smiles. "You think he will come with you?"

"No, I don't think he will. He is very close to his family. He said he didn't know what to do in America, but I'll tell him about Lake Michigan and that he can be a fisherman. Then . . . it's up to him." I stare into my empty teacup. "In America, do people worry about which class they fit in . . . like here?"

"Do you mean is it possible for a farmer's daughter to marry a fisherman?" Hendrik chuckles.

My cheeks are burning.

"Yes, you can marry a fisherman where I live." Hendrik answers.

"And the church . . . ?" I'm hesitant to ask.

"Most people marry people who go to the same church, but not always."

It must be a whole different world out there.

"Have you considered what you will do if he won't come to America? Will you still go?"

"I can't go back."

"I know." He looks at me with concern.

"And I always wanted to travel. I've longed to learn a new language, and this is my chance. Even if Machiel can't join me, I'll still look forward to exploring America and learning new ways."

"We can't waste any time then. I'm leaving in fifteen days and it would be best if we could travel together." Hendrik takes the plates to the kitchen.

"As soon as Neeltje comes back, we'll leave for Rotterdam. We need to get you a visa at the American consulate. After we have your papers, we'll go to the Holland America Line office to get you a ticket for your passage to America."

An hour later, Hendrik and I board the train to Rotterdam.

During the train ride, I can't stop questioning Hendrik about the boat ride, the farm in America and Jack, his boss. Hendrik is easy to talk to, as if I've known him for a long time. What will I call him, I wonder? Uncle Hendrik? Father? I shouldn't worry about that now.

From my window, I watch farmland pass by and small towns with church spires and clusters of houses until the train reaches the tall buildings in the port of Rotterdam. On the bus ride to the consulate, my eyes have difficulty absorbing the many cars, shops displaying colourful signs with gold lettering and people walking on the sidewalks in fancy clothes and black suits.

The port of Rotterdam was bombed by the Germans during the war to force the Dutch government to capitulate. Most buildings are new and modern looking with tall glass windows. At the American consulate, we ride the elevator to the second floor. My stomach drops as the elevator lifts off, and my heart pounds — or sings. The whole time, I feel that my heart is ready to burst, and I don't have enough eyes to take in all these new impressions.

Despite the lineup, it takes only an hour before I hold my visa in my hands.

Next, we ride the bus to a tall building close to the harbour in which the Holland America Line houses their offices. I strain my neck to look up at the top floors.

"Get used to it," Hendrik says. "When we get to New York, the buildings are even taller. They're called skyscrapers."

"They must be tall if they can scrape the sky." I try to visualize these buildings with brushes on the roofs, scraping the clouds away.

Hendrik persuades the lady at the ticket window to give us two second-class cabins right beside each other for our passage to America. After answering many questions and filling out forms, we finally succeed and Hendrik holds up two tickets.

On the way home, Hendrik tells me about the luxury liner SS *New Amsterdam*. "Did you know that during the war, the British Ministry of Transport requisitioned this ship? She transported over three hundred and fifty thousand troops. The ship returned to Rotterdam in 1946 to be turned back into a great ocean liner."

"I find it hard to imagine. It must have been a big job to rebuild the ship after the war."

"Yes, there was so much damage that it took eighteen months to rebuild, refurbish and refinish the vessel to look as luxurious as before. You'll love the crossing, if you don't get seasick, that is. We'll reach New York in seven days."

"What about the cost?" I watch Hendrik's smiling face.

"It's about time I spent some money on my daughter," he chuckles.

By the time we return to Roseville, my head is filled with images of the ocean liner and with big dreams about the huge farm in my future country.

"The telephone is for you," Aunt Neeltje says as we walk in the door. "It's your mother."

I take the receiver. "Mother."

"Do you realize what you've done by running away? You are only making things worse for our family and Luuc's. It doesn't solve anything. You *will* marry Luuc. Now come home so we can get this wedding organized. . . . Are you listening?"

"Mother, you have to listen to me. I'm not coming home. I'm . . . going to America with Hendrik." I can't believe it myself, but now that I've said it out loud I know it is true.

"You're what!" Mother bristles. There's a long pause. "I better talk to your Father."

"Mother," I say in a choking voice, realizing I'll never see my family again.

But the line stays quiet.

"Mother," I repeat.

"Will we see you before you leave?" my mother asks in a much softer voice.

"Do you want to see me after what I've done?"

"You better come home. You'll have to deal with Luuc's family, especially his mother."

"I'll come home tomorrow."

"I'll stay one more night at the neighbour's then," says Aunt Neeltje, placing a pot with stew on the table.

"I'm starving," Hendrik says. "Thank you, Neeltje. I haven't had stew with potatoes, sausage and endives for a long time."

"I see that Klara looks much happier. You need to tell me about your day." My aunt takes the lid off the pot.

After my aunt goes next door, I muster the courage to ask Hendrik about my mother.

"When did you go out with my mother?"

"You know that Gilda's parents didn't have children for a long time?" Hendrik clears his throat. "Martin, her father, was a well-respected veterinarian, and Rosa, her mother, volunteered for many good causes in town."

"Oma has told me a little about my grandparents."

"At age forty-five, Rosa gave birth to your mother, but unfortunately she died during childbirth. Your grandfather, Martin, raised Gilda, and he often took her with him on his rounds to the farms. She was in my class at school. Jannes is two years older." Hendrik pauses and looks out the window as if he's looking into the past.

"Just like her father, Gilda was really good with animals," he continues. "I remember how she calmed the animals when they were nervous, when her father had to do some procedure." He looks away.

"She helps the vet when there are problems with calving," I add. "She also knows when an animal isn't well."

"Oma often set two extra plates when the two of them were on the farm during the noon or evening meal. We got to know them well." He stares in the distance.

"My mother treats animals when they're sick, often with home-made remedies." I love that about her.

Uncle Hendrik smiles and nods.

"How did you and my mother . . . fall in love?"

Hendrik fidgets in his chair. He avoids my gaze.

"I . . . we didn't . . . we did . . . but that doesn't answer your question." He takes a deep breath. "Jannes started to see Gilda, and everybody agreed that they were the perfect couple. Does that sound familiar?"

My throat tightens.

"I was the only one who didn't agree — because I had discovered I had feelings for Gilda. But I had nothing to offer her. Jannes would inherit the farm. As the second son, my job was to find a farmer's daughter who had no brothers so I could marry a girl with a farm." He pauses. His hands clasp and unclasp on his knees.

"One night, when Gilda was visiting and Jannes wasn't home, I made a terrible mistake. I told her how I felt."

"But my mother . . . was she . . . in love with you?"

Hendrik nods. "Jannes found us. . . . He threatened to kill me if I didn't leave town the next day."

I can easily imagine Father's anger.

"I would've done the same thing if our roles had been reversed."

I have no words. I watch the emotions on Hendrik's face.

"Now you know what the big fight was about and why I left. I had nowhere to go." He finally looks at me. "What I didn't know . . . and nobody ever told me . . . was that Gilda got pregnant that night."

"Oma knew," I say softly.

"She wrote me that your parents had gotten married soon after I left. In October a daughter was born, six weeks early."

I watch the pain in his expression. "When you were coming to visit us, Father told Mother that she had to tell you I was your daughter," I say softly.

"She did." Hendrik looks away. "I admire Jannes for marrying your mother and sparing her the humiliation she would have experienced if the community had found out."

37

Saying Goodbye

EARLY TUESDAY MORNING, I take the bus to the ferry. *Now comes the hard part.* My heart feels heavy when I think of leaving Oma, Mother, my siblings and Dora.

The trip home goes by fast, as my mind keeps running to the future. A sliver of hope keeps sneaking into my heart when I allow myself to think of Machiel. I wrote him a long letter last night, asking him about his injuries. I told him about the opportunity to be a fisherman in Michigan, that I obtained my visa and a ticket on a really big ocean liner, that we're leaving on the thirtieth and that I hope and wish with all my heart to meet him before the end of the month.

My bicycle waits in the bike rack beside the ticket kiosk in Harbour Town. I cycle home — anticipating my welcome.

Adriaan spots me first. "When are you leaving?" he asks. "What will you do in America?"

I meet Father outside when I park my bicycle in the new shed. He doesn't say anything; his expression is stern but not angry, I notice.

Mother and Oma are in the kitchen preparing the meal.

"I can't believe you went against our orders." Mother stirs the soup ferociously.

"I'll miss you, Klara," Oma says. "But I'm also glad that Hendrik will have family in America."

I can tell that Rosa has lost her animosity toward me, but even though I've somewhat forgiven her, I'm still so mad that her jealousy got Machiel hurt.

During the noon meal, when my younger siblings come home from school, there are even more questions about how I'll travel, how much money the passage costs and where I'll be living.

As soon as we clear the table the phone rings. I'm close to it, so I answer. "Yes, Mrs. van Borselen. This is Klara. . . . For a fitting? No, Mrs. van Borselen. I've decided not to marry Luuc. I'm going to America with my uncle." When it stays quiet at the other end, I look into the receiver. After a moment of silence an explosion of words thunders across the telephone line. I hardly understand what Luuc's mother is saying except for something about the wedding dress.

"I'm sorry I spoiled your family's reputation, Mrs. van Borselen," I say when Luuc's mother pauses to take a breath. "You can talk to my mother about the dress." I hand the receiver to Mother, who has followed the conversation closely.

"Yes, Mrs. van Borselen. . . . We couldn't persuade her to change her mind. . . . We've decided it'll be better for everybody's reputation that Klara disappears to America with her uncle." My mother looks at me. "The dress . . . of course we'll pay for the dress. I'm sure there is enough material to make outfits for our little girls."

I can't believe that Luuc's mother is making us pay for the dress.

"I agree, Mrs. van Borselen," Mother continues. "We realize the shame and humiliation that Klara's decision has brought upon your family and ours. I'm —" my mother stares into the receiver, surprised — "She hung up on me."

The next days are filled with packing, and my apprehension grows as the departure date draws near.

Oma knits me a warm sweater. "I've heard it can get quite cold in the winter in Michigan," she says. "They get a lot of snow."

"I'll love the snow, but I will miss you so much." I hug her close, fighting back my tears.

"I'll pray for you and Hendrik." Oma dabs her eyes.

"What did you and Uncle Hendrik talk about?" Adriaan asks during the evening meal.

"We talked about the farm," I answer. "He told me about the cattle he has to take care of and the many hectares of land the farms in America have. Even the lake is as big as the sea."

"I'd like to see that," Adriaan says.

"Maybe in the future, it'll be cheaper to go by airplane to America," Father responds. "Maybe we can all visit Klara and Hendrik."

I look at him and smile. I have to assume that he has accepted the fact that I'm not marrying Luuc and that I'm going to America.

That night when I tuck in Clasina, she clings to me. "Will you take me to America?"

"I wish I could, but the trip is too far, and you need to stay with Mother and Father and . . ." I hold her close.

"I'll go with Adriaan when he goes on a plane to visit you." Clasina squeezes my arms.

"We can write to each other."

"But I can't write." Her lip trembles.

"You can draw pictures for me, and I'm sure Liesbeth will write down what you want to tell me. Uncle Hendrik promised that he'll buy me a camera, so I can take photographs and send them to you." We hug for a long time before Clasina lets me tuck her in.

On my seventeenth birthday, the phone rings and Rosa answers.

"She's here," she says, motioning for me to come to the phone. "Machiel," she whispers.

"Machiel!" I sing his name. "I'm so glad to hear your voice. Did you get my letter? Can I see you?"

"That's why I'm calling," Machiel answers. "I'm not good at writing. And happy birthday."

"How badly were you beaten?"

"I'm all right," he answers.

"Will you come to America now that you can be a fisherman?"

There's a pause. I hear him clear his throat.

"I can't get away. My father is ill, and I have to help out."

"So . . . you won't come?" My hope vanishes.

"Klara." His voice is hoarse. "Have a safe trip and write to me when you're in America."

"Will you write back?"

"I'll do my best."

"Will I see you before I leave?"

"I wish . . . I can't . . . I . . . They're calling me. Klara . . . you're my angel."

I bite my lip, holding back the tears.

Rosa watches me when I hang up.

I run up the stairs, close the door and fall on my bed.

Alone in my room, the tears run freely. If I'm honest with myself, my hero coming with me to America was a fairy tale. Machiel has a strong obligation to his family. He will never let them down.

For him, I'm Cinderella with the wild curls, another fairy tale. But my world is real, not magical. I wash my face and look in the mirror. A sad face full of determination looks back at me. The distant shores are calling. Despite my sadness, I smile back at myself.

"What is this world coming to," Father remarks later that evening when the little ones have gone to bed. "First, the war and now the flood. Life here on the island will never be the same. I can't keep up anymore."

"You will have to go with the times." Mother smiles at him.

Hendrik comes to pick me up in a rental car because my suitcase weighs a ton. "Here's your belated birthday present." He hands me a new camera. "I suggest you take pictures of your family right now."

It becomes a chaotic spectacle before everybody is in the photograph.

"You need to remember us," Martin cries.

"I'll miss your stories," Jacob adds.

"I'll come visit you on the plane with Adriaan." Clasina kisses me so hard she almost chokes me. The little ones don't understand, but Neeltje and Sara are generous with their kisses.

Liesbeth can't speak.

"We'll write," I tell her.

Rosa's eyes fill, but I throw my arms around her. "Maybe you can come visit," I try to console her. I'm so glad we're sisters again.

It's difficult to say goodbye to Mother. I read in her eyes that she knows Hendrik told me her secret. I forgive her, knowing she had no choice all those years ago.

Oma can't stop drying her eyes.

"I'll send you pictures and write every week, every day, if I have time," I promise.

Father takes my hand. "Work hard in America and do us proud, and may the Lord look after you in this far-away country."

"I promise," I say in a thick voice.

Hendrik takes my suitcase and places it in the trunk of the car. Before I know it, we're on the road. The farm becomes smaller and smaller, my life on the farm with my family farther and farther away.

38
Far Away Shores

FROM THE DOCK, I look up at the SS *New Amsterdam* — the ocean liner is enormous.

"More than twelve hundred people are sailing on this ship." Hendrik picks up both suitcases and starts up the gangplank. Overcome by many mixed emotions and feelings, I follow him.

In awe, I watch men, women and children of all ages fill the decks.

Hendrik and I find the way to our cabins on the first deck.

"Let's go to the second deck, so we can watch our departure from the harbour." Hendrik puts my heavy suitcase in my cabin, locks the door and hands me the key.

With hundreds of others, we watch the commotion on the quay. Still more people walk up the gangplank — travellers and crew members, it doesn't seem to end. When the last person boards, the gangplank slowly turns away from the ship. The horn blasts its adieu, and the ship inches away from the quay where family and friends wave goodbye to their loved ones, some, like me, embarking on a new life.

As the ship moves out of the harbour, I watch tall cranes loading large freighters. They look like long arms waving and reaching for the sky. Row upon row of warehouses line the wharf, and people look like working ants from my spot on the second deck. Fields of oil tanks that supply the vessels with fuel sit on opposite sides along the harbour.

Small and large boats, long tankers, tugboats and cargo ships all sail toward the English Channel.

A breeze picks up, and I shiver as I watch the coastline getting smaller. A big lump lodges in my throat, and I glance at Hendrik.

He meets my gaze and places his hand on my arm. "This is the hard part, Klara. Watching your fatherland slowly disappear."

"Did you leave on an ocean liner years ago?" I ask in a thick voice.

"I left in January and worked for my passage on one of those large cargo ships. I couldn't afford this." He gestures at his surroundings.

"We should check out the swimming pools. I've heard that the indoor pool on E-deck has Delft-blue tiling."

"I don't have a bathing suit, but I would like to see the pool." I can't believe all this luxury. It's like I'm traveling in a dream.

My cabin is small but cozy. There's just enough room for a bed, a dresser and a sink. I move my suitcase underneath the porthole.

In the following days, I try foods I've never seen or tasted before, like calf's tongue and soup of asparagus. I have a hard time keeping the tiny, round green peas on my plate and not spilling them all over the white linen. My favourite dessert is what they call petits fours, tiny little cakes covered in marzipan.

"Get used to it, Klara." Hendrik points at my bowl of cereal. "We eat cornflakes for breakfast on the farm, too."

I laugh. "The first time I saw these flakes, I didn't think you could eat them. Father would say it's rabbit food. Oh . . . I forgot. He isn't . . ."

"But he is, he was," Hendrik responds. "For seventeen years he was your father, and I'm not used to being called 'Father.'" He smiles. "Call me Hendrik. It makes it easier."

"It's still so new." I take a bite of my fried eggs with bacon. "Not bad. I can get used to that. I especially love the fresh squeezed orange juice they serve with breakfast."

The tables in the dining room are set with white linen and china. Sparkling chandeliers hang from the ceiling, and waiters dressed in white serve the many guests. Every morning when I wake up, I pinch my arm. Every night I write about all the new impressions and experiences in my notebook. I want to feel and remember that this journey was real.

Hendrik asks many questions about school, my friends, work on the farm and what my favourite things are.

After breakfast, we walk the decks and watch the people. There is a tennis court and a golf course on the first deck. There are shops and cafés where you can drink coffee, tea or beer and wine. When the weather is cool, we spend the rest of the morning in our cabins, and I write letters to my family, to Machiel and Dora. Hendrik writes to Jack about his daughter, who's coming to help out on the farm.

After we pass England, the Atlantic becomes a little rough as northwestern storms move across to Europe. Many passengers become seasick, and in the dining room, several tables stay empty.

We both escape the illness, and I start to look forward to the meals with exotic foods like roasted chicken and plum pudding with brandy sauce. There is an abundance of fruits during breakfast and dinner. I taste grapefruit for the first time, but I'm not sure I like these citrus fruits.

After the evening meal, we dress warmly and watch the sunset from the upper deck.

"I have one piece of advice." Hendrik's expression is serious. "Don't compare every American boy with Machiel, but give them a chance."

I sigh. "I'm done with boys for a while. I want to focus on my new life, a new language and having a father all to myself."

I wonder if my mother ever wished she had followed Hendrik to America, or what her life would've been like if she'd studied and become a veterinarian like her father? But I don't remember her ever complaining. The mother I know is mostly kind, except when it comes to the family's reputation. She defended Father when he ranted about her sin.

On the sixth day of our journey, it rains hard, and the wind is brutal. Hendrik suggests we go to the movie theatre to pass the time.

"I've never been to a theatre. Father was convinced we would be exposed to evil." Hendrik laughs, and I can't help joining him. We enjoy two silent movies, one with Charlie Chaplin and the other with two funny actors named Stan Laurel and Oliver Hardy.

I can't remember if I've ever laughed so hard in my life. "My stomach hurts," I cry.

"I love those two characters," Hendrik chuckles as we make our way to the dining room.

"I'll wake you early," Hendrik says before turning in. "We'll go to the upper deck. I want you to experience your new homeland slowly coming into view."

The next morning, I'm awake and dressed well before the knock on my cabin door.

We climb the stairs to the upper deck. Just as Hendrik promised, the shoreline slowly comes into view. The early morning sun illuminates the skyline of New York City. I can't believe we're this close.

The tall buildings are etched against the morning sky. My heart lifts from the cage it's been confined to for the last six months. I'm like a butterfly opening my cocoon and feeling my wings for the first time. I smile up at Hendrik and recite, "The call of the breakers, crashing the coastline, makes me yearn for faraway places where mysterious shores call my name."

Hendrik returns the smile. His eyes sparkle. "There in the distance is your mysterious shoreline. I can hear it calling your name."

Now it's my turn to smile.

"Those tall buildings on the faraway shores are the skyscrapers." He places his arm around my shoulders.

A warm feeling envelops me, and my heart soars.

"And there . . . to the right, is the Statue of Liberty. Welcome to America, my daughter."

AUTHOR'S NOTE

The story of Klara is a work of fiction based on true events. I became inspired from a visit in September 2012 to the Watersnoodmuseum (Flood Museum), which is in the province of Zeeland, in the southwestern part of the Netherlands.

That's why this story is set in the Zeeland. The province consisted of several islands and Zeeuws Vlaanderen and Zuid-Beveland, which were connected to the mainland. Sea dikes protected the islands from the water. All the islands were below sea level. The dikes had been terribly neglected during and after the Second World War.

During the evening of January 31 and through all of February 1, 1953, a full moon and high tide combined with a strong northwestern storm to cause a so-called spring tide. Most dikes breached and the islands of Zeeland and parts of the provinces of North Brabant and South Holland flooded. The island of Texel also suffered extensive damage. France, Belgium, Scotland and England also suffered from this flood disaster. The water came so suddenly that most people drowned in their sleep and had no chance. Many families who woke to find the main floors of their homes flooded escaped to the second floor, the attic and even onto their roofs. The winds blew with hurricane strength and forced the water into cities and towns, with devastating results. The lack of communication by radio or phone (most people didn't have phones) resulted in more devastation as people could not be warned or reached. In 1953, people didn't have computers, internet, cell phones or televisions.

One hundred thousand people were evacuated, and two hundred thousand hectares of land flooded; 1,836 people drowned, and 20,000 cows, 1,200 pigs, 1,750 horses, 2,750 sheep and goats and 165,000 poultry were lost. It took many years for the islands to recover and for their inhabitants to rebuild. An enormous sea defence project was built called the Deltawerken (Delta Works).

Today, the islands are well protected from the sea, but the emotional scars will never heal.

Sixty years after the flood, a program called the Oral History Project invited survivors to tell their stories and experiences. Although the characters in this novel are fictional, their experiences are based on facts and on recordings and interviews made for the Oral History "1953" project. Visit the website of the flood museum at www.watersnoodmuseum.nl to see footage of the flood and its devastation, to learn about the Oral History project and to take part in many online events.

To move my story forward, I took some liberties and made Klara's family return to their farm in August of 1953. The animals arrived that same fall. In reality such events didn't happen until the following year. On October 30, 1953, the SS *New Amsterdam*, did not sail to New York, but for the ending of this novel, I needed to bend the facts a little.

Klara's community was steeped in tradition and ruled by social control and the church. The Biblical quotes and texts used in this novel are from the King James Version (KJV) and World English Bible (WEB). But in the 1950s, in the Netherlands, Father and the ministers would probably have read from the more traditional *Statenvertaling Bijbel*, a bible that had been translated into the Dutch language directly from ancient Greek and Hebrew.

The Dutch have battled storms and the sea from the beginning of time, and they continue to fight rising sea levels due to climate change. The Deltawerken is an ongoing storm surge defence project that will hopefully protect most of the country from future flooding. The next twenty years will be crucial and will show us if the reinforcing of dikes and pumping stations will be sufficient to protect the land. For more information on the Deltawerken, visit www.rijkswaterstaat.nl.

HISTORICAL NOTE

Chronology of events: how the flood and devastation unfolded

SATURDAY, JANUARY 31, 1953

A strong northwestern storm blows all day and the evening forecast calls for hurricane-force winds. It's the fifteenth birthday of Princess Beatrix, the oldest daughter of Queen Juliana and Prince Bernhard. People complain that it is impossible to fly the Dutch flag in honour of the princess's birthday. All day, the rescue boat *Wilhelmina* assists ships in trouble off the coast.

In the afternoon, water levels in various harbours on the islands of Zeeland are reported as higher than normal. All ferry service between the islands is cancelled by four o'clock that afternoon. At eleven o'clock that evening, the people in the town of Zierikzee discover to their horror that the water level at *low* tide is as high as the typical water level at high tide.

FEBRUARY 1, 1953

Around midnight, the authorities in many communities forecast that some of the dikes will not hold back the water. In many places, waves wash over the dikes, submerging quays and streets even with the flashboards closed. In villages and towns where the water has come over the dikes, volunteers are called up, sirens from the fire departments are turned on and church bells chime to wake the population. Men try to fill the holes with sandbags where the dikes have already breached, but the waves are too strong; the sandbags wash away as soon as they are put in place. Many polders are flooding; farms become isolated, and the water rises so fast that people retreat upstairs. But many citizens drown in their sleep, because they couldn't hear the warning signals. Farmers who own telephones are called to cut loose their cattle. Older houses crumble like cardboard structures. Many roads wash out, and volunteers who try to rescue people with cars and trucks become stranded and have to abandon their vehicles. By four o'clock in the early morning, the first spaces for evacuees are opened in churches and city halls. By five o'clock most telephone lines have been destroyed.

Sunday morning at eight o'clock, the national radio broadcasts the first news of the flood in the southern and coastal provinces.

By four o'clock on Sunday afternoon, a second spring tide brings more damage and destruction. Buildings that survived the first wave collapse and people and animals drown.

FEBRUARY 2, 1953

The Monday newspapers report on the devastation, and the estimated death toll is 150. The National Disaster Relief Fund is established. The Red Cross starts collecting clothing, blankets, water and food. Members of the royal family prepare for visits to the flooded areas. A pilot who flew over the flooded areas makes an emergency landing and raises the alarm with the authorities about the situation. Slowly, rescue efforts get underway. Amateur radio operators contact their colleagues all over the country and report on the scale of the disaster. Fishermen who waited out the storm start to evacuate stranded citizens with rowboats and small motorboats. People build rafts from debris. At four o'clock in the afternoon, the first members of the military service arrive in Zierikzee, but an attempt to evacuate 350 citizens of that town fails. During the war, the Germans had bombed the dikes and flooded the area in an attempt to stop Allied troops from invading the country. Many citizens were evacuated and when they returned home, they found their homes had been looted. This was the reason the citizens refused to leave their properties.

The evening news reports the drowning of 400 casualties. Refugee centres open up in the cities of Bergen op Zoom and Roosendaal. The government announces that action is needed instead of debate.

FEBRUARY 3, 1953

Fishermen from all over the country assist in the evacuation of the devastated areas. Planes drop rubber boats. Rescue teams set up shelters in the Ahoy Hallen, in the seaport of Rotterdam, for the victims. In the town of Zierikzee, too many volunteers arrive, and the harbour is plugged with boats. The rescue efforts come to a halt until a member of the Ministry of Interior Affairs takes charge. Marines arrive to assist with the rescue operations. The first DUKWs (vehicles that can be used on land as well as in water) arrive from Germany. The evening news announces that the number of casualties has risen to 653, and the town of Renesse reports the first incidents of looting.

FEBRUARY 4, 1953

Queen Juliana, her mother, Princess Wilhelmina, and the Royal Commissioner Governor all visit Zierikzee and try to persuade the inhabitants to evacuate, but to no avail. The population refuses even though the city is in chaos. The Red Cross reports that their warehouses are overflowing with donations of clothing and furniture, but there is a need for blankets and financial aid.

Everywhere in the world, donations of money and relief supplies is being collected. NATO sends military service men and materials. The evening news announces that the death toll has risen to 1,233.

FEBRUARY 5, 1953

In many areas, the evacuation is now complete, and the search for casualties of this flood begins. Small towns are overflowing with soldiers, and a curfew is installed for fear of looting. Prince Bernhard is appointed chair of the National Disaster Relief Fund. By this time, 7 million guilders (approximately $5 million CAD) has been collected. The Dutch people have been asked to donate the equivalent of one hour of their salaries. This activity is very successful. Soldiers and students arrive to help with the improvised closure of the dikes. The number of casualties has risen to 1,320.

FEBRUARY 6, 1953

Prince Bernhard makes one more attempt to convince the people of the town of Zierikzee to leave, but they refuse for fear of looting. Many communities implement a curfew from seven in the evening till seven in the morning. In the town of Oude Tonge, thirty bodies are buried in a mass grave. The newspapers announce that the repairs on the dikes are slow and primitive. The National Disaster Relief Fund announces that 11.5 million guilders (about $7 million CAD) has been collected so far. The number of casualties has risen to 1,355.

FEBRUARY 7, 1953

Mr. Beel, the Minister of Interior, Affairs visits Zierikzee to pressure the inhabitants to leave, but again the citizens refuse. There is an enormous problem with stealing and looting in the town.

FEBRUARY 8, 1953

A day of mourning is declared for the entire country. Queen Juliana speaks on the radio. In the devastated areas, funerals are held in churches, schools and cafés. In Zierikzee there is another desperate call for evacuation as 5,000 people now occupy an area that is two hundred by a thousand square metres, which is forty-nine acres or twenty hectares of land (approximately the size of forty football fields).

FEBRUARY 10, 1953

A new stamp is developed to help the victims of the flooded areas. In some towns, it is now law to keep cats and dogs inside because of the many cadavers and the fear of spread of disease.

FEBRUARY 11, 1953
Queen Juliana visits many devastated communities. As compensation for their losses, children receive a rabbit from the queen.

FEBRUARY 13, 1953
English soldiers help with the closure of a major hole in the dike on the island of Schouwen-Duiveland. The Ministry of Interior Affairs announces a forced evacuation of the people of Zierikzee. Many citizens go into hiding. The government wants to reduce the number of people from 5,000 to 1,500, but only 820 people are evacuated instead of the planned 2,500.

FEBRUARY 19, 1953
The first groups of volunteers, mostly women known as "silt and soap crews," arrive at one of the towns where the water has receded, but a layer of sand and dirt has covered houses and streets.

FEBRUARY 20, 1953
Three thousand people remain in the town of Zierikzee, but tensions remain.

END OF FEBRUARY 1953
Many holes in the dikes have been repaired and the focus is now on the large breaches.

MARCH/APRIL 1953
The first evacuees are allowed to return if a minimum of two rooms in their house have been cleaned. By Easter, more families have returned to areas where the devastation hasn't been as severe. Queen Juliana visits the islands to observe the progress on the dike repairs.

APRIL 21, 1953
After the dike has been repaired in the Reyersbergse polder, railway services connect the island with the rest of the country.

MAY 1953

After two months of cleaning, people in Oude Tonge may return to their homes.

JUNE 1953

Many homes are condemned after the salt water corroded the foundations and walls.

AUGUST 27, 1953

A large hole in the dike at Schelpbroek is closed with caissons from Normandy. In 1944, Allied troops used caissons — concrete cases — to build harbours out in the ocean.

NOVEMBER 7, 1953

Queen Juliana and Prime Minister Drees attend the final dike closure at midnight, when the last caisson is put in place.

JANUARY 1954

After almost a year, the last evacuees are allowed to return to their homes on the island of Schouwen-Duiveland.

ACKNOWLEDGEMENTS

Many people supported me during the long process of writing this novel. My late friend, Marla Hayes, advised me not to put a large family in my story as I wouldn't remember who is who. Dear Marla, you must know that I didn't take your advice, but insisted on writing about a family with nine children and making it work. Jacqueline Guest, my mentor during those early drafts, I am so thankful for your insight and invaluable suggestions. Heather Stemp, for guiding me through the many stages of this story, I am forever grateful for your encouragement and friendship. Dear friend and fellow writer, Rebecca Upjohn, you helped me overcome the darker parts of this novel. Thank you, Karen Upper, I value your enthusiasm for children's books, for sharing books by Canadian authors with students, and for being a friend. Donna Sinclair, author, creative writing teacher, mentor and dear friend. Thank you for guiding me through the uncomfortable parts of this story. Wendy Atkinson and Kevin Welsh, thank you for all your support for this novel. Robyn So, thank you for your insight and amazing editorial advice. A great big thank you to the late Ronald Hatch, for believing in this story. To my family for their love, support and inspiration, thank you.

ABOUT THE AUTHOR

Born in the Netherlands after the Second World War, Martha's novels for children and young adults are based on family experiences and historical facts.

Martha's young adult novel, *A Time to Choose*, won the Blue Heron Book Award and was shortlisted for the Geoffrey Bilson Award for Historical Fiction. *Hero*, a middle-grade novel, won the Elementary Teachers' Federation of Ontario Writer's Award, was nominated for the Silver Birch Award, and has been translated into the Frisian language by a Dutch publisher. *Awesome Wildlife Defenders*, a middle-grade novel, is about endangered species, young activists and mental health.

You can find more information at www.marthaattema.com